"Is there any way Ray this to himself?" I asked.

"Doesn't look like it," Lieutenant Binder answered.

I cleared my throat and asked the question I'd been dreading. "How long will we be closed?" I felt selfish asking. A man was dead. But the future of our business depended on the answer.

"Certainly you'll be closed tomorrow. After that, it'll be day-to-day."

The Snowden Family Clambake was teetering on the brink as it was. Every day we were shut would bring us closer to financial ruin. And to losing this island. Which I was convinced would break my mother, still recovering from my father's death. That's why I'd come home. To save the business that provided for my family. And to save Morrow Island for my mother.

"Lieutenant, we have a short season here on the coast. Every day we're shut—"

"I understand, Ms. Snowden. I do. But we need to process the scene. We also need to make sure the island is a safe place for you and your guests."

A safe place? "You think this could have something to do with the island?"

It was another question I hadn't wanted to ask, though it was all I had thought about for a couple of hours . . .

Books by Barbara Ross

CLAMMED UP

BOILED OVER

MUSSELED OUT

FOGGED INN

Published by Kensington Publishing Corportion

CLAMMED UP

Barbara Ross

KENSINGTON PUBLISHING CORP.
http://www.kensingtonbooks.com

ISBN-13: 978-0-7582-8685-7
ISBN-10: 0-7582-8685-6
First Kensington Mass Market Edition: September 2013

eISBN-13: 978-0-7582-8686-4
eISBN-10: 0-7582-8686-4
First Kensington Electronic Edition: September 2013

10 9 8 7 6 5 4 3

Printed in the United States of America

*This book is dedicated to Bill Carito,
my best friend, the love of my life,
who has supported me in everything I've ever done.
Honey, I'm sorry I got annoyed at you for breathing
while I was trying to write.*

Chapter 1

She hadn't seemed like a Bridezilla. Not in the least. Most brides who would celebrate their wedding with a clambake on an island in Maine were pretty relaxed. Just think about all that broth and butter, and the dress-staining properties of blueberry grunt. We were making the first run of the day out to Morrow Island with the wedding party, well almost all of the wedding party, and the bride had a grip on my upper arm like a blood pressure cuff that tightened with each swell our boat steamed over.

"Julia. Turn. The Boat. Around," the bride, a willowy brunette named Michaela, demanded.

I shook my head. "Not a good idea. We've discussed this. We'll get to the island and unload the food. Then the boat will head right back to the harbor."

My eyes swept the deck, searching for the maid of honor. Wasn't calming the bride her job? But she was off in a corner of the stern with the bridesmaids, gossiping vigorously. I knew exactly what they were talking about. The best man wasn't onboard. Neither was the groom.

Back at the dock, when the best man hadn't shown up at the appointed time, there'd been some nervous joking. The night before, after the rehearsal dinner, a group had gone out to Crowley's, the noisiest tourist bar in Busman's Harbor, and evidently, the best man had gotten pretty hammered. Nobody remembered walking him to his hotel. He must have been the last member of the wedding party left in the bar.

As time had ticked by, his continued absence wasn't so funny. His hotel door had been pounded on. His cell phone had been tried, though service was pretty spotty in the harbor. I called from my phone, which would at least get a signal, but his end went straight to voice mail.

"We have to get going," I'd finally told Michaela. "If we don't get the food over to the island soon, you'll have a lot of hungry guests." The hold of the *Jacquie II* was filled with live lobsters, clams, and sweet corn that still needed to be shucked so only one thin layer of husk remained.

Michaela had agreed. "Julia's right. Ray can take the later boat with the guests."

The groom, Tony, who up to then had been relaxed and smiling, shook his head. "You guys go along. Get to the island, get settled, fix your hair, or whatever it is you've gotta do. I'll find Ray and bring him on the later boat."

"But—" Michaela had started to protest, but then the reality of the situation hit her.

The other groomsmen were her teenage brothers. Tony's father was slightly disabled by a stroke and Michaela's dad had died years before. The ancient minister wasn't up to searching the harbor. Michaela's mother, Tony's mother, and the bridesmaids were already dressed and in high heels. The rest of the passengers included the DJ and my crew, the cooks, waitstaff, and general helpers who made the clambake run smoothly. As far as I knew, none of my folks had ever seen the best man. There was really no one but the groom who could look for him.

"Don't worry." Tony kissed Michaela on the forehead. "I'll be there. Ray and I will both be there." And then he'd walked down the gangway and off the dock.

At the time, I'd thought Michaela took it pretty well, but now she had a wild look in her eyes and seemed perilously close to a meltdown. To anyone watching, we must have looked like quite a pair. We were the same age, thirty, but Michaela was tall, exotic-looking, and already dressed in her beautiful gown. I was blond, small and wiry, and wore my new uniform of faded jeans, work boots, and a sweatshirt. I'd thought about dressing differently in honor of the occasion, but putting on a clambake was hard, physical work. Thank goodness I'd kept up my gym membership for the nine years I'd lived in Manhattan.

I'd known Michaela vaguely, years ago, as a friend of a friend in New York City, but we'd never been close and I didn't know what to say to her now.

From across the deck, my brother-in-law Sonny made a face at me that simultaneously said *Now look what you've got us into* and *I told you so.* I rolled my eyes at him.

Back in early spring when I'd explained my idea to "expand" the Snowden Family Clambake business—I'd deliberately avoided the inflammatory word *save*—by adding private parties, company picnics, weddings and the like, Sonny was dead set against it. And when I told him private catering would require an expanded menu, he'd lost it.

"The bake is the bake!" he'd yelled. "Twice a day we haul two hundred tourists out to the island, feed them steamers, lobsters, corn, potatoes, an onion, and a hard-boiled egg, all of which we cook in a hole in the ground, the same way the Indians taught our Puritan forefathers. The Maine clambake is sacred. Don't mess with the bake!"

"Sonny, Indians didn't start the bake. My father did. In 1979. And since the economic crisis, there aren't two hundred tourists on that boat twice a day. Sometimes there are fewer than two dozen. In Maine, we've got exactly four months to make our money. Four months. So if you think I'm going to stand by and lose my father's business because you can't be flexible, you're wrong!"

We'd retreated to our separate corners, knowing we'd be going a few more rounds. Sonny was more right about some of it than I was. My father had started the Snowden Family Clambake Company, but he certainly didn't invent the clambake. As to the Native Americans, we knew they ate a lot of shellfish, as shown by the giant, prehistoric piles of oyster shells called middens just up the road in the Damariscotta River. And we knew the Puritans ate lots of clams, or even more would have died during those early winters. But the rest was as much mystery as history. One thing I was sure of. The Indians didn't teach Sonny's Puritan forbearers how to do a clambake. If his ancestors were anything like him, no one could teach them a damn thing.

Just as Morrow Island came into view, the maid of honor, whose name was Lynn, finally woke up to her duty. She gently pried the bride off my arm and walked her to a seat. "Ray is just a jerk," I heard Lynn say, but Michaela shook her head no.

I rubbed my arm to restore the feeling to my tingling fingers, moved to the bow, picked up the cable, and got ready to land.

Morrow Island. I still couldn't believe Sonny had

almost lost it. The island had been in my mother's family for a hundred and thirty years. It was a great piece of rock, really. Thirteen acres, with good deep-water dockage, and that rarity in Maine, a small sandy beach. On a high hill at the center of the island stood Windsholme, the summer "cottage" built by my great-great-grandfather at the height of the Gilded Age.

As our captain maneuvered the *Jacquie II* into dock, the island's caretakers, Etienne and Gabrielle, hurried to meet us. The mansion was abandoned during World War II, when no one had servants to run the place or fuel to get there. The family money was long gone by then, anyway. After the war, my grandfather built a modest house by the dock. That's where my mother had spent her summers, and where she'd fallen in love with the boy from town who delivered groceries in his skiff.

Now Etienne and Gabrielle lived in the little house all summer. Etienne was our bake master, managing the fire pit where the clambake was cooked. Gabrielle ran the kitchen and made the deep-dish blueberry grunt we served to guests at the end of the meal.

I jumped onto the dock. A steady breeze blew from the south and I wished the temperature were a couple degrees warmer for Michaela's big day. In spite of what the Busman's Harbor Tourism Board would have you believe, mid-June was still pretty early for coastal Maine. I closed my eyes for just a second and breathed in deep. Etienne had already started the towering hardwood fire that heated the stones to cook the meal. The smell of burning oak, sea air, and a slight tang from the scrub pines clinging to the rocks was Morrow Island to me. No matter where I went or what I did, it would always mean home.

Etienne and Sonny helped the rest of wedding party onto the dock and we started the long trudge up the great lawn toward Windsholme. Constructed in stone, in deference to the sea winds, the mansion had twenty-seven rooms, not counting bathrooms, storerooms, and pantries. Inside, it was gracious and unexpectedly airy. The double front doors opened into a three-story grand foyer with a staircase that rose, turning back on itself, all the way to the top floor.

We didn't use Windsholme for the clambakes, though we allowed guests to relax in the rockers lining its deep front porch. Sadly, the inside wasn't in great condition and we didn't want customers getting hurt or lost. But to host weddings I knew there had to be a place for people to dress or fix their hair and makeup. The mansion's 1920s-era knob and tube wiring had long been turned off. In a fit of optimism, I'd hired electricians to rewire a couple rooms on the main floor to handle modern hair dryers and makeup lights.

As we walked up the lawn, the discussion going on behind me was about the best man, Ray Wilson. He was selfish, irresponsible and immature, the maid of honor insisted. "He had one job to do for this wedding. Show up and bring the rings. And he couldn't get that right."

"Ray's changed," Michaela responded. "Really, he has. I'm worried about him. Something's wrong."

"I'm sure he'll be here." I tried to sound confident.

And he was. When I threw open Windsholme's great front double doors, Ray Wilson hung by a rope around his neck from the grand staircase. Dead.

Chapter 2

Of course, I didn't know who he was then. But I had a strong inkling when Michaela crumpled to her knees, shrieking, "Ray! Ray! Ray!" Instinctively, I herded the guests outside and slammed the door. I could tell there was nothing we could do for that poor man.

Once were were back on the porch, I couldn't catch my breath. My heart banged in my chest as adrenaline surged through my body. I was responsible for these people and for Morrow Island. I took a deep gulp of air to steady myself, then hollered for Sonny and Etienne.

They were down by the fire which makes its own noise, but by the third bellow they heard me and came running. After Sonny took a quick look inside, he and I had a whispered argument about who to call. The Busman's Harbor Police, the State Police, the harbormaster, the Coast Guard?

We decided to call Busman's Harbor PD and let them sort it out.

Sonny ran back to the *Jacquie II* to raise the police department via the radio. He also radioed his wife, my sister Livvie, who worked in our ticket kiosk, so she could let the wedding guests know the boat wouldn't be coming back any time soon.

I ordered everyone back aboard the *Jacquie II*. They couldn't be in Windsholme or roaming around the island, so the boat seemed like the best place to keep the wedding party and our employees confined. Once aboard, they clustered as Maine people do in the summer—locals to one side of the top deck, people "from away" to the other—both groups talking like mad. Several got out their cell phones, wiggled and jiggled them, and held them to the sky in the direction of some imaginary satellite. The local people knew it was pointless, but they did it, too.

Michaela sobbed, her mother and the maid of honor on either side of her. I felt terrible. This was supposed to be the happiest day of her life and now no wedding would take place. And she must have so wished Tony was with her during this awful experience. But he was stuck in the harbor, just as we were stuck on the island.

The first person to arrive was Jamie Dawes. I have never been so happy to see anyone in my life. Jamie and I were best buds as children. Until I went away to boarding school, we waited for the bus together every day, and we worked together at the clambake every summer through high school and college. In the few months since I'd been back in town, I'd been so buried in work I hadn't reconnected with him. According to my mother, over the winter, he'd been appointed full-time to the Busman's Harbor Police Department.

An officer I didn't know steered their borrowed motorboat. Jamie jumped out before it stopped moving and I ran to meet him. He put a hand on my shoulder and looked directly into my eyes. "Are you okay?" He was tall and broad through the chest, but he still had the same blond hair, sky-blue eyes, dark lashes, and open, expressive face he'd had as a boy. I swallowed hard and nodded yes.

We walked up the hill to Windsholme and Jamie and his partner went to take a look at the body. They were only inside a few minutes. When they returned, Jamie signaled for me, Sonny, and Etienne to gather around him. "We have to call in the medical examiner and the state police major crimes unit," he said in a low voice.

"Major crimes! Surely the poor man killed himself." I said it because I wanted to believe it.

"You don't know that, Julia," Jamie responded. "It's an unattended death with a boatload of question marks around it. Officer Howland and I will stay on the island to secure the scene."

It didn't matter to me why Jamie was staying, I

was just glad he was. He knew us and he knew Morrow Island and that's what counted.

Four more members of Busman's Harbor's police department arrived to help. The town only had nine sworn officers, and four of those were part-time. Two state police detectives arrived an hour or so later, hitching a ride out with the harbormaster. The medical examiner came on a commandeered lobster boat. Our island looked like it had been invaded by a tiny, mismatched flotilla.

The detectives and medical examiner went up to Windsholme. It felt like we waited for hours, though I was sure it wasn't that long. Sonny banged around the *Jacquie II* in a barely concealed rage. "Weddings," he muttered under his breath, as if holding wedding receptions at a clambake was the craziest idea anyone ever had. And then louder, "I hope you're happy."

Happy? I wasn't even supposed to be there. I was in Maine because of a panicked call from my sister Livvie.

In January, Livvie intercepted a call from the bank to her husband Sonny, who'd run the clambake for the five years since Dad died. The bank was calling our loan. Not only could we lose the clambake, but Sonny had persuaded Mom to put up her house in town and Morrow Island as collateral on the loan. We could lose it all.

"Livvie, how could you let this happen?" I'd yelled into my cell phone.

"I didn't *let* it happen. Mom is a mentally competent adult. It's her property. She can do what she wants!"

I let it go. There was no point in fighting about it by then. The money, borrowed during good economic times, was long gone, used to rebuild the dock, outfit our ticket booth for online sales, and replace the slate roof on Windsholme, which was desperately in need. Slate roofs were incredibly expensive and any work you had done on an island cost three times more.

Then the stock market crashed and the recession hit. The first summer wasn't so bad. Lots of people canceled flying vacations to take driving vacations and Busman's Harbor is a day's ride from the most densely populated part of the country. But the second summer was a disaster. Driving vacations turned into stay-cations and to top it off, the weather was awful. In the harbor, restaurants and inns were half empty. Most of the art on the walls in the galleries and the clothes on the racks in the shops were the same ones at the end of the summer as were there at the beginning. The next two summers weren't any better. No one was spending money and the Snowden Family Clambake Company was dying.

Livvie begged me to give up my venture capital job and my life in Manhattan to come home and run the business with Sonny. "You're trained for this. You went to business school. Helping entrepreneurs is what you do. Julia, please. I don't know what's going to happen to us."

I promised Livvie I would give it one summer, which was all the bank had agreed to anyway. In March, I'd moved back to Busman's Harbor.

Happy. What a concept. I didn't respond to Sonny. I'd had enough experience this spring to know it wouldn't be productive. I tried to keep the guests and employees calm . . . and I waited. Finally the detectives emerged from Windsholme and made their way down to the dock.

"Who's in charge here?" the older of the two yelled up at the boat.

I glanced at Sonny. The question went straight to heart of the issues between us. When he didn't say anything, I stepped forward. "I am."

Chapter 3

"Where can we go to talk?"

I led the state cops through Gabrielle's pin-neat kitchen to the front room of the little house by the dock. It had always been a comfortable place for me, cozy inside with views to Spain out every window. I sat on the window seat with my back to the view. The detectives pulled straight-backed chairs from the dining room and sat opposite.

"I'm Lieutenant Jerry Binder, Commander, Major Crimes Unit." He had a bald spot stretching in a narrow strip from his forehead to his crown. Right away, I liked that he didn't attempt to disguise it with some elaborate comb-over or shaved head. I sensed in him the same straightforwardness of character he displayed with his hairstyle. The fringe of hair he did have was medium brown with flecks of gray. The round brown eyes staring out over the ski-slope nose showed just a few wrinkles. I put him in his mid-forties.

"This is Detective Tom Flynn," Lieutenant Binder said. Flynn was younger, early thirties I thought. He had the kind of body that only comes from hard work at the gym. Unlike his partner, Flynn had plenty of hair follicles, but the hair itself was cut so short I only had an impression of its sandy color. He had a New England accent, though it wasn't quite Maine. Boston, or maybe even Providence. He sat with his back ramrod straight. The whole package—the hair, the posture, the toned body—said ex-military to me.

Binder was polite, even empathetic. He asked me about the island and the business. "Tell me about finding the body."

I described step by step what had happened. Was I apprehensive when I threw open Windsholme's heavy front doors? I couldn't have been. But in the movie in my head, I hesitated, hand on the doorknob, knowing what awaited me.

"What happens next?" I asked when we'd finished.

"We'll question everyone here and then let you take them back to the harbor," Detective Flynn said. "From what you say, we should talk to this Etienne person next. Two of our colleagues are with your sister on the mainland. They're getting information from the wedding guests. We'll take their contact information and let them go back to their hotels. Same with these people here. Another officer in the harbor is talking to the groom right now."

The groom. Poor Tony. Not only had he lost his wedding day, he'd also lost his friend.

"Is there any chance Ray Wilson could have done this to himself?" I asked, because more than anything, that was what I wanted to believe.

"Doesn't look like it," Lieutenant Binder answered. "Preliminarily, the medical examiner thinks he was hung up there after he was dead."

I'd only looked at the body for a few seconds, but I closed my eyes and let myself see what my mind had been denying. The dried blood covering the front of Ray Wilson's pink polo shirt. "Is that where the blood came from? From when he died?"

Neither of them answered. Flynn brushed imaginary lint from his trousers.

I cleared my throat and asked the question I'd been dreading. "How long will we be closed?" I felt selfish asking. A man was dead. But the future of our business depended on the answer.

"No way to know," Flynn said.

Binder followed, a little more sympathetically. "Certainly you'll be closed tomorrow. After that, it'll be day-to-day."

The Snowden Family Clambake was teetering on the brink as it was. Every day we were shut down would bring us closer to financial ruin. And to losing the island—which I was convinced would break my mother, still recovering from my father's death. That's why I'd come home. To save the business that provided for my family. And to save Morrow Island for my mother.

"Lieutenant, we have a short season here on the coast. Everyday we're shut—"

"I understand, Ms. Snowden. I do. But we need to process the scene. We also need to make sure the island is a safe place for you and your guests."

A safe place? "You think this could have something to do with the island?" It was another question I hadn't wanted to ask, though it was all I had thought about for a couple hours. *Why here? Why on the island?*

Chapter 4

I climbed back aboard the *Jacquie II*. The name of the boat was a bit of a joke. My mother's name was Jacqueline, but I couldn't imagine anyone, even my father, calling her Jacquie. My father had purchased the boat seven years ago, when the economy was flying high, to replace the refitted minesweeper that had been the *Jacquie I*. It was a logical thing to do at the time, even a necessity, but when Sonny took out the new loan, he'd rolled the boat loan into it to get a more favorable rate. So the boat was part of the giant debt endangering my mother's property.

People seemed to have accepted we'd be stuck aboard the boat for a while. Sonny had opened up the bar and was serving water and soft drinks, no alcohol since everyone still had to be questioned—though I'm sure some people could've used it. He put all the snack food we normally sold on the boat—chips, candy bars, small bags of cookies—out on the bar for people to help themselves. It was a small financial hit for us to take, compared to the enormity of what might come.

When Etienne came aboard the *Jacquie II* after meeting with the state police, Sonny and I huddled up with him in the pilothouse to compare notes.

"I told them no one landed a boat at our dock last night. No way." Etienne's English still rolled with the soft syllables of his native Quebec. Even in his late fifties, he was a powerful man who did hard, physical work every day. The hair that was left on his head was mostly gray, and he had great, bushy eyebrows and a mustache. He'd come to work for my dad just a few years after the company started, so I'd known him for as long as I could remember. I trusted him with my business and property, and, if it ever came down to it, I would have trusted him with my life.

"You were asleep," Sonny challenged, running one of his big hands over his forehead and through his buzz cut.

"*Non, non,*" Etienne insisted. "We leave the dock lights on all night. Look how close the house is." Etienne pointed from the cottage to the dock as if Sonny and I didn't have the whole island memorized. "Gabrielle right now is telling the police the same thing. No one landed on the dock." His voice was insistent and I was afraid he and Sonny would be off on another one of their arguments.

There'd been tension between Sonny and Etienne all spring. I couldn't figure out what the problem was. They'd worked together for a dozen years, the last five without my father, and somehow they'd gotten on. But not anymore. I thought maybe my presence in the business exacerbated the tensions between them, especially since Etienne almost always took my side.

When Paul Simon sang that orangutans were skeptical about changes in their environments, he'd described my brother-in-law perfectly. Sonny even had the flaming orange hair and barrel chest to go along with his deep suspicion of anything new or different. Etienne had proved much more flexible when it came to saving the clambake, ready to try anything. The only idea of mine he'd opposed was rewiring the two rooms in Windsholme, which he'd argued was a terrible use of our severely restricted cash. But I'd gone ahead and done it.

For once, perhaps because of the weight of the events of the day, Sonny didn't push his disagreement with Etienne further. Instead, he looked at me. "If not the dock, could he have landed on the beach?"

"It's possible, I guess." Our little beach was on the other side of the island, as far from the dock as it could be. It's a long walk, but we kept a path cleared for clambake customers who wanted to explore. You could land a small boat there, if you were very skilled.

Sonny nodded. "A local then. Knows the harbor, knows the island."

A chill ran through me and I huddled into my sweatshirt. I nodded toward a cluster of college students on our waitstaff. "What do they say?" Fed and talked out, they were sunning themselves on the top deck.

Sonny answered. "Some of them have friends who work at Crowley's. What's going around is Ray Wilson was at the bar last night at closing time, drunk off his ass and picking fights. Chris Durand threw him out of the bar, loaded him into his cab, and drove him away. Nobody saw Wilson after that."

Sonny and Etienne looked at each other, and I could tell they were thinking the same thing I was. *Chris Durand. Local.* Knew the harbor well. And he knew the island. Thanks to me.

Chapter 5

Back in March, when I returned to town, I moved in with Mom because I only planned to stay for a few months. But sometimes living and working with family, all day, everyday, got to be too much, especially since Sonny and I had been at each other's throats from the beginning. When I'd been home about two weeks, I'd slammed down the phone after an argument with Sonny and stomped out of my mother's house.

Mom and Dad's house in the harbor was a five-minute walk to the town dock, so I hadn't bought a car yet. That meant I was stuck. Then I remembered Gus's. I walked back over the top of the hill and down the other side and followed a long path past the boatyard to a low wooden building jutting over the water.

Gus's restaurant had an old gas pump with a round top out front, like something out of an Edward Hopper painting. Inside, you climbed down a long set of stairs into the main room where you found a candlepin-bowling lane on your left and a lunch counter on your right. In back was a dining room with the best view of Busman's Harbor anywhere.

Gus looked up from the grill when I walked in and growled, "Get out. No strangers." He was governed by the same public accommodation laws as any restaurant owner, but nevertheless had an ironclad rule. He didn't serve diners unless he knew them personally or someone he did know vouched them for. I have no idea how he got away with it.

"Gus, I'm Julia. Julia Snowden. I've been coming here all my life. For goodness sake, I was born here in the harbor."

Gus looked at me appraisingly. "Now Jul-ya, just because kittens are born in the oven don't make them biscuits." But then he said, "What'll ya have?" and I knew I was in.

His fare was simple in the extreme—hamburgers, cheeseburgers, BLTs, hot dogs, lobster rolls, and fried clam rolls—all served with the best French fries on the face of the earth. He bought his beef from Maine farmers and ground it fresh daily. He only served Maine clams and potatoes.

You would never see the word *artisanal* on Gus's menu. In fact, aside from the scrawl on the blackboard behind the counter, you'd never see a menu. Gus didn't prepare food that way because he was some kind of a locavore. He did it because that's the way he'd always done it. He'd missed the era of frozen food entirely, and now he was right back on trend. You had to reserve a slice of Gus's wife's scrumptious pie when you placed your meal order, because Gus didn't like to be surprised later. I ordered a cheeseburger, cherry cola, and a slice of three-berry pie.

It was late for lunch by harbor standards and I had the dining room to myself. Since my last visit, someone in town had placed signs around that said things like GUS DOESN'T SERVE HORS D'OEUVRES. HE DOESN'T BELIEVE YOU NEED FOOD WHILE WAITING FOR FOOD, and YOU CAN ASK GUS FOR SALAD. YOU'LL NEVER GET IT, BUT YOU CAN ASK FOR IT. I'd just settled back to sip my soda and stare dreamily at the view, when I heard the slam of a car door. I looked out the street-side window just in time to see a pair of work boots and jeans clattering down the stairs. I'm embarrassed to admit I recognized those legs before the head they were eventually attached to ever came into view. *Chris Durand.* I'd had a crush on him in junior high so strong I still felt its echoes.

Busman's Harbor's small junior high and high schools were in the same building. In seventh grade, I was assigned the locker next to Chris's. He was a junior and so handsome I'd go weak in my thirteen-year-old knees whenever he came near. If we happened to be at our lockers at the same time, I could barely breathe.

Chris, football player, reputed wild man, was kind to the shy girl with the crush. "Hey, beautiful," he'd say, while I fumbled with my lock or dropped my books. "How's it going?"

We went along like that for two years, until he graduated and I went away to boarding school. For a while, whenever I went home, I'd pump Livvie for the details of Chris's life. Who was he seeing? How was that going? She was sympathetic, but discouraging. I could tell she felt I wasn't in his league, so I eventually stopped with the questions.

I sat in my booth blushing furiously at the memory.

Chris placed his order—fried clam roll and coffee to go—and asked Gus, "Anybody here?"

"Julia Snowden. In the back. Take her these." Making patrons deliver food was just one of Gus's many charms.

I wasn't sure Chris would remember who I was. He'd never worked at the clambake, though he'd done just about every other job in town. But I was the only person in the dining room.

"Julia," Chris said, handing over the red gingham paper boats almost all Gus's food was served in. "You home now?"

"Just for the summer to help out with the business."

"Yeah, lots of people have moved home." For some reason, Chris having the idea I'd crawled back to live in my Mom's basement mortified me, but I couldn't figure out how to explain that wasn't the case without sounding defensive. It was such a longer story.

"What are you doing now?" I asked, the best defense being a good offense.

"Oh, you know." He rolled his impressive shoulders. "This and that. I own Harbor Cab. I landscape in season. And I'm still the bouncer at Crowley's."

I could believe it. The impressive shoulders were paired with an impressive set of biceps and a broad chest that tapered to a narrow waist and those long legs—

Geez, Julia. Get ahold of yourself. "That sounds great," I stammered.

I was saved by Gus calling to Chris that his order was ready.

"See ya around." Chris turned and walked away, proving the part about the landscaping. You don't get a backside like that from driving a cab. I hunkered down in the booth and ate every morsel of Gus's delicious meal, including the pie.

Since then, whenever we'd end up at Gus's at the same time, which seemed to be every Tuesday,

Thursday, and Saturday, Chris and I ate lunch together. It wasn't a thing, exactly. I'm not sure what it was. Chris became my sounding board, the person I poured my heart out to, cataloging my troubles, confessing my fear I wouldn't be able to save the clambake. He was the only person I ever talked to who wasn't a family member, an employee, or a vendor—in other words, who wasn't depending on the Snowden Family Clambake financially.

At least, he'd never been a vendor until I'd hired him to help Etienne and Sonny clear the winter's damage off Morrow Island and get it ready to open for the summer. So Chris knew Morrow Island. Really well. And he'd apparently been the last person in the harbor to see Ray Wilson alive.

Chapter 6

It was late afternoon by the time Lieutenant Binder told us we could return to town. Jamie came along on the *Jacquie II* and I was grateful for his presence. He'd worked at the clambake for so many summers it was like having another member of the crew. Somehow I'd missed him on my last couple holiday visits to the harbor, but we'd been so close as children, we fell right back into being comfortable with one another. He was a grown man, very much the cop, but I still saw the boy—long blond hair, nose perpetually peeling, baggy surfer shorts—when I looked at him. Jamie was like a cousin to Livvie and me.

On the ride back, I tried to get him to tell me something, anything, about the investigation. "Do they know yet if Ray Wilson was killed on the island or brought there dead?" I hoped my tone conveyed appropriate concern, not panic or morbid curiosity.

Jamie shut right down. When he was in his new police role, he wasn't the kid who waited for the school bus with me. He was all business. "You know I can't tell you that."

"It's just . . . I keep wondering why the island? Whoever took him there, killed him, and hung him up went to a lot of trouble. Why go through all that? What was the point?"

Jamie's blond brows rose, providing an even better view of his sky-blue eyes. His look communicated clearly he was getting a lot more out of me asking questions than I was going to get from him by way of answers.

"Just tell me this," I persisted. "How long do *you* think we'll be shut down?"

That did get me a look of sympathy, which scared me more than his just-the-facts-ma'am persona. "Julia, I'm sorry. I'm sure Lieutenant Binder told you it will take as long as it takes."

When we pulled into the harbor, the dock was in chaos. The wedding guests surged toward the boat, shouting questions, while the passengers rushed to get off. Sonny and Jamie immediately took charge, helping people disembark one at a time.

Michaela ran down the gangway and fell weeping into Tony's arms. He held her close, whispering into her hair. Around them, the crowd quieted, all eyes on the couple. At some point during the afternoon, Michaela had changed out of her wedding gown into a pair of tailored white trousers and a fitted navy blouse that must have been her "going away" outfit. She'd thought she'd be wearing those clothes as she and Tony sailed off as man and wife after their wedding reception. I wondered if she'd ever be able to wear them again.

Damn. That reminded me I had to cancel the little boat I'd hired to take them away.

The crowd shook itself alive and the low throb of chatter resumed. As Tony walked Michaela off the dock, my sister Livvie came out of our ticket booth, searching the crowd for Sonny and me. When she spotted us, she trotted over and hugged us each in turn.

"Oh my God, oh my God, oh my God." She let me go and stared at the two of us. "Oh, my God!"

"What's it been like here?" I asked.

"Insane." Livvie cocked her head toward the ticket booth, which I took to mean we should speak more privately. The three of us crowded into the little space, which was claustrophobic for one person . . . and Sonny was a big guy.

"It was awful," Livvie said. "There were police cars at the entrance to the dock, so people knew right away something was up. They'd walk up looking kind of uncertain and scared by all the uniforms and the people milling around. The state police took names from everyone and asked their relationship to Michaela and Tony. They said someone had died on the island and there wouldn't be a wedding. The police never exactly said it was a murder, but people aren't stupid. If it was an accident or a heart attack, why would cops be taking names and asking for their contact info?"

"Did the police question you?" Sonny asked.

Livvie nodded. "They asked a lot about Michaela and Tony. What did we know about them? Why did they hire us to do the reception? Did I know this Ray guy? I told them they had to talk to you, Julia. You were friends with them in New York."

Friends was a strong word for my relationship with Michaela, let alone Tony. Michaela and I had run on the periphery of the same crowd when I first got to New York. I assumed that's how she'd heard I'd moved to Maine to run a place that could host wedding receptions. But she and I had never been close—never been alone just the two of us, that I could remember. Tony was even more distant. Over the last couple of years, I'd seen him with Michaela at big parties, places far too noisy for conversation. I'd gotten to know them only slightly better while we were planning the wedding, but we definitely weren't friends.

I'd never met Ray at all. For all I knew, he was mixed up in something criminal in New York. I didn't wish anything worse for Tony and Michaela than they'd already been through, but I fervently hoped if Ray's death was a homicide, that it was trouble that had followed him to town. As much as I wanted to believe that, I couldn't reconcile the idea of a criminal from New York taking a man out to our island in the dead of night, landing a boat on our little beach, and then murdering him. Why go to so much trouble? I couldn't make sense of it.

Out on the dock, the crowd slowly dispersed.

"We should go back to Mom's. She and Page will be worried," Livvie said.

"You two go ahead. I'll be right along." I had a few things to take care of.

After Livvie and Sonny left, I called the lobster pound and canceled my order for the next day. I hoped they'd be able to sell some of what I'd contracted to other customers. We still had two hundred lobsters stored in the cold water under the dock on Morrow Island, and I didn't know when we'd be able to use them. I also canceled the clams, the eggs, and the produce.

I was pretty sure, small-town grapevines being what they were, all our employees, let alone every-one in Busman's Harbor, knew we wouldn't be opening tomorrow. I sent a group e-mail just in case, grateful this form of communication demanded brevity. No explanations or predictions about the future required.

As I locked up the ticket booth, Sarah Halsey approached. She was one of Livvie's closest friends and a teacher at Busman's Elementary. Both she and her mother worked summers at the clambake. Neither of them had been booked to work at the wedding—the smaller crowd meant a lighter staff—but they were both scheduled to work the next day, which should have been the first day the Snowden Family Clambake was open to the general public.

"No work tomorrow, huh?" Sarah said it pleasantly, but I could hear the tiny bit of worry in her voice. Teachers in Maine don't get paid much, and she was the single parent to a nine-year-old son.

"Not tomorrow, Sarah."

"What do you think about Monday?"

What indeed? "I'll let you know as soon as I know."

"Thanks, Julia. Take care."

"'Bye, Sarah. See you . . . soon."

Chapter 7

I walked the block from the town dock to my mother's house. Perched at the peak of the hill that formed the residential part of Busman's Harbor, the house was a solid foursquare with a cupola on top of its flat, mansard roof. The house was painted a deep yellow with dark green trim and you could see it from anywhere around, land or sea. I always felt it was like a bright beacon leading me home.

My father bought the house for my mother before I was born. A town person marrying a summer person was unusual, but even rarer when my parents wed thirty-two years ago—especially a union between a high school educated boy and a girl from a family who owned an island. My father built the Snowden Family Clambake Company because he loved my mother. He understood that even though she loved him, she wasn't prepared to be poor. Her hopes and dreams weren't outlandish, but she expected a roof over her head, heat in the winter, and to give her daughters the same kind of education she had received. So my father built the clambake company to provide all that, and to keep Morrow Island in the family. For my mother, who loved it.

When I came along, I dutifully followed the path my parents set for me. Prep school in New Hampshire, college in Massachusetts, business school in New York City followed by a job at a top venture capital firm, each step taking me farther in every way from Maine.

My sister Livvie, two years younger, rebelled at every chance. She'd finally flunked out of so many prep schools my parents relented and let her finish high school in the harbor. At eighteen, she got engaged to Sonny Ramsey whose father was a local lobsterman. She got married and got pregnant, though not, as she'll cheerfully tell you, "necessarily in that order." She gave birth to my niece Page.

Our life trajectories seemed set. Livvie stayed in Maine with her little family and she and Sonny joined the clambake business. My life was in Manhattan. But then came Dad's awful diagnosis and his death, followed by the recession, and finally, the frantic phone call from Livvie. So, I was back in the last place I expected to be.

I found Mom in the kitchen with Page, my nine-year-old niece. Mom stood at the counter chopping vegetables for salad. She was small like me. Or rather, I was small like her. Livvie got my father's height and athletic build and auburn hair. I got Mom's petite blondness. But that was where our resemblance ended. My mother was all romance. I was all practicality.

Page folded dinner napkins at the kitchen table, her head bobbing up and down to a tune playing in her head. She had Sonny's fiery red hair and Livvie's tall, swimmer's build. She'd be a gorgeous adult, but I feared in the next few years she'd grow to hate her bright hair, lightly freckled skin, and height. I hoped with all my heart she'd mature through that phase and remain the special person she was. Page's warmth, innocence, and humor had held our family together during my Dad's illness and gave us all, especially my mother, a reason to go on afterward.

"Julia, how are you?" Mom's eyes slid meaningfully toward Page. I understood we weren't to discuss murder in front of my niece. Ray Wilson's death would be the talk of our little town for weeks to come, so Livvie and Sonny would have to find a way to explain it, but later, in their own home.

I responded, "Fine," in the same chipper tone my mother had used. "What's for dinner?"

"Lobster mac and cheese." Mom indicated the contents of the heavy glass pan bubbling away in the oven.

"Oh—"

"Livvie made it this morning before she went to work."

Thank goodness. My mother was a terrible cook. Livvie, on the other hand, was world-class, and lobster mac and cheese was one of her specialties.

"Why don't you let Page and I finish up?" Mom said.

The rich aroma of sweet lobster meat and sharp cheese filled the room. My tummy rumbled in response, reminding me I'd eaten next to nothing all day.

I grabbed a Sea Dog ale from the fridge and joined Livvie and Sonny on our wide front porch. The heavy, wood-framed windows were still up and I looked through the wavy glass out toward the harbor and its six tiny islands. Morrow Island was farther out, beyond the harbor's mouth. My mother claimed she could see it from the cupola at the top of our house. Sonny, Livvie, and I knew that was impossible, but in the years since my father's death, we'd given up arguing with her.

"I'll take these porch windows down tomorrow, put up the screens," Sonny said. "Might as well. No work."

"So what do we think?" Livvie asked from her seat on the porch swing. "Who did it?" Like most Mainers, Livvie was nothing if not direct.

"From the questions the cops asked you, sounds like they think it's trouble Wilson brought with him from New York," Sonny answered. He turned toward me. "Were these people into something shady there?"

"I don't know. I barely know Tony and I'd never met Ray." I flashed on the body hanging from the grand staircase at Windsholme.

"So that's it then," Livvie was as eager as I was to pin the murder on outsiders.

"But why on the island?" I asked them the question that had bugged me from the beginning.

When no one had an answer, Sonny offered an alternative. "Chris Durand was the last to person in the harbor to see the dead guy."

"I'm sure Chris had nothing to do with it," I responded, a little too vehemently.

"Julia, I know you and Chris have this *thing*," Sonny said. "But that doesn't mean he couldn't have done it."

"What *thing*?" I glared at Livvie. *Betrayer.*

"That thing where you eat lunch with him at Gus's three times a week," Sonny answered.

Oh, that thing. I remembered what I hated about living in a small town.

Sonny continued relentlessly. "I know you have a big blind spot where Chris Durand is concerned, but that doesn't mean he isn't involved."

"I don't know what you're talking about."

"You do," Sonny insisted. "He's been in and out of trouble since high school."

I looked at Livvie to see if she was going to give

me any help, but she sat on the swing, apparently in agreement with her husband.

"Chris is a respected citizen of Busman's Harbor." My voice rose. "He owns three businesses in this town. God forbid if we were all judged by the things we did in high school. You especially, Sonny."

"You don't live here, Julia," Sonny raised his voice to meet my own. "I do. I hear stuff. Current stuff."

"What stuff?" I demanded. I'd been arguing with Sonny so long and hard all spring, it was reflexive. I yelled, he yelled. Such a well-worn road.

"Dinner."

The three of us had been so caught up, we hadn't heard Page open the front door. "What are you guys fighting about?"

"Nothing important, honey," Livvie jumped off the swing and moved toward her daughter. "You know how Daddy and Aunt Julia are."

"Always yelling," Page grumbled.

Livvie put an arm around Page and escorted her into the house, followed by Sonny. I brought up the rear. Passing him on the way into the dining room, driven, as always, to have the last word, I hissed, "Even if Chris had something to do with it, which I totally discount, it still doesn't answer the question *why on the island?*"

Chapter 8

Livvie's mac and cheese was the perfect comfort food at the end of a long, horrible day. I ate heartily, savoring the rich tanginess of the cheese combined with the sweetness of the lobster. The tastes and textures perfectly complimented one another—the springy noodles and toothsome lobster along with the crunchy panko breadcrumb topping. People asked if I ever got tired of lobster. I'd discussed this with the family who owned the ice cream parlor in town, who fielded similar questions. The simple answer was no. If you loved something, you loved it.

After dinner was cleared up and Livvie, Sonny, and Page finally went home, I climbed the back stairs to my room and fell exhausted onto my bed. I wanted nothing more than to sleep. But once I was cleaned up and properly tucked in, sleep didn't come. I couldn't stop worrying about the clambake.

In the clambake business, when a day was lost, it was lost forever. The income projected for this weekend was gone, our ability to make it up later severely hampered by the short Maine summer season. I knew if we were still closed on Monday I'd have to have a conversation with our banker. And I knew it wouldn't be pleasant.

I lay awake, doing calculations in my head. What if we were still closed on Monday? On Tuesday? Wednesday? Being shut down through the next weekend would be catastrophic. I was certain if that happened, the bank would call our loan. I tossed and turned and started calculating again.

Eventually, counting our potential losses had the same effect as counting sheep, and I nodded off. But then, in that split second of twilight between conscious and unconscious, a vision of that awful, inert body hanging from the stairs leaped into my brain. My eyes flew open and I was wide-awake again. I couldn't stop picturing how dead Ray Wilson was. Even in the few moments I'd stared at his body, I'd known there was no spark of life.

I started the counting again, and the cycle repeated—the nodding off, the awful vision, the wide-awakeness, then back to the counting. I don't know how many times it happened, but it felt like most of the night. I must have slept some, but even those periods were disturbed by a dream where I ran from place to disconnected place—

Manhattan, Busman's Harbor and towns I didn't recognize—struggling to tell people a man was about to be killed, but unable to produce a sound.

At dawn, I gave up and climbed out of my girl-hood bed. Sunrise came early in coastal Maine. I looked longingly at the door connecting my room to Livvie's old bedroom, wishing she were there so I'd have someone to talk to. I dressed quickly, though I had nowhere to go.

I considering putting on coffee and making breakfast, but the house felt like a cage. I had too much energy to be indoors. I headed out, not thinking about where I was walking, but somehow making a beeline for Gus's.

The restaurant was packed with lobstermen, fishermen, the crew who ran the whale watch, and the ferrymen who took people to the summer colony on Chipmunk Island. Was it my imagina-tion or did the noise level fall when I walked into the place? The murder on Morrow Island was the biggest news to hit Busman's Harbor in years. It had to be the main topic of conversation, but no one came up to ask questions. No one spoke to me at all, a benefit of that famous Maine reticence.

I looked around hopefully for Chris Durand, but he wasn't there.

Jamie Dawes was, however, sitting at a round

table with the officer who'd taken him out to the island. They were in uniform, which I thought was a hopeful sign, ready to get to work nice and early. I briefly debated whether it would be weirder if I walked over to their table, or weirder if I didn't. I decided on weirder if I didn't and approached.

"Hey, Jamie."

"Julia. This is Officer Howland. I'm not sure if you met yesterday."

"Not properly. Hello, Officer. I think you were in my brother-in-law Sonny's class at Busman High."

Howland grunted in my direction around a mouthful of eggs.

"Are you going out to Morrow today?"

Jamie gestured toward the empty chairs at their table. "Yep. Waiting for the state police detectives and the crime scene team to get here from Augusta."

"Thanks."

As I walked back toward the counter, I was grateful for Gus's "no strangers" policy. At least I wouldn't run into any of the wedding guests, though I had to admit that was unlikely so early in the morning. I grabbed a stool at one end of the C-shaped counter.

Behind it, Gus unhurriedly fried bacon and made pancakes, despite the size of the crowd. He didn't vary his pace for anyone. "You're up early," he said as he poured my coffee.

"Couldn't sleep."

"Ayup. Clam hash?"

Among the cognoscenti, which is to say the locals, Gus's clam hash was famous. Like any hash, it's made with lots of onions and potatoes, but he uses clams instead of beef or corned beef. The fresh, diced clams give the hash a salty-sweet taste that cannot be beat. And if you ask for it, he will top the hash with one or two perfectly poached eggs.

"Yes, please. With one egg."

"Because one egg is un oeuf." Gus repeated the oldest joke in the world.

Sitting diagonally across from me on the long side of the counter was a man dressed differently from everyone else in the place. He had on a tweed sports coat and a tailored blue shirt, and was reading, my heart went pit-a-pat the *New York Times*. He was one of my people.

Suddenly, I was homesick for Manhattan. It was all I could do to keep from hiking out to the highway and sticking out my thumb. Back to the land of fresh bagels, high salaries and, best of all, no family responsibilities.

I stared at the backside of the man's newspaper. It had to be yesterday's. It would be hours before the Sunday *Times* made it to our end of the peninsula. But no, he was reading the wedding notices from the *Times* "Sunday Styles" section. My favorite part of the weekend. Where had he gotten hold of it?

"Do you two know each other?" Gus asked. "Quentin here's from New York City, too."

"Not everyone in New York knows everyone else," I said more grumpily than Gus deserved. I knew he didn't think that.

He put my order down in front of me. I cut into the egg and watched its exquisitely cooked yolk run onto my hash. I put a fork full into my mouth and felt my mood lift.

The man waved at me across the counter. He was pleasant looking, somewhere in his mid-forties, with dark blond hair, expensively cut. "Quentin Tupper."

Tupper. That explained his presence at Gus's. Like me, he was a legacy. The Tuppers were an old Maine family with many branches. If my father had been alive, he could have given me a complete genealogy and told me whose son Quentin was. But I'd never be able to ask my dad those kinds of questions again.

I leaned across the counter and stuck out my hand. "Julia." I left off my last name in case he'd already heard about the murder at the Snowden Family Clambake. It was the last subject I wanted to talk about.

Quentin asked me where I lived in the city, and I told him. As was so often the case when Manhattanites were out of town, we discovered we lived four blocks from one another and shopped at the same delis, lingered in the same coffee shops. While I sopped up the end of my egg with a piece of toast, we had a long chat about our neighborhood. I even forgot for one brief moment about the events of the previous day.

Gus's was all but empty by the time I finished eating. The harbor workers had places to go and it would be a couple hours before the after-church crowd arrived. Quentin Tupper finished his coffee and paid his bill. "Lovely to meet you," he said.

I said the same and he took off, leaving me alone at the counter with Gus.

The only people still in the dining room were Jamie and Officer Howland. I couldn't help myself. I approached them again. "Still waiting, huh?"

Jamie nodded. "They called. They were too late to have breakfast with us, but they're here now. We're meeting them at the station house."

"You know it's really important to me to be up and running again as soon as possible, right?" I tried to keep any hint of whine out of my voice, though I'm not sure I succeeded. Officer Howland gathered up his trash and stomped off toward the barrel.

"Julia, I get it." Jamie stood to leave. "I told you yesterday, you can't rush this."

"Well, if you think I can open tomorrow, can

you try to let me know in time for me to place food orders?"

"I'll make sure the state police are aware of your time constraints," Jamie answered formally. Then, in a friendlier tone, he added, "Honestly, that's the best I can do."

What could I say to that? I thanked him, returned to the counter, and asked Gus for my check.

Chapter 9

Just as I was about to say good-bye to Gus, a familiar pair of legs came galumphing down the restaurant stairs. "Hey, beautiful," Chris Durand called.

The place was empty except for the two of us. And Gus, of course. I looked down at my new uniform—Snowden Family Clambake sweatshirt, jeans, and work boots. Clearly, "hey, beautiful," was a meaningless greeting as far as Chris was concerned.

"Keep me company while I eat breakfast?" he asked.

"It's the middle of the day for you."

"The cops want to see me again at nine. I figure I better get something in my stomach. Might be there for a while. My day is shot, anyhow."

While Chris placed his order, I went to the dining room and sat down in the booth that, somehow over the last couple months, I'd come to think of as "ours."

Chris came in and sat across from me. He was so handsome that even all those years past my seventh grade crush, he took my breath away. He had light brown hair worn a little too long and the most astonishing pair of green eyes. His strong chin, covered with a day's growth of beard, had at its center, God help me, a dimple. At thirty-four, his face had weathered from outdoor work, but that only added to his charm.

"How are you doing?" I asked.

"Moved down to my boat on Saturday." Chris owned a beautiful wooden sailboat, the *Dark Lady*, a thirty-three foot Maine-made Hinckley he kept in the marina just around the bend from Gus's place. He also owned a lakeside cabin he'd purchased from his parents when they couldn't take the winters anymore and fled south. Every summer, he rented out the lake house for the season and moved onto the *Dark Lady*. Even with three jobs, it was the only way to afford both.

"That's not what I meant." I could tell he hadn't misunderstood. He was deliberately avoiding the topic of the murder.

"I know," he admitted.

I'd discovered Ray Wilson's body on Morrow Island, and Chris had, apparently, been the last person known to see him on the mainland. The two events were separated by time and geography, but it still felt to me like we'd shared a traumatic experience. My sense was we needed to talk about it.

"Okay," Chris said as if reading my thoughts. "You first."

I walked him through that morning. Waiting for Ray on the *Jacquie II*. Tony leaving to search for him. Michaela's nervousness on the boat. The moment when I opened the doors at Windsholme and saw what I saw.

"So he was just hanging there? That's tough."

The sympathy in his voice brought tears to my eyes. It was the first time, awake and fully conscious, I allowed myself to feel the horror of what had happened . . . because I felt so safe when I was with Chris.

I focused on lining up the salt and pepper shakers, the sugar, syrup, and catsup bottles in a row and managed not to cry. "But what about you? The state police want to see you again?"

"Two hours yesterday. More today. You heard I drove the victim back to his hotel Friday night in my cab? Of course you did. Everyone in town knows it."

In a bigger town, it might be considered a conflict of interest for the bouncer in a bar to have the power to take away a patron's keys and then load that person into a cab the bouncer owned. But in Busman's Harbor everyone wore multiple hats and we thought nothing of it.

Gus dropped a huge plate of blueberry pancakes and a side of bacon in front of Chris. "Thanks." Chris was genuinely surprised. Gus didn't believe in table service.

"Don't get used to it."

Chris picked the plastic maple syrup dispenser out of the little formation I'd created and applied its contents to his pancakes.

"Tell me, from the beginning," I said.

He dug into his pancakes and ate. The moment stretched and I wondered if he was going to say anything. Finally, he spoke. "They all came into Crowley's about ten, a little after. Since it's so early in the season, I was the only bouncer on, working just inside the door, checking IDs. From there, I can keep my eye on the bar and the dance floor, pretty much the whole place."

"And by 'they all' you mean . . . ?"

"The bride, the groom, the best man, and three bridesmaids."

The entire wedding party, except Michaela's teenaged brothers, who were too young to go out to a bar after the rehearsal dinner. By three bridesmaids, Chris meant the maid of honor and the two others. I didn't correct him.

"Were they drunk?"

"Not when they arrived. A couple of the brides-maids were a little silly, but I've seen people come

in a whole lot worse. The bride wasn't drinking—
she had seltzer and lime—and the groom nursed
one beer the whole time he was there."

Made sense, the happy couple would have
wanted to be bright-eyed for the big day.

"And Ray Wilson?"

"I'd have sworn he was stone cold sober when
he came in, but I must be losing my eye, because
after a couple drinks, he was completely gone.
And you know the drinks at Crowley's."

Over-priced and watered-down, especially for
tourists. And more watered-down later in the
evening. "So what happened?"

"The best man and the bridesmaids all got
pretty happy. There was a lot of dancing, initially
as a group, but later with some of the other customers."

"Many local people there?"

"Aside from the employees? Just a few."

Crowley's is mostly too expensive for the na-
tives. "Any of my people?"

"*Your* people?" Chris grinned, but he knew what
I meant. "I don't think so."

But then, he paused. I sensed there was something he wasn't telling. "What? Who?"

"Sarah came in about 10:30."

"Sarah Halsey?"

"She works for you."

"Yeah. I'm just surprised. A schoolteacher with
a kid at home—"

"She's not allowed to blow off a little steam?"

"Sure, I guess." I indicated he should go on.

"The groom left after about half an hour."

"Wait. Tony left?" It seemed odd for the groom to leave his own party so quickly. "Why?"

Chris shrugged his shoulders. "No idea. I didn't think about it at the time. Anyway, not too long after that, the best man started drinking heavily, getting handsy with the women on the dance floor, stumbling. At a little before one, the bride and bridesmaids wanted to leave. The bride told Wilson to go back to his hotel and go to bed. He refused. She was pretty mad. They were both yelling. So I stepped in and told her I'd take care of him."

"And?"

"The ladies left. It was almost closing and the place had really emptied out, so I left the bartender to close up, put the best man in my cab, and drove him to the Lighthouse."

The Lighthouse Inn was a large hotel about five minutes from Crowley's. It was called the Lighthouse because, rumor had it, from one of its thirty-eight rooms, if you leaned as far over the balcony as was humanly possible, you could see Dinkums Light. Ray and a number of the wedding guests were staying there.

"Did you walk him inside?"

"Nope. Now I wish I had. I wish I'd tucked him into bed, to tell you the truth. I thought he could make it on his own. Last I saw him, he was stumbling

out of my cab toward the lobby." Chris rubbed a
hand over the stubble on his chin. The chin with
the dimple. "That's all I got."

He glanced over my head at the big clock over
the threshold between Gus's dining room and the
counter area. I've always felt the clock was Gus's
way of saying, "You've finished eating. Now get
the hell out of here."

"Can't keep the cops waiting." Chris stood and
I did, too. I wanted to go with him to the police
station, but figured that wouldn't look good, what
with him being the last to see Ray and me finding
the body. I wanted to give him a hug, but we'd
never actually touched. So I walked him to the
front door and wished him good luck.

"Earth to Julia."

I realized I was standing in the front room of
Gus's, my mind a million miles away, while Gus
refilled the saltshakers and the catsup bottles and
got ready for the post-church rush. I grabbed a
gallon jug of syrup from behind the counter and
helped out. Preparing to feed a big crowd was
something I knew how to do.

We worked in silence for a while, then Gus said,
"I'm sorry for your trouble. Is it bad?" He knew
the murder was bad. He was asking about the
business.

"I don't know when they're going to let us open.

Every day that goes by is killing us financially."
And increasing the chances the bank would call
our loan. "That's assuming anyone will want to
come party on an island where there's been a grisly
murder."

"Don't worry. You'll probably get so many of
those rubberneckers out to see where it happened, you'll make more money than ever."

"Maybe." I wasn't comforted. I didn't like the
idea of profiting from Ray Wilson's death.

"The police know who did it?"

"I don't think so. From the questions they
asked her yesterday, Livvie thinks it's got something to do with the people from New York who
hired us to do their wedding reception."

"The state police think people from New York
City took a man out to your island in the middle
of the night and strung him up on your staircase?"

"Absurd, isn't it?"

"State cops. They don't know this harbor." In
Gus's opinion nobody from out of town knew
much of anything, but he had a point. Busman's
residents knew how hard it would be to take
someone out to Morrow in the dark, but would
state cops know?

"I think this murder will finally bankrupt the
Snowden Family Clambake," I said. "And the worst
part is, there is not one thing I can do about it."

That did seem like the absolutely worst part. I'd
put my career and my life in New York on hold.

I'd worked like a dog all spring and battled with Sonny. And none of it was going to matter. We were going to succumb to something completely beyond my control.

Gus wasn't having any of it. "Now Julia Snowden, I don't want to hear you talk that way. Your business is too important to this town. We can't be losing any more employers. You say there's not a thing you can do? Do you know these people who hired you to do the wedding, the ones from New York?"

"Vaguely."

"Do you know them better than the state cops do?"

"Maybe, but—"

"And do you know Morrow Island better than the state cops do, and who might have business there?"

"Of course, but—"

"And aside from the dead man's family, is there anyone who has more interest in getting this murder solved than you do?"

"Probably no, but—"

Gus wagged a finger at me. "'Not a thing you can do about it.' We don't talk that way in Busman's Harbor, Maine, missy. I'm sure you if think about it, you'll know exactly what you have to do."

Chapter 10

I climbed the steps from Gus's restaurant to the street. Gus was right. Nobody in town cared as much about solving the murder of Ray Wilson as I did. But that didn't mean I knew what to do.

I did absolutely know what I *didn't* want to do. Yet, inescapably, it was the thing I had to do next.

A couple months earlier when they booked the reception, Michaela and Tony had given me a deposit for half the wedding costs. Yesterday morning, before the whole day exploded, they'd given me a check for the balance. Depositing the second check would be wrong. Our contract gave me the right to, but Michaela and Tony hadn't, at the end of the day, had a wedding. The circumstances were so extraordinary I didn't think it was the right time to be a stickler for legalities.

But I was already out of pocket for more than the original deposit check covered.

I needed to have a conversation with Tony and Michaela about money, and much as I didn't want to have it on the day after their best man was found murdered and their wedding spoiled, I did want to have it in person. That meant catching them while they were still in town.

I dialed their hotel room from my cell.

Michaela picked up and told me they'd just returned from another interview with the state police. They'd meet me in the hotel dining room for coffee.

Michaela and Tony had stayed overnight in the honeymoon suite at the Bellevue Inn, a rambling wooden structure on the other side of the harbor from the hotels and B&Bs where their guests were staying. I'm sure the isolation had seemed like a great idea when they made their reservation, though I wondered how they were feeling about it now.

The breakfast crowd had almost cleared out of the dining room by the time I got to the Bellevue. I spotted Michaela and Tony in a quiet corner and rushed toward Michaela to give her a hug. She stood and returned it. Even more than I had with Chris, I felt like she and I were comrades who'd been to war together, and talking about money seemed even more uncomfortable. But once I'd sat down and poured a cup of coffee from the carafe on the table, Tony leveled his gaze at me and said, "You're here about the bill."

I knew they were paying for the wedding themselves, and I'm not sure why, but I had the impression Tony was the source of most of the funds. I nodded, indicating I was, indeed, there to talk about the money.

"How much are you out of pocket over and above our original deposit?" Tony asked.

"The lobsters are alive, stored under our dock," I said. "If the police give us permission to open tomorrow, I can use them. And I can resell the liquor. But the rest of the food, the flowers, and the fuel for one roundtrip on the *Jacquie II* . . ."

I gave a figure and, to his credit, Tony didn't flinch. Across the table, Michaela remained silent, though she did sigh softly when I mentioned the flowers. I was sure she was thinking about her hopes for a beautiful day and all she'd lost.

"And the labor cost?" Tony prompted.

That was the part of the conversation I dreaded. People were the biggest expense of running the clambake. True, most of the employees hadn't actually worked. But they'd lost the day and most couldn't afford to lose the wages. I gave Tony the amount.

"And the gratuity?"

A service charge would have been added to the bill to be pooled and split by the employees. But that was the problem. There had been no service. I hesitated.

"Just tell me how much." Tony sat, pencil poised over the paper napkin he'd been taking notes on. "I want to pay it all. There's no reason for your employees to suffer because of what happened."

I named another figure. Tony wrote it down. As he added up the numbers, I studied him and Michaela. If long-term couples grow to look alike, they had a significant head start. Both were dark-haired and dark-eyed, and each possessed a pair of perfectly arched eyebrows. His were not in the least feminine, and hers were not at all masculine, but both pairs were striking in their shape. Each had a gender-appropriate version of the same long-limbed body, and they moved with the kind of casual grace the rest of us noticed and envied. As I watched them, Tony reached across the table without even looking at Michaela and grabbed her hand as if he always knew by some sort of built-in sonar where every part of her body was in relation to his own.

I genuinely liked Michaela, but something about Tony caused me to keep my guard up. I was relieved he was willing to pay the employees. It would be much harder to manage the clambake if word got around we'd stiffed people. But he was being too agreeable. Too generous. Why? Did he want to get this sad business over and done? Or did he have some other reason to care whether the citizens of Busman's Harbor thought well of him?

"What are you planning for the rest of your day?" I asked.

"The police said we could leave, so we're headed to Bath to spend time with Tony's parents." Michaela's dabbed at her eyes with her napkin.

I looked at Tony. "You're from Bath?" That was a surprise. Bath was just a twenty-five minute drive south along Maine's jagged coast.

"Both Ray and I are. Were," Tony replied. "We grew up together."

How could I not have known? I could've sworn when Tony introduced me to his parents on board the *Jacquie II*, he said they'd just flown up from Florida. Then again, that wasn't an unusual migration for an older Maine couple.

"That's why we chose your place for the wedding," Michaela said.

"I thought it was because you knew me in New York."

Michaela shook her head. "No, no, no. Tony picked your place."

Tony signaled for the waitress and signed the bill for our coffee. "We've got to get going and pack the cars," he said to Michaela.

"Cars?" I said. "You didn't ride up together?"

"Michaela came up early to meet her family," Tony answered. "I was supposed to drive up with Ray, but when he came to pick me up, he had a big camp trunk taking up the whole backseat of his Porsche. There was no way his little car was going to fit me, Ray, his luggage, and all my luggage for the wedding and the honeymoon. So I drove myself up." Tony shook his head and smiled. "Freakin' Ray."

Big camp trunk? Wasn't that a little odd? "What did he say was in the trunk?"

"He didn't. Some stupid thing would be my guess." Tony smiled again indulgently. "Some prop for the best man speech or some other prank."

"Did you tell the police about the trunk?"

"They didn't ask. But they took all the stuff from his hotel room into evidence and towed his car from the lot at the Lighthouse Inn, so I guess they've found the trunk by now."

Chapter 11

On my way back across the footbridge, I stopped halfway, took off my sweatshirt, and tied it around my waist. The day was still cool, but the sun was beginning to work its magic. A perfect day for a clambake. It was supposed to be our first day open to the general public for the season. I didn't want to think about it.

I put my elbows on the rough wooden handrail and stared across the harbor, past its little islands to its mouth. Ray was from Bath, Maine. That increased the odds tremendously that he had the skills to get himself out to Morrow Island in the dark. It also meant he knew people who lived not too far away from Busman's Harbor. For the first time, I began to believe Ray's murder was the result of some trouble that had followed him to Morrow Island.

Even if some out-of-towner, whether from New York or Bath, had killed Ray, I still couldn't imagine why the murder was committed on our island. And why had Ray's body been left hanging in Windsholme?

I looked out at the harbor. Over the last few months, it had come alive. When I arrived in March, there'd been no boats in the frozen water. By the end of April, most of the working lobster and fishing boats were out or at least being readied for the season. In May, the tour boats came—day boats and whale watchers, the ferries to Chipmunk Island, and our own *Jacquie II*. Now the pleasure boats were beginning to arrive— cabin cruisers, beautiful sailboats, catamarans, and the yachts. Some came from Florida or the Caribbean, others from just down the coast. It felt great to see the harbor bustling, and I stood for a moment and enjoyed it all—the sun, the salt air, the *clang-clang* of the warning buoys out on the water.

On a map, Busman's Harbor looked like the silhouette of the head and claws of a lobster dangling from the Maine coast into the sea. The residential part of town was built on the lobster's head, my parents' house sitting at its highest point. Off the lobster's right shoulder was the inner harbor, lined with hotels and restaurants. On the other side, off the lobster's left shoulder, was the back harbor where the working boats were anchored. The boatyard was there, with Gus's restaurant nestled just beyond it. The points of land that made up the lobster's claws surrounded the big outer harbor as if holding it in an embrace, and left an opening to the ocean just wide and deep enough for commercial traffic. These points, where the millionaires lived, were called Eastclaw and Westclaw.

As I stood on the footbridge, drinking in the sights and sounds of the awakening harbor, I was surprised to see the Boston Whaler we kept at Morrow Island speeding toward the town dock. I squinted to see who was in it. The royal blue baseball cap and matching windbreaker told me it was Etienne steering the small boat. I hurried the rest of the way across the footbridge to meet him.

Etienne tied up the Whaler and was just coming up the dock when I got there.

"Hey there," I called. "What are you doing here?" I tried to sound chipper, as though my question was motivated by simple curiosity, but that's not the way I felt. I wanted to say *I was counting on you to stay on the island and make sure those people from the crime scene investigation team don't destroy it.* Or, *I'm surprised the police let you off the island.* Or, *You hardly ever leave the island during the summer.* But I didn't say any of those things.

"The lieutenant wants to talk to me again."

So Lieutenant Binder isn't out supervising the crime scene team on the island. He must be the one Chris,

Tony and Michaela had their interviews with this morning. I said to Etienne, "I'm sorry this has been such an ordeal for you."

"The police are convinced I must have heard something that night. To tell you the truth, I am happy to be off the island. They have asked us to stay in the house. Out the windows, we see them searching every blade of grass, stomping in and out of Windsholme with their dirty boots. It is like a violation. I could not stand to watch. That sergeant said to come to town. So I have."

I believed what Etienne said, he couldn't stand to see the state police having their way with the island. He probably also couldn't stand sitting in his house. Being still wasn't one of his talents. He was built for constant work.

Etienne and Gabrielle had a nice house on the mainland where they spent the off-season. It was an old farmhouse with a pond, just a couple miles out of town. During the winter, he toiled in his woodshop making large wooden animal sculptures that were sold in shops up and down the coast. She hand sewed quilts that fetched breathtaking prices in the same stores. They always rented their farmhouse out for the entire summer season. The same family had taken it for years.

"How's Gabrielle doing with all this?"

"Not well. I tried to get her to come to town with me, but she doesn't like to leave the island in the summer. She's lying down."

Gabrielle lying down in the middle of the day? I could barely imagine it.

She had always been shy and far more self-conscious about her English than was warranted. It was actually quite fluent when you got her talking, but that was rare. An angular woman with graying hair cut in a neat pageboy, she wore dresses, never pants, and sensible shoes. I couldn't remember ever seeing her, morning, noon, or night without an apron on. When we were little, Livvie and I had giggled about Gabrielle wearing her apron to bed. She had a vast collection, mostly floral prints, bib-front style, she'd made herself.

Livvie had told me Gabrielle's shyness had become even more severe in recent years. She was too wedded to her routines and her places, Livvie thought. Changes in plans and unexpected events made her anxious and there had been so many unexpected events on Morrow Island in the last two days.

"She waits for him," Etienne said.

His expression was so sad I reached out and touched his shoulder. It was solid muscle. "I know."

Etienne and Gabrielle's son, Jean-Jacques, had been a year ahead of me in school. He was quiet like his mother and a hard worker like both his parents. We'd grown up together on the island and worked at the clambake every summer. Jean-Jacques and I had had an easy day-to-day relationship, like siblings. But he was hard to know.

At school, his parents' foreignness made him something of a curiosity. We had that "outsiderness" in common. He with his Québécois parents, and me with the mother who'd been a summer person. Following high school, he'd gone to the University of Maine, but it didn't take. He drifted back, worked different jobs in the harbor, and joined the army after 9/11. He stayed in for two tours, first to Afghanistan, and then Iraq.

Six years ago, his parents held a party for him when he was home on leave. I wasn't there, but my parents were, along with Livvie and Sonny. Jean-Jacques had accepted everyone's well wishes in his quiet way, then walked out of the house, down the road, and was never seen again. At least, as far as I or anyone in my family knew. Perhaps Etienne and Gabrielle knew more, but they didn't say.

It might have seemed strange to many people that Gabrielle waited for Jean-Jacques in a place with no phones or cell coverage, a place that could only be reached by boat. But I understood her vigil. Morrow Island was where Jean-Jacques had spent every summer of his childhood. It was as much in his blood as it was in mine. That's where he would return.

Etienne and I stood in silence for a moment, lost in our own thoughts.

"I'll walk with you."

"To the police station?"

"Now that I'm sure Lieutenant Binder's there, I want to ask him again when we can open."

Chapter 12

The police station was part of Busman's Harbor's relatively new fire department-town offices-police complex. The huge bays for the fire department rigs—one each for ladder truck, pumper, and ambulance—dominated the front of the building. Etienne and I cut around the side to the police department entrance. Normally, it was a sleepy little place. The two full-time officers on duty on each shift were always off on patrol, and if you were lucky you might catch the chief at his desk doing paperwork. Today, the place hummed with activity. State cops, local cops, and cops from the county sheriff's office were all crammed into the small room, working two and even three to a desk.

I waited while Etienne gave his name and was led off into a small warren of cubicles by a policeman in plainclothes.

"Good luck!" I called after him, then wondered

if that was the wrong thing to say. Did it imply he needed luck?

I gave my name to the harried-looking female civilian employee behind the desk and asked to see Lieutenant Binder.

"Sorry, he's in a meeting. Can't be disturbed."

"Even if I know who killed Ray Wilson?"

The woman looked up sharply. "Do you?"

"No," I admitted. "But I really need to talk to him."

The woman got up and went through the door behind her into the giant multipurpose room where our town meetings were held. I caught a quick glimpse as the door opened and closed behind her. Chris was still there, sitting across the table from Binder. I had only a partial view of his back, but I recognized him instantly—the curve of the face in profile and the clothes. It was definitely him. How long had he been there? He'd left Gus's more than two hours before.

The woman reappeared. "Sorry, Lieutenant Binder can't be interrupted."

I turned and left the police station discouraged, heading toward home.

As I passed the Snuggles Inn, a B&B across from my parents' house, Michaela's maid of honor Lynn stomped out onto the porch, struggling with a rolling suitcase, a garment bag, and a tote. She looked frazzled, to put it mildly. Her hair was in the same up-do she'd had yesterday for the wedding. She'd obviously slept in it. She was wearing yoga pants and a pink T-shirt and her pink-painted toes were shoved into flip-flops.

"Let me give you a hand." I took the garment bag and tote so she could concentrate on pulling the suitcase along the inn's uphill front walk. She needed the help, but I also thought it might be my only chance to talk to her. Gus's challenge from this morning still rung in my ears. I had to solve my own problems.

"That's my car." Lynn nodded toward a mid-sized convertible with its top down parked in front. She put the suitcase on the backseat, turned toward the front door of the Snuggles, and screeched, "Beanie, get your butt out here! I am leaving in five minutes."

Lynn grabbed the garment bag from me and tossed it in with the suitcase. "There's five hundred bucks I'll never see again. What do you think it would get on eBay? 'Murder gown for sale?' Too tacky? Beanie! I mean it!"

I didn't know where to start or what to ask. It was easy for Gus to tell me to solve a murder, but it was much harder for me to do it. Lynn and I stood awkwardly on the sidewalk waiting for the unseen Beanie, who I knew was one of the bridesmaids. Michaela had thought it would be fun to put them all up together at the Snuggles, like a pajama party. She'd stayed there with her attendants the night before the wedding.

"Headed back to the city?" I assumed Lynn lived in New York, but it seemed best to be sure.

"Yes, thank God. The cops finally told us we could go. Beanie!"

"I just came from seeing Michaela and Tony. The cops told them the same thing." Lynn had to be a close friend of Michaela's. She was the maid of honor, after all. That probably meant she also knew Tony pretty well. But what about Ray? "Was Ray Wilson a friend of yours?" I asked.

Lynn stomped a flip-flopped foot in disgust. "Freakin' Ray. Freakin', freakin' Ray," she said, echoing Tony's words, but in a very different tone. "Immature. Irresponsible. Still acting like a frat boy. Always ruins everything. Always. I certainly wasn't his friend. I don't see how Tony could stand him. And Michaela. I warned her a hundred times that man would bring her nothing but grief. *Beanie!*"

Though everything Lynn said was consistent with the feelings she'd expressed about Ray the day before, it was a little shocking to have her speak so badly about someone who'd just been murdered.

"Michaela's taking it pretty hard," I pointed out, thinking regardless of her feelings about the deceased, it was the job of someone close enough to be her maid of honor to support Michaela, not to go badmouthing her choice of friends to relative strangers.

"I bet she is," Lynn smirked. "Tell me, you say you just saw them. Who was taking it harder, Michaela or Tony?"

I hesitated for a moment. People show grief differently. True, Tony had been calm and businesslike, the much less affected of the two. When he'd talked of Ray, it was with fondness, not sadness—which might have been a little odd, considering he and Ray were best friends and grew up together. But maybe Tony had some macho inhibition about showing his emotions, especially to someone he barely knew. Who was I to judge? And what was this woman saying? That Michaela cared about Ray too much? More than she cared about Tony? It seemed absurd.

Lynn, however, took my silence as agreement. "My point exactly."

Beanie, also looking like she'd slept in her clothes, appeared at the front door of the Snuggles carrying an overnight case and a garment bag identical to Lynn's. She jogged to the passenger side, threw her bags in the back, and jumped into her seat.

Before I could ask anything else, Lynn slid behind the wheel. "No offense, but I hope I never see you or this godforsaken place again," she said just before they zoomed off, leaving me standing on the sidewalk.

Chapter 13

I looked across the street at my mother's house where Sonny, good as his word, was taking down my mother's porch windows. It was a terrible job. Twenty huge, wooden windows ran the length of the porch. They were ungainly and ungodly heavy, as I knew well, because it had always been Livvie's and my job to carry them to the garage once Dad had them off the house. The porch was high, so you had to stand on a ladder when you took the windows off, carrying them down one at a time. If that wasn't bad enough, the windows were old, a little warped, and covered in layers of paint, so removing them always involved a lot of shoving and swearing, which is exactly what Sonny was doing as I came up the walk.

"Hey!" I called softly, hoping not to startle him.

"Hey, yourself." Sonny paused on the ladder before starting on another window. He was red in the face and his dark green T-shirt was soaked with perspiration. "Man, I hate this job."

"Dad hated it, too."

When you think about men who've hauled lobster traps, chopped wood for towering bonfires, and disposed of the lobster shells, corn cobs, and clamshells left by four hundred people a day, it says a lot about the rottenness of the window job.

"Times like this, I really miss him."

I nodded, thinking about how few the years had really been, between when Dad had accepted Sonny as a permanent fixture in Livvie's life, and when he'd died. For those few years, Dad had help with the windows.

"I checked the Internet reservations," Sonny said. "We're almost full up for tomorrow."

"Really?" I'd turned the reservation system off for today, but I'd left it on for tomorrow in the hope that we'd be cleared to open. Mondays were usually decent days in the clambake biz. Lots of people came to Maine for three-day weekends. But full, in June? "Ghouls," I said.

"Julia, you don't know that. Maybe it's people who wanted to go today, but couldn't. That's why we're full."

"I doubt it."

"Well, it doesn't matter why they're coming. The position we're in, we have to take their money."

And who put us in that position, Sonny? "We don't even know yet if we can run."

"I heard the cops have Chris Durand back for a second round of questioning today. He's been there at least a couple hours."

Why did I bristle at that? Was Sonny implying if the police were questioning Chris, they'd end up arresting him and our troubles would soon be over? If that was what he meant, he probably would have just said it. Sonny was not a subtle guy. I wasn't surprised he knew Chris was at the police station. In Busman's Harbor, at times it felt like everybody knew everything.

"I think Chris is being interviewed because he was the last person in Busman's Harbor to see Ray Wilson alive," I said. "Turns out, Ray and Tony grew up in Bath."

"Really?" Sonny clearly understood what that meant. Maybe nobody from the harbor was involved.

"Yup. Tony told me himself this morning."

Sonny climbed down off the ladder with the heavy window in his hands. "Still doesn't answer the question why the body was left like that."

"I know. That bothers me, too." Neither of us had the answer, so I said, "Let me go upstairs to my office and check the reservation system. Then I'll come back and help carry these windows into the garage."

* * *

"Jul-ya!"

I was still in my office, going through tomorrow's reservations, adding up the money we'd flush down the drain if the cops didn't let us open. I'd called Jamie at the station house on the hope he was back from Morrow Island. The woman at the desk told me he wasn't around.

"Jul-ya, state cops are here for you!" Sonny was still out on the front lawn and evidently felt no hesitation about announcing it to the whole harbor.

"I'll be right down."

Lieutenant Binder and Detective Flynn stood on my mother's front porch. Sonny had finished taking the windows down and was humping them to the garage.

I led Binder and Flynn to a corner of the porch and sat them on the wicker furniture. Binder looked more tired than yesterday. The creases around his deep-set brown eyes were more pronounced, and he sat down heavily on the settee. Flynn, though considerably younger, didn't look much better. He was slightly stooped as though it was tough to carry his bodybuilder muscles. Both were dressed in dark slacks, white shirts, sports jackets, and boring ties. They had on ugly cop shoes, and I could tell just by looking that Detective Flynn had been out on Morrow Island while Binder had stayed in town. Flynn had a tiny patch of wet sand clinging to the top of the rubber sole of his right shoe where it met the leather upper.

"I thought you'd call me down to the station when you were ready for me."

"We needed the walk," Binder said.

"Coffee?"

"No thanks." He hesitated. "Unless you want some." I didn't, but they looked like they could use an afternoon pick-me-up, so I went to the kitchen and brewed a pot. My mother always had some store-bought cookies around "for Page," as she said, as if the nine-year-old in our lives was the only one who ate them. I put a plate of cookies next to the coffee mugs on a tray.

"Thanks," Binder said when I returned to the porch.

"No problem. What else can I do for you?"

"You can take us through yesterday. Again," Flynn answered.

So I did.

Their questions were more specific. They'd obviously gathered a lot of information since our interview the day before. Did the bride seem hungover or maybe even still drunk? The groom? Any of the attendants?

I answered honestly. "No."

I was aware of Sonny down on the lawn. I couldn't see him, but caught glimpses of the tops of window frames gliding past as he went back and forth to the garage. I was sure he was eavesdropping, though he, like the cops, had heard it all before.

"I know this is difficult, Ms. Snowden. But before you opened the door to Windsholme did anyone, anyone at all, give you the slightest indication they knew what was behind it?"

I replayed the horrible discovery in my mind. "No one."

"Well, you let us know if you remember anything else." Binder switched subjects. "I understand Christopher Durand worked on the island this spring." I nodded and he continued. "What did he do for you there?"

"I wasn't on the island everyday. Etienne Martineau or my brother-in-law Sonny Ramsey can be more specific, but generally . . ." I went through the litany of opening-up chores—clearing brush, raking the beach, repairing winter damage to the buildings and dock, bringing out the picnic tables and other furniture. It was three weeks worth of hard work for three men. "He also painted a couple rooms for me in Windsholme because I was getting ready for this wedding."

"Did anyone else work on the island this spring? Or maybe last fall?"

"The electricians." I'd forgotten all about them. "I changed the service and had two rooms at Windsholme rewired in May." I gave the names of the father and son who did the work. Flynn wrote down the information. "Do you think they could have something to do with Ray's murder?" I couldn't imagine what. They lived two towns up the coast, in the opposite direction of Ray's hometown.

"Just covering our bases," Flynn answered.

"Can I ask, did you find anything on the island today?"

The corners of Binder's mouth turned up in amusement. "That's a pretty broad question."

"Like a boat? Did you figure out how Ray Wilson got to my island?" Now that I knew Ray was from somewhere nearby and could have gotten himself to the island, I wanted to know how he'd done it.

Binder's smile faded. "We didn't find a boat. But I don't think that's meaningful. Wilson could've arrived on the island with his killer, who then left with the boat. Or Wilson and his killer could have come to the island in separate boats and Wilson's was carried out by the tide later. We won't know with certainty whether Wilson was even alive when he arrived on the island until we get the medical examiner's full report tomorrow."

I tried to picture a killer carrying Ray's body up the long, steep path from the beach to Windsholme. It seemed impossible. It would require two killers. Maybe three. Gangs of marauding murders on Morrow Island? It was too terrible to think about. "You should check Westclaw Point for the boat. There's a little inlet almost directly across from the island." That's where the inflatable balls, tubes, and rafts Livvie and I lost off our little beach when we were children always ended up. Eventually. "Did anyone report a boat stolen?"

"No, but it's early in the season. Lots of people aren't here yet. We're checking as best we can, but it will take time. The killer could have gone to the island in his own boat." Binder shifted forward in his seat and put his hands on his knees. "We do have some news. The crime scene team is done on your island. You can open tomorrow."

I practically jumped out of my seat. "Why didn't you tell me right away?" My mind raced forward. I had to let the staff know, buy the food, check the boat.

"Because we knew the moment we told you, you wouldn't be able to pay attention to anything else." He smiled his crinkly-eyed smile. "You can use the island for your clambakes, but please, keep everybody out of the mansion. We have it secured. Windsholme is still an active crime scene."

"Of course. Don't worry. I'm just so relieved. So you think the murder happening on the island was just random? Why was his body left there?"

"Think about it," Lieutenant Binder said. "Seeing that body had a powerful effect on more than just you."

Michaela. Of course. How could I have been so self-absorbed? She was the most hurt by seeing Ray hanging at Windsholme on her wedding day. And the maid of honor had dropped those not so subtle hints that Michaela and Ray were close. Too close. That could explain why Ray's body was left for Michaela to find.

"Thank you, Lieutenant for telling me this. It's a huge relief." It all made so much more sense. Tony and Ray were from Bath. Ray's body was hung up at Windsholme to send a message to Michaela on her wedding day. It was an unspeakably awful thing to do and I couldn't imagine why anyone had done it. But it had nothing to do with us.

"Thank you, so so much. You don't know what this means."

Binder grinned. "Oh, I think we do. Your friend, young Officer Dawes made sure we did."

Sonny and I stood on the porch and watched the retreating backs of Binder and Flynn as they walked down the hill.

"Did you hear all that?"

"Most of it. Seems like they're looking at Ray Wilson's life."

"And Michaela's." My eyes fell on a thick newspaper, neatly folded, sitting on a side table. "What's that?"

"I forgot to tell you. Quentin Tupper III dropped

it off for you. Said he was driving back to New York tonight and didn't want to 'schlep' it. He said he thought you'd appreciate it."

Quentin Tupper from Gus's this morning? It seemed like an odd thing to do. He didn't know where I lived. I hadn't even told him my last name. Of course, he could have asked pretty much anyone in town. Lots of people knew who I was and everybody knew the Snowden house.

Nothing sounded better than curling up on the porch swing with the Sunday *New York Times*. But I had a lot of work to get done if we were putting on a clambake tomorrow.

Chapter 14

I worked at my desk well into the evening to make sure everything was set for the clambake the next day. The sounds of Mom banging around in the kitchen traveled up the back stairs.

"Come down and eat," she called.

"Eat what?" I tried to keep the suspicion out of my voice. I realized I hadn't eaten since my early breakfast at Gus's.

"Leftover mac and cheese."

Thank goodness. Not something my mother had concocted. I felt terrible that I hated my own mother's cooking, but there it was. I knew it wasn't her fault. Goodness knows, she had tried.

Her mother died when she was young and Mom grew up in an all male household that included her father and a distant cousin. My grandfather didn't cook at all. When he had visited our house, he never crossed the kitchen threshold, expecting to be served his meals—even the bowl

of cold cereal he always ate for breakfast—in the
dining room. As far as I could tell, there'd been
no beloved, long-term housekeeper/mother substitute in Mom's life, just a string of Gerta-
Colleen-Consuela-Brigittes who were rarely
mentioned and who had left, at best, erratic
marks on my mother's culinary skills.

Mom had tried to teach herself to cook. Alone
in her kitchen, she attempted to reconstruct
half-remembered meals prepared by the Gerta-
Colleen-Consuela-Brigitte contingent. Her desire
to be the supportive helpmate she imagined Dad
expected matched his desire to provide the mate-
rial comforts he thought she needed. But she
never did get the hang of it. It didn't help that
our little grocery store in those days had such limited stock, especially in the winter. My mother had
no compunctions about substituting tomato soup
or catsup for salsa, or mayonnaise for hollandaise.
The results were dreadful.

It was one of the great ironies of our lives that
in summer, fed by the clambake and by Gabrielle's sumptuous cooking, we ate like kings. And
then we suffered all winter long.

For years, led by my father's dutiful example,
we ate, or at least pushed the food around on our
plates, and didn't complain too much—until
Livvie rebelled, as she did in all things. But in this
case, her rebellion was constructive. She spent
time in our neighbors' kitchens, learning their

best dishes. She spent hours with Gabrielle. And we were saved from starvation.

I finished up my work and went down to join my mother at the kitchen table.

"The clambake's running tomorrow," I said brightly when she'd put the food in front of us. Too brightly? All spring, Sonny and I had been careful about what we said to Mom. Of course, she knew I was home to help with the clambake because it was in financial difficulty. But we'd never given her the details, never told her how close to the edge we were. And she never asked. We didn't want her to worry and I thought she really preferred not to know.

"First day of the season," I continued. "Why don't you come?" My mother, who'd spent the first fifty summers of her life on Morrow Island, had not set foot on it since the day my Dad's cancer was diagnosed. I knew she loved the island, and I thought it would help her to go there and face whatever it was that kept her away. "C'mon," I urged. "I'm sure Gabrielle would love to see you."

It was a mild play on my mother's feelings of obligation, though I didn't push it and say, "I'm sure Gabrielle would love to see you because she's been traumatized by the murder on the island." I had no wish to remind Mom about the murder, though I doubted it was far from her mind.

She and Gabrielle were as close as my mother's

WASPy reserve and Gabrielle's natural shyness allowed. Their husbands had been best friends and Jean-Jacques, Livvie, and I were all close in age. I know Mom cherished having another woman, another mother, living with us on the island when we were young.

But then life got complicated. Jean-Jacques disappeared and less than a year later my father died. Gabrielle reacted to her tragedy by spending as much time on the island as possible. My mother reacted by never setting foot on Morrow Island again. Grief drove them to separate corners.

I thought it would do my mother good to see her friend again. Especially now that her best friend, my father, was gone. I wanted Mom to be happy. To heal. To go to the island. But I knew she wouldn't.

"Maybe later in the summer," she said. "Give Gabrielle my love."

We ate the rest of the meal in silence. Though my mother couldn't cook, she'd nurtured Livvie and me in so many other ways. My parents' marriage was a great love story, but it wasn't the kind of relationship that crowded everyone else out. Livvie and I always had my mother's complete attention and support. And though she could seem standoffish with others, within the family she was warm and loving, the stable support that balanced my father's work-hard, play-hard personality. My dad was the builder; my mother the quiet foundation on which all was built. Even five years after his death, she still seemed lost.

We cleaned the few dishes like the practiced team we were. My mother went off to the little sitting room off her bedroom to watch television and I returned to my office.

As I entered the room, my eye fell on the *Times* dropped off by Quentin Tupper for reasons I didn't understand.

I pulled out the Sunday Styles section, my favorite part of the paper. "The single woman's sports pages," Carrie Bradshaw had called it. I opened it, ready to savor the Vows and Modern Love columns. I noticed the corner of one of the pages was dog-eared. Turning to the page, I saw a photo of Michaela and Tony, their perfect eyebrows aimed directly at the camera. The article beneath the photo said:

MICHAELA CARPENTER, TONY POITRAS

Michaela Joan Carpenter and Anthony Robert Poitras were married Saturday on Morrow Island in Busman's Harbor, Maine.

Ms. Carpenter, 30, is an assistant buyer at Saks Fifth Avenue. She graduated from SUNY Binghamton. She is the daughter of Elizabeth Carpenter and the late Giles Carpenter.

Mr. Poitras, 35, is a graduate of the University of Massachusetts. He is a partner in the firm of Poitras and Wilson. He is the son of Flora and Edward Poitras of Bath, Maine, and Fort Myers, Florida.

Reading the wedding notice submitted to the paper weeks before made me sad. Sad about Michaela and Tony's ruined wedding day. Sad that whenever someone typed *Morrow Island* and *wedding* into a search engine, they'd get dozens of news articles about the murder before they'd get to this happy announcement.

I wondered about Quentin Tupper, the stranger who'd gone out of his way to leave me the newspaper. Had he turned down the corner on the page so I wouldn't miss the wedding announcement? There was no other explanation. It seemed a little mean. Why would someone I'd never met before want to taunt me?

Chapter 15

By the next morning, as I walked to the town dock, I was feeling pretty good about the world. A full night's sleep will do that for you. Yes, a horrendous thing had happened on Morrow Island, but the police had let us open the clambake. Reservations were strong and the weather was perfect. It was Opening Day.

Just before I arrived at our ticket booth, my cell phone rang. I grabbed it from the pocket of my sweatshirt and stared at the display. *Damn.* It was Robert Forman Ditzy, our banker. *Ugh.* I'd been hoping to avoid him. I hit the TALK button. "Hello."

"Julia. Bob Ditzy."

"Hi Bob. How are you?"

"Actually, I'm calling to see how you are. I heard you had a tragedy there at the clambake."

I rushed to reassure him. "Yes. But the police

have cleared us to open and we're full for both lunch and dinner."

"Good. Good. Because I don't think I need to remind you, Julia, it's going to take every cent you can earn to dig out of the hole you're in. As you know, the business plan you gave us when we renegotiated your loan the last time allowed for only five closed days during the season. Every day you're shut down makes it that much harder. At some point we approach mathematical impossibility that you'll be current on your loan by the end of the summer."

A warm flush rose from the base of my neck. Nobody knew those figures better than I did. What was he talking about, anyway? It was only the second day of the season and Tony and Michaela's wedding reception had never been included in the figures I'd given the bank.

"We've been closed exactly one day. You can't blame us for what happened." I tried to keep my voice calm, but I could hear the slight vibrato that meant I wasn't being entirely successful.

"It's not a question of blame, Julia. It's not your fault when there's a nor'easter and you lose three days to stormy weather. And it's not your fault when lobster hits six dollars a pound wholesale. And I'm sure this . . . this . . . death . . . is not your fault, either."

Why did he make it sound like that was a question?

"It's just that, as you know, you have a razor

thin margin of error. Of course, if it were up to me . . ." he continued, secure in the knowledge it absolutely was not.

My father had dealt with First Busman's Bank from the day he'd set up the business. They'd supplied the initial loan, and in our family we were brought up to be loyal to First Bus. But in the past decade they'd been bought by a regional bank that was swallowed up by a bigger bank that was swallowed up by a bigger bank still, like so many fish. A European financial conglomerate now owned First Bus. I was sure no one at corporate headquarters in Madrid could find Busman's Harbor on a map if they had a gun to their head. Something I admit, I'd occasionally fantasized about. Whenever we talked, Bob made it clear he had to answer to his corporate masters on the loan committee and their problems around the globe meant they could care less about the loss of fifty seasonal jobs in coastal Maine.

"I get it, Bob," I said, and I did. "Thanks for your concern."

I ended the call before it could go any further, my buoyant mood shot to pieces. As I'd reassured Bob, I knew the numbers—how much we had to clear every day and every week until Columbus Day—as well as I knew my own name. I also knew the consequences of failing. The Snowden Family Clambake would shut down. We'd lose the *Jacquie II*. Fifty people including Sonny and

Livvie, Etienne and Gabrielle would lose their livelihoods. Most likely, they'd have to move out of town to get work. I'd put the money I'd saved from my years in venture capital into the business when we'd renegotiated the loan. So I was all in, too.

Worst of all, if the loan was called, my mother would lose her house in town with all its memories, the place where'd she'd lived her entire married life and raised her family. And we'd lose Morrow Island. Though Mom hadn't been on the island since Dad died, I thought, somehow, losing it would kill her, or at least change her profoundly and not for the better. I had the same compulsion my father did when he founded the clambake—to keep Morrow Island for my mother. It was a part of her and she was a part of it. The two could not be separated.

By the time I finished the phone call and the black thoughts that came from it, I'd reached our little ticket booth. Livvie was already hard at work, selling seats for the dinner cruise and handing out will-call tickets to the Internet purchasers for lunch. I stood for a moment, absorbing the bustle of the town dock, the heat of the sun on my face, and the excited chatter of our passengers. My mood began to shift back. It was the first day of clambake season!

* * *

I stood on the quay, collecting tickets as the passengers climbed the gangplank. The sun cast everything in the flat, bright light that brought so many artists to Maine. The crowd seemed like the usual mix of sunblock-slathered tourists, with a tilt heavier to retirees than families because many schools in the northeast were still in session. Most passengers had heeded the warning on our Web site to bring layers of warm clothing. No matter how toasty it felt in the harbor, once we motored out of its protective arms into the North Atlantic, the weather would turn cool and breezy. In every crowd, there was at least one family who dressed not like they were traveling on a wild ocean to get to a rustic island, but like they were going on a Disney ride with the same theme. We kept blankets aboard the *Jacquie II* for the midriff-baring teens and sun-suited babies.

The news of Ray Wilson's murder had been all over the Maine media—the television news, Sunday papers, and the radio. But tourists often traveled in a magic news-blackout bubble, especially if, as was common in the harbor, they were staying at B&Bs that don't offer in-room TVs or Internet service. As I came aboard the *Jacquie II*, I had high hopes it would be a normal day with a normal group of customers.

But the moment my foot hit the deck, Sonny stepped beside me and hissed, "Three in the bow."

I looked toward the front of the boat where a trio of college-age boys was seated on the bench along the bulkhead. They laughed loudly and shoved each other so boisterously the woman sitting next to them moved her little boy protectively to her lap.

Sonny nodded toward the boys. "They already tried to buy beer. I asked for IDs and they backed off."

Clambake customers were usually self-selecting. Spending four hours on a boat and an island doesn't attract a rough crowd. But once in a while there are problem people, and we can usually spot them before we leave the dock. When you work with the public, and in particular, when you sell alcohol, you develop a sixth sense. As Sonny and I watched, the middle boy in the group pantomimed looping a noose around his neck, then reached above his head, pulling the imaginary rope tight. His head lolled to one side and his tongue stuck out while the other boys hooted and hollered.

"That's *it*," I said under my breath and marched over to the boys. I'm tiny, but they were seated so I stood over them. "Get off." I kept my tone conversational, but I didn't say please.

"Why?"

"We were just foolin' around."

"You can't kick us off. We paid!"

I walked calmly to the bar, opened the till and extracted a wad of twenties from under the money tray. I returned to the boys, peeled off three for each of them, slightly more than they'd paid, and repeated, "Get off. Now."

The middle boy looked like he wanted to argue, but then shrugged and slunk off, followed by his friends. "Bitch," he said once he was safely on the gangplank.

There was a smattering of applause from the crowd. Sonny gave me a nod that said he approved of my actions, despite his pronouncement yesterday about taking every dollar we could, even from the ghouls.

George, our captain, started the *Jacquie II*'s engines and I released the last of the lines holding us to the dock. I stood, paying close attention to set a good example, while Captain George went through the safety speech. And we were off.

We toured the inner harbor as far as the footbridge while Captain George pointed out the sights—the hotels, restaurants, and the biggest of the yachts. Across from The Lobster Deck, he tooted our horn and they echoed back with their giant ship's bell. "If you don't get enough lobster at the clambake," Captain George intoned into the mike that carried his voice throughout the ship, "The Lobster Deck has it any way you could want it, bisque, fried, salad, sandwich, baked and stuffed, and over pasta. You name it. They also have a full menu including clams, mussels, oysters, and Maine rock shrimp!"

The harbor businesses supported one another. The more tourists who came to the area and had a great experience, the more business there was for all of us. The Lobster Deck displayed our brochure prominently where the long lines of customers formed to place their orders.

The *Jacquie II* swung around to the back harbor, past Gus's restaurant and the shipyard. Most of the boats were out, either fishing or hauling lobster traps, but enough were still moored to give our customers a feel for the working side of Busman's Harbor. The crowd on the *Jacquie II* was happy—drinking, chatting, and taking photos of the harbor and each other. It was a beautiful day and almost all the passengers were crowded onto the open top deck. We headed out to the big bowl of the outer harbor.

Busman's Harbor had six islands, three with structures on them. Chipmunk was the largest by far. It housed a summer colony, complete with its own ferry. The hundred houses there were passed from family member to family member or were snapped up by neighbors. They almost never came on the market.

From Chipmunk, we sailed toward Bellows, a towering piece of rock with a deserted stone monastery on top. Our guests oohed and ahhed at the harbor seals. The tide was low, so most of the seals were hauled out, sunning themselves on the rock ledges. The many pups were still small and especially adorable. They would grow quickly on their mother's rich milk and in another month most of our visitors wouldn't be able to tell the babies from the others. Captain George steered around Bellows twice to make sure everyone got a good look. He cut the engine so we could hear the social animals on the island barking at one another, even as the social animals on our boat did the same. "Get in the shot!" "Get out of the shot!" "Stand next to your brother!" "Stop hitting your brother!" The happy, familiar sounds of summer at the bake.

The final island before the mouth of the harbor was Dinkums Light. As it came into view, the "lighthouse people" rushed to the bow, snapping photos and chattering as excitedly as if they were birders adding to their life lists. Dinkums was worth the excitement. Though not tall, the light was picturesque, with its stone keeper's house, boathouse, and fuel house still intact.

From Dinkums, we passed through the mouth of the harbor into the Atlantic. Morrow wasn't far, two miles southeast along the coast. We never lost sight of land, but the wind came up and the passengers pulled on their hoodies or windbreakers.

Then, just when they were ready for the trip to be over, it was. The dock on the Atlantic side of Morrow Island came into view, and the guests could see the bonfire where their food would be cooked. The crowd buzzed with excitement.

Chapter 16

I tossed the lines to one of our employees on the dock, then stood quietly while Captain George made the second safety announcement of the day, the island version. Morrow was a relatively safe place, or it had been until Saturday, and George hadn't yet worked, "Please don't get yourself hung from our staircase," into his spiel. We did have some rules—watch your children, stick to the paths, and, of course, stay out of Windsholme. Looking up the great lawn from the dock, I was relieved to see the mansion's front porch wasn't hung with yellow crime scene tape. Whatever the state police had used to secure the big front doors was much subtler.

Windsholme stood at the highest point on Morrow Island, facing the open ocean. Below it was a wide plateau of land that was once the formal gardens. It held the badminton net, bocce court, horseshoe pit, and croquet field with picnic tables scattered around the periphery.

Also on the plateau was the pavilion that contained the bulk of seating for our guests. It had a roof and clear plastic curtains that rolled down, so we could run the clambake even on cool or rainy days. Sunny days were better, but many people thought there was nothing like a bowl of creamy clam chowder and a lobster to ease the pain if bad weather happened to interrupt their Maine vacation.

Attached to our pavilion was the commercial kitchen where Gabrielle reigned. She and her small staff prepared everything that wasn't cooked on the fire. Also attached to the pavilion were the bar, the little gift shop where my mother had worked during her clambake years, and the public restrooms. Our water and electricity came over from the mainland in big conduits. The town of Busman's Harbor turned them on in mid-April and off just after Columbus Day.

Behind the pavilion was Gabrielle's glorious vegetable garden, which produced some of the best food I'd ever eaten. With no deer or rabbits on the island, and not even many land-based birds, the garden thrived.

The guests exited the *Jacquie II* and scattered. Some took the footpath across the island to the little beach, others headed for the playing fields.

Some lingered at the picnic tables with a beer, soda, or glass of wine.

As always, the bonfire drew a crowd. The fire was in a little cove a ways from the dock. It meant the kitchen staff had to carry the trays of un- cooked food a fair distance, but we had to keep the fire away from everything else. A fire on an island wasn't funny. It wasn't like you would get the trucks from the local department rolling down the street.

As he supervised the clambake, Etienne wiped the sweat from his brow with the blue bandanna he always kept in his back pocket. Then he care- fully explained to the customers what he was doing. Early this morning, on a concrete slab, Eti- enne had placed kindling and oak logs in layers alternating with rocks that had to be the exact type and size so they heated through but didn't explode. When most of the wood had burned away, he and his crew stepped in to rake out the charcoal and debris and then repiled the rocks that would actually cook the meal. Some bake masters don't actively participate in this hot, dangerous job, preferring to supervise from the sidelines. But Etienne wasn't that type of man or boss. Sonny worked silently next to him, his face glistening with sweat.

As soon as the rocks were piled up, the kitchen crew came running with the trays of clams, lob- sters, sweet corn on the cob, Maine potatoes, onions, and eggs. Once all the food was on the pile, the men covered it with rockweed, a North Atlantic seaweed, and then with canvas tarps.

"You see the eggs?" Etienne held one up to the crowd while his crew hosed down the tarps. "They are magic eggs!" He played to the children in the crowd. "How are they magic? As your food cooks, I reach into the pile and pick out one egg, open it and eat it. If the egg is perfectly hard-boiled, your meal is ready. Time to eat."

I gave Etienne and his crew a wave and turned away. While I had the chance, I wanted to take a quick tour around the island to see if there were any visible signs the crime scene techs had been there. I started toward Windsholme.

The big double front doors were secured with something that looked to me like a garbage bag tie. I didn't test it. I was sure it was stronger than I was. Same with the French doors to the dining room along the side porch. I walked around to the back of the house. Though it looked from the front like Windsholme was three stories tall, in the back the land sloped away and you could see that it was really four. The ground floor housed the great furnace, storerooms, and laundry as well as the first level of Windsholme's two-story kitchen. While I was at the back of the mansion, I tried peering through the windows, but I couldn't see anything and didn't want anyone to catch me.

From Windsholme, I started down the path toward the beach, but then thought better of it and took a branching path to the playhouse.

When it was constructed in 1890, the playhouse stood on the edge of the great lawn, but that part of the side yard had long since reverted to deep woods. A perfect, tiny imitation of Windsholme, the little house had two rooms, a parlor complete with a fireplace and a bunkroom for sleepovers. As I approached it through the trees, I thought of my mother's mother playing there in the 1930s, in a place bigger than the cottages where many harbor families lived.

During the summers, when our family lived in the house by the dock where Etienne and Gabrielle lived now, they stayed with Jean-Jacques in the playhouse. It didn't have a bath or a true kitchen. They used the commercial kitchen and the public restrooms back at the pavilion. My father had tried to talk them out of staying there, but Windsholme itself was uninhabitable, and thrifty Etienne wouldn't consider giving up the money they made renting out their house on the mainland for the summer. Besides, he pointed out, he needed to be on the island early and late for the clambake. My mother, who'd grown up playing in the tiny house, thought it was a great place to live. In truth, at times I envied Jean-Jacques.

In recent years, when there'd been so little money, none of it had been spent on maintenance of the playhouse. It was overgrown with vines, its screens broken and porch sagging. Sonny worried it was an "attractive nuisance" and muttered from time to time about bulldozing it, but there was no money for that, either. The last time I'd been in the playhouse, it had been full of dead leaves and spiderwebs. I gave the front door a shove.

The inside was astonishing—swept clean, furniture neatly arranged and a fire lay in the hearth. I tiptoed into the front room, half expecting to see three bowls of porridge on the dining table. Looking around, I noticed the glass in the windows had been repaired. I shivered in the gloom of the little house. The dense woods let little light in through the windows. *Who could have done this?*

The state of the playhouse freaked me out a little, but I had to explore the other room. The bunkroom was as tidy as the parlor. There was a mattress on one of the bottom bunks with an old wool blanket folded at the end of it. The original mattresses had moldered away years ago and we'd never replaced them. One thing you didn't want to do when you employed as many high school and college kids as we did was supply places that invited people to party and have sex.

My mind was still whirling, wondering who could have done this, when my eye caught three letters carved into the wooden side of a top bunk. CJD.

CJD. Christopher John Durand. I knew those initials

as well as I knew my own because I'd written them over and over in my junior high notebooks. CJD loves JMS. Christopher John Durand loves Julia Morrow Snowden. Mrs. Christopher John Durand. Julia Snowden Durand. And so on, ad infinitum. Ad nauseam. I ran my hand over the initials. The wood was still raw. The carving was new.

I breathed easier, my pulse dropping. That explained it. Chris must have cleaned the playhouse this spring when he was working on the island with Etienne and Sonny—not a stranger. Chris.

But why had he never mentioned it? And what had the police made of the neat dwelling—and the initials?

From the pavilion, a gong sounded, signaling lunch. I left the playhouse, closing the door carefully behind me. Time to get to work.

Chapter 17

Our guests gathered at the picnic tables for the first course, Gabrielle's New England clam chowder. For my money, it was the absolute best chowder on earth. Some chowder was so thick with cream and potatoes, a spoon would stand up in it, while some was so thin, it couldn't possibly satisfy the working fisherman it was invented for. Ours was the perfect consistency, hearty, yet creamy, flavored with onions, bacon, and thyme. And absolutely no tomatoes. Locals still talked about how in 1939, a bill to make tomatoes in clam chowder illegal was introduced in the Maine legislature. It didn't pass.

Chowder was always served with small, hexagonal oyster crackers. The Snowden family upheld this tradition, though I wasn't a fan myself. The crackers were tasteless and added nothing to the soup. They were sealed in little cellophane packets that made them as difficult to open and eat as the lobster.

As the guests finished up, the servers cleared away the paper bowls. Then the whole staff, including Etienne's team from the bonfire, the kitchen crew, the waitstaff, even Captain George pitched in to deliver the main course while it was hot.

Every customer got a plastic tray containing two bright red, pound-and-a-quarter lobsters, a string bag full of steamed clams, an ear of corn, a potato, an onion, and an egg. All the accoutrements—the bib, the nutcrackers for opening the claws, a pick for getting the meat out of small places, a dish of melted butter, and a cup of clam broth—were also piled on the heavy tray. Once the food was delivered, a temporary hush fell over the crowd as everyone got down to work. Though I'd seen it all my life, I still found it funny to see nearly two hundred adults wearing bibs.

I circulated among the customers looking for people who needed help, playing the host as I'd watched my father do for most of my life. I'd learned over the years it was best not to make assumptions. People speaking foreign languages might be expert lobster eaters, while people dressed head to toe in L.L. Bean—the uniform of Maine—might have no idea what they were doing.

The clambake got its name from the steamers,

the small, soft-shelled clams that opened as they cooked. Knowledgeable diners grabbed the clams by the neck, dredged them in broth to remove any remaining sand, dipped them in the butter, and swallowed them whole. Though the lobsters were the alleged stars of a Maine clambake, my heart belonged to the clams, which tasted salty and delicious, like you were eating the sea itself.

For some of our more experienced guests, the ritual of eating the lobster was as important as the food itself. Those customers had strong opinions about how lobster eating should be done and provided commentary on everyone else's approach. "You're putting lemon on that? *Blasphemy!*" Some people ate only the big front claws. Others ate almost everything but the brain and the shell, picking through the body and the small claws, determined to get every bite.

On the other hand, some of our first-time guests reminded me of the restaurant scene in *Splash!* where Darryl Hannah, playing the mermaid, picked up the lobster and bit directly into its shell. I approached a middle-aged couple and showed them how to use the nutcrackers to open the claws. Visibly relieved, they thanked me profusely.

"First time in Maine?"

Mouths full, they nodded enthusiastically.

"What do you think?"

The husband swallowed and dabbed melted

butter from his chin, another lobster-eating ritual. "To tell you the truth, we've been trying to figure out all day how to move here."

I nodded and smiled. It was a common reaction to a great vacation. But it wasn't as easy as it looked on a lovely June afternoon.

As the servers cleared away the plastic trays with the lobster carcasses, clamshells, and corncobs, the guests sat back, groaning about how full they were. But somehow they still managed to eat dessert.

Gabrielle's blueberry grunt was an intense concoction made from the tiny, low-bush berries for which Maine was famous. It was baked with a sweet, dumpling-like top. In June, the grunt was made from berries picked last summer and lovingly frozen by Gabrielle in single layers on cookie sheets then transferred to plastic bins.

Every Maine family had multiple recipes for blueberry desserts—duffs, grunts, slumps, crunches, crisps, pies, and coffee cakes. Throughout New England and the Maritime provinces of Canada, it was possible to get into quite a lively discussion about which was which, with some people insisting a slump was a grunt and vice versa. Whatever you called it, with vanilla ice cream melting over it, Gabrielle's blueberry grunt tasted like heaven.

As the meal ended, the guests drifted back toward the dock with full tummies and the memory of a beautiful day spent with family or friends. At least that was our goal.

After a headcount, the *Jacquie II* took them back to Busman's Harbor where it picked up the dinner crowd.

Chapter 18

Like most of the staff, I stayed on the island between lunch and dinner. The truth was this lull between the meals was my favorite part of the workday. It reminded me of one of my best memories of growing up—Livvie's birthday parties. Livvie was born on Patriot's Day, a holiday in April celebrated only in Massachusetts and Maine, as a former part of Massachusetts—though bizarrely it was spelled Patriots' Day in Massachusetts and Patriot's Day in Maine. It was the last gasp holiday in coastal Maine when families could relax and celebrate together. After that, the lobster traps went in the water, shops brought in their summer inventory, and everything in town had to be painted, planted, or repaired to prepare for the tourist season. Livvie's party always included Jamie and his parents, Etienne, Gabrielle and

Jean-Jacques, the aunts, uncles, and cousins on my father's side, and all Livvie's little classmates at the elementary school.

When the official party was over and the class-mates had been collected by their parents, my father would yell, "The OPK are gone!" Other People's Kids. That was when the beer and wine came out, the steaks and burgers went on the grill, and the adults settled in for the real party. That was my favorite part of the day, too—wild games of tag with Jamie, Jean-Jacques, and the cousins. The adults, focused on their own fun, were much less occupied with our behavior than when the OPK were there.

I always felt the same way during the interlude between the first and second seatings on Morrow Island. The tourists were gone and it was just the staff working hard and then eating a meal together. It was our time to catch up on one an-other's lives and the latest gossip.

Though I loved the clambake, it was a well-kept secret the very best meals on Morrow Island were the ones Gabrielle and her kitchen staff cooked for the help. If the dinner guests had any idea what we were enjoying while they motored to the island on the *Jacquie II*, they would be jealous. In honor of the first day of the season, Gabrielle always made *tourtières*, traditional French Canadian meat pies. You could have as many arguments about what made up a traditional tourtière as you could about blueberry slumps or grunts—probably more. Toutières always had ground or diced pork, except when they had beef, veal, game, or salmon. They always included diced potatoes, except when the potatoes were mashed. They were always spiced with some combination of cinnamon, clove, nutmeg, and allspice, except when they were spiced with a combination of rosemary, thyme, and sage. The arguments went on and on, but they didn't matter to me. Gabrielle's tourtière—diced pork, diced potato, cinnamon, and clove—was the best I'd ever eaten. And the best I would ever eat, I was sure.

I cut a generous slice of the meat pie and helped myself to a salad made from soft Boston lettuce, fresh peas, and leeks from Gabrielle's garden then carried my plate to a picnic table where Sarah Halsey sat alone.

I took a fork full of tourtière and brought it to my mouth, anticipating the taste of one of my favorite foods. I chewed.

Something was terribly wrong. The meat pie was absolutely delicious, but it wasn't Gabrielle's. The taste of Gabrielle's tourtière was so distinct to me, so bathed in nostalgia I sensed the fraud instantly. I was certain Gabrielle had not made this tourtière.

I swallowed my disappointment along with the

meat pie and turned to Sarah. We talked about her son Tyler, and her mother Marie, and about Livvie and Page. Other people came along and joined in the conversation.

In some ways, the staff at the clambake was quite hierarchical. At the top were Etienne's men who ran the fire pit, the women who worked with Gabrielle in the kitchen, Captain George and the boat crew, the bartender, and, it must be said, the family. Then came the college kids who made up the bulk of the waitstaff, anchored by a few long-term employees like Sarah. Finally, at the bottom of the pecking order were the high school kids, the jacks-of-all-trades or JOATs as we called them, whose job was to run, run, run—answering the calls of "More butter!" "More chowder!" "More iced tea!"—and to get those items to the table while they were still hot or cold, whichever it was supposed to be. But at staff dinner, we all sat together with no distinctions between us.

Eventually, the conversation at our table turned to the murder. It was like we couldn't help ourselves. It was the biggest thing that had happened in Busman's Harbor in ages and the clambake was involved.

"I hear you were in Crowley's Friday night when the wedding party came in," I said to Sarah.

Her pale face turned an instant scarlet and she stammered, "I–I . . ."

"Really?" someone farther down the long the table called out. "Tell us *everything*."

Sarah was still tongue-tied. I hadn't meant to embarrass her. As Chris had said, she was a grown woman entitled to a night out. Did she think we were somehow judging her?

"Nothing much to tell," she finally managed, and the conversation moved on.

I was sure that wasn't the end of it. She'd be getting questions all night, maybe longer. I was sorry for my part—that I'd been the one to let people know she'd been there. But really, what did Sarah find so embarrassing? Had she overindulged? Was she there with someone she shouldn't have been? A married man? Crowley's wasn't a bad place to hide in plain sight, with its tourist trade and high prices that kept the locals away.

Marie Halsey arrived at the table and sat in the only open seat, right next to her daughter. If she noticed Sarah's discomfort, she gave no sign of it.

"Did you like the tourtière?" Marie asked me. "I made it. My own recipe."

"You made it? Not Gabrielle?"

"She wasn't up to it. Opening day. You know."

Wasn't up to it? Gabrielle had been there for twenty-seven opening days. Had some crisis occurred in the kitchen? From where I'd stood among the guests, our first day had seemed remarkably glitch-free. Sure there were some hiccups. At one point, I'd witnessed a JOAT literally running in circles while customers shouted orders at him. For the most part, though, I thought our training sessions, plus a high percentage of returning employees, had kept things pretty calm.

But there'd also been a murder and police all over the island. Normally, making a traditional dish like tourtière was an activity that soothed Gabrielle. Something she would turn to in times of stress. If she couldn't even manage to cook, she must be deeply unsettled by the events on the island. I couldn't blame her. There'd been a vicious murder a few hundred yards from where she'd been sleeping.

I cleared my place and worked alongside the rest of the staff, setting the tables for our dinner guests. Etienne loomed beside me. I glanced down at the fire, which was burning well.

"Do you think Sonny can handle the bake tomorrow at lunchtime?" he asked. "The police want to interview me in the morning."

"Again? Etienne, it will be your third time."

He shrugged. "I know. They believe I must have heard something that night, but I did not."

I called Sonny over and he agreed to help out right away. "I already checked in with Livvie. Reservations tomorrow are strong for a Tuesday— but it's still a Tuesday. I can handle it." Tuesdays were always the slowest day of the week.

We talked some more about logistics, getting Sonny out to the island early. As our conversation ended, we saw the *Jacquie II* maneuvering toward the dock with the dinner crowd aboard.

"Back to the salt mines," Sonny said.

Chapter 19

Greeting the guests coming off the boat, I was surprised to see Lieutenant Binder, Detective Flynn, and Jamie Dawes, the last three to disembark. "What are you doing here?"

"Heard so much about this famous clambake, thought we'd check it out," Binder answered. "Unofficially."

"Uh-huh."

Jamie was in jeans, a polo shirt, and sneakers. Binder and Flynn had sort of tried for casual. Their ties were gone and their shirtsleeves were rolled to mid-forearm, but the ugly cop shoes weren't fooling anyone. From behind them, Jamie gave me a whatya-gonna-do grin and I rallied.

"Well, gentleman, you're in for the best meal of your lives. Jamie, you know the drill."

Jamie led them off toward the bocce court.

We did it all again. The later crowd, as usual,

was mellower, less interested in exploring the island and more interested in alcohol, which was good for the bottom line. Binder and Flynn seemed to enjoy themselves and devoured every consumable piece of their twin lobsters. They must have been telling the truth about being off duty, because each of them, Jamie included, had a beer. I personally delivered their blueberry grunt. Binder groaned, but still picked up his spoon and took a bite. "My God, this is the best thing I've ever tasted."

While they ate, I watched Le Roi, the island cat, as he wound his way from table to table. Le Roi was a Maine coon cat and had their distinctive big-boned body and long hair. He was named Le Roi, which means the King, after Elvis Presley. When Gabrielle adopted him eight years ago, he had the sleek muscularity and swively hips of a young Elvis. Now he looked a lot more like Vegas-era Elvis, but he was still the undisputed king of the island. Could there be anything better in this world than to be the sole cat on an island where over a thousand pounds of seafood was served per day? Maine coons were generally known for their caution around strangers, but Le Roi was past all that. As I watched, he casually rubbed himself against the legs of an elderly woman who reached down and fed him a large chunk of lobster in return for the affection.

After dessert, most of the guests drifted off to

the point on the west side of the island to watch the sunset. You don't get many over-ocean sunsets on the East Coast of the United States and Morrow Island's was spectacular. Tonight, the sun was like a giant fireball sinking into the sea. The clouds above echoed bright pinks and blues onto the water below. Couples who probably rarely had time to watch sunsets held each other, and a man hoisted a sleepy toddler onto his shoulders. Sometimes I just loved what we did.

Around me, the staff cleaned up quickly. Most of us would leave with the guests on the *Jacquie II* as soon as the sun was down. I noticed Lieutenant Binder hadn't gone over to the point with the other guests, but lingered at his picnic table. I couldn't resist approaching him. "How's the case going?"

"Fine."

I smiled. "You're going to have to give me more than that."

Binder smiled back. Lobster and beer will do that for your mood. But before he could say anything, I heard a shout and saw Etienne pointing at something behind me. I whirled around. The side porch that ran the length of the Windsholme was engulfed in roaring flames.

Chapter 20

"Move guests to the boat!" I yelled to Captain George, but he and some of the more experienced staff were already herding our customers toward the *Jacquie II*. It was the safest place for them, and if the fire spread, Captain George could pull away from the dock and be out in open ocean in minutes. A few people protested or lagged behind to watch, but most of the guests were models of calm cooperation.

I sprinted for the fire hose and picked up the nozzle. We practiced with the hose when we drilled the staff every summer, but far as I knew, it had never actually been used on a fire. It was kept near the pavilion because the commercial kitchen was the most likely starting point for a fire. Supposedly there was enough hose to get up the hill to Windsholme. I ran with the hose toward the mansion, while Sonny and Etienne struggled to open the big valve. The expression, "No man is an island," was ironically never truer than when you were actually *on* an island. We all had to depend on one another. It would be a long time before help arrived.

About ten feet from the flames, I stopped and waited, desperately hoping there was enough water pressure to get up the hill. Windsholme's side porch was completely consumed by the fire. I backed up a foot or two because my cheeks and the end of my nose felt like they were burning. Smoke clogged my nose and mouth and I coughed and sputtered. I tried to steady my hands.

The water came with such force I staggered backward and almost dropped the hose. I felt strong arms at my back and Jamie's voice shouting, "I got you." I trained the water toward the fire, desperately wishing I knew what I was doing. Do you aim toward the center of the fire, or work your way from the outside in? How could I not know?

The fire roared. With a crash, part of the side porch roof plummeted onto the burning deck. The French doors to the dining room began to burn. Soon, the fire would be inside the house.

I rushed forward, aiming a torrent of water on the doors, but quickly fell back, half pulled by Jamie, half driven by the heat. Around us, burning embers filled the air and I could feel Jamie behind me beating them off my shoulders and back. The fire blazed on, impervious to the water I directed at it.

"Jamie, what should I do?" I shouted.

"Rockland Fire Department. Let me take it." The man who'd had the boy on his shoulders reached in and took the hose with such authority I immediately handed it over. "Count the guests and employees. Make sure everyone's accounted for," he shouted.

Oh, my God. "Do you think someone could be inside?" It hadn't occurred to me.

The man didn't answer. He was completely focused on the fire, which was already responding to his expertise.

I ran to the *Jacquie II* to make sure all the guests were onboard. Along the way, I directed every employee I passed to get on the boat. They all wanted to help, to do anything they could to save Windsholme. Gabrielle outright refused to go aboard. I understood her refusal. Unlike all the others, the island was her home. In the end, all the other employees did as I asked. The *Jacquie II* pulled out of our dock with everyone on board except Sonny, Etienne, Gabrielle, Jamie, Lieutenant Binder, Detective Flynn, the firefighter, and me.

The Coast Guard fireboat and the harbormaster's boat carrying the Busman's Harbor Fire department arrived at the same time. Sonny had reached them on the radio. By then, the fire was under control. Two men in full fire gear finally took the hose from the exhausted Rockland firefighter.

"Thank you!" Without thinking I embraced him.

He smiled wearily. "I wanted to show my in-laws a real Maine clambake. I didn't count on the after-dinner show."

"You and your family have free passes to the clambake for life. We were so lucky you were here."

"You were lucky in a lot of ways. Lucky this happened during a damp spring instead of a dry fall. Lucky for those thick stone walls and slate roof. If that structure had been wood, the whole thing would have gone up."

Windsholme's stone walls and slate roof. I'd never felt lucky about them before. I'd felt only their crushing financial burden. I'd always seen the house as an albatross. But in that moment, I realized losing Windsholme would leave a mansion-sized hole in my heart. Behind us, Detective Flynn unlocked Windsholme's front doors and firefighters wearing flashlights on their heads tromped inside.

* * *

About 3:00 A.M. we all climbed the Boston Whaler to head back to the harbor. Binder finished up a whispered conversation with Sergeant Flynn, the Busman's Harbor fire chief, and my hero firefighter, then touched my arm. "You're closed down again until we can determine if this is another crime scene."

I'd known right along we wouldn't be open tomorrow. We'd need to get the building inspector out to the island to assess the damage. Best-case scenario, if there were no structural problems inside Windsholme, we could get the porch secured so it wasn't a safety hazard for the clambake guests and be open the following day. The crime scene issue could cause a further delay. "You think the fire was set?"

"That's what I'm about to find out," Binder answered.

"How long will it take?"

His mouth was set in a grim line. "As long as it takes."

More devastating than the fire itself was what it represented. I'd been happy all day believing Ray Wilson was murdered by a stranger, his body strung up to scare or intimate Michaela. Morrow Island was barely involved.

Clearly, Binder was no longer sure about that scenario. The fire caused him to take a second look at our island. If it was set, who could have set it? Was there a stranger lurking on our island even now? Whatever had happened, we were closed for business again. And ever closer to financial ruin.

I sat in the Whaler, looked up at the beautiful stars, and tried to absorb the blow.

Chapter 21

When daylight crept into my room the next morning, I wanted to cover my head. What was there to do, now that the clambake was shut down for a second time?

The answer was there was so, so much to do. I had to contact the town offices to arrange for the building inspector to go out to the island and tell us what to do about the ruined porch. Most important, I had to talk to my favorite banker, Robert Forman Ditzy. I wanted to call him first thing, before he called me.

I got cleaned up, dressed, and took my coffee upstairs to my office to wait for Sonny. On the long boat ride home, we'd agreed to do the call together. Sonny was the "good cop," or should I say "good old boy," who'd originally put the loan together with Bob the Banker. I was the "bad cop" who'd charged in from out of town at the eleventh hour, demanding that the loan be renegotiated and hammering out the agreement we were operating under now. The phone call required both cops to get through it.

I looked at the clock. Still way too early to call the bank or the town. The minutes ticked slowly by. The office where I sat was originally my dad's. I hadn't changed it much since I took it over. For one thing, I hadn't had time. For another, sitting in the same room where he'd run the Snowden Family Clambake, with its familiar piles of paper and metal filing cabinets, made it feel like Dad was watching over me. "What would you have done?" I'd asked the air so many times that spring, longing for my father.

His big oak desk sat in a rectangular bay of windows at the front of the house. From it, I could see the full expanse of the inner harbor where the *Jacquie II* was bobbing quietly in her berth. Bobbing quietly, instead of being cleaned and prepped for the clambake.

I read through a few e-mails, most from suppliers confirming we'd canceled our orders—again—and expressing sympathy or shock we'd had such a run of bad luck. I stood up from the desk and stretched. Craning my neck, I peered down the steep hill at our ticket kiosk on the dock. If Livvie was there, it would mean Sonny had dropped her off and would be at the office any minute. It was empty.

The *New York Times* Quentin Tupper had dropped

off for me sat on a pile of invoices, forgotten where
I'd left it Sunday night. I stared at it, longing to sit
in the coffee shop around the corner from my old
apartment in Soho and read the paper. Or even
to be back at my job in venture capital, when the
businesses I worked with weren't my own with the
exhausting emotional cost *that* involved. I had to
admit if I'd been brought in as a consultant to
assess the Snowden Family Clambake, I would've
advised shutting it down.

I picked up the *Times* and shuffled through it.
The fat paper even included the New York area
local sections we normally don't get in Maine.
How had Tupper gotten his hands on it?

I pulled out the real estate section. It wouldn't
hurt to look. A girl could dream. I'd given up my
expensive Manhattan lease back in March. I stole
another look at our ticket booth. Still no Livvie. I
had time. I opened up the paper and started fan-
tasizing about New York City apartments.

"That's right. Leave when the going gets tough.
Like you always do." Sonny stood in the open
doorway to the office, his red brows set in a scowl
over his deep-set blue eyes.

I frowned. *What on earth is he referring to?* "Oh,
the real estate section," I mumbled, setting down
the paper. I let it go. I didn't need to explain or
apologize. And there was no advantage to getting
into an argument. We had to save our fighting
spirit for the phone call.

"Let's get this over with," he said.

I pulled the speaker phone forward on the desk and punched in the bank's number, including Bob Ditzy's extension, which I'd memorized during our almost daily phone calls when I'd first arrived in the harbor.

Ditzy answered on the first ring.

"Bob? Julia Snowden and Sonny Ramsey here."

"Julia. Sonny. I was just about to call."

I bet you were.

"I'm sorry for your trouble—"

"Thanks." I wanted to underline any goodwill or pity he felt.

"—but I think we need to discuss practically what this means for the business."

I was prepared. "I don't know what you've heard, Bob, but the fire was confined to Windsholme's side porch. I'll get a building inspector out today. Then we'll just have to do a little demolition and we're good to go. A day or two at most."

"That sounds awfully optimistic."

It was. For one thing, demolition and disposal would be complicated on the island. More important, it was actually Lieutenant Binder who had shut us down, in addition to the town. But I wasn't telling Bob Ditzy unless he asked. My only interest was in buying time, so I reassured him.

He wasn't convinced. "Still. You lost Sunday and now you're saying you'll be closed today and probably tomorrow. At some point, your projections go right out the window."

"Our plan allowed for five lost days," I said.

When I'd gotten Livvie's panic-call, Sonny had already renegotiated our loan once and the bank was threatening to call it again. I'd stopped them, or rather stalled them, by presenting a business plan that projected how much we'd make— revenue and profits—every day from mid-June to Columbus Day. My plan said we'd be current with our loan payments by the end of the summer. The business plan and the renegotiation with the bank were the reasons Sonny suffered my being there. I was the perfect person to do it. Like me, Sonny and Livvie knew the clambake business, but my venture capital training meant I could build spreadsheets and business plans in my sleep.

Fortunately, I had not only Sonny's rather slipshod records from the last five years, but all my father's ledgers as well. I'd studied them with the fervor of a pirate looking at a treasure map and could tell pretty much to the person how many people would be on each run of the *Jacquie II* every single day during the season. I knew it mattered how many snow days there had been over the winter, which affected when school got out and family vacations began. It mattered what day of the week Fourth of July was and what date in September Labor Day fell on. I had factored all of that and more into the elaborate projections I'd given Ditzy. I'd thought to dazzle him with detail.

But I couldn't control the one thing every Mainer wishes they could—the weather. Even with the pavilion to shelter the guests and the enclosed lower deck on the *Jacquie II*, I wasn't crazy enough to assume we would run the clambake every day of the summer. Based on historical averages, I'd included three days of no revenue to allow for a nor'easter or hurricane and then added two more as a contingency. Five lost days.

I wasn't sure Ditzy really understood the business plan. I thought, in retrospect, maybe I'd gone over the top and made it too complex, too clever. I'd coached Ditzy on it endlessly, because he was the one who had to sell it to his superiors at the bank. He'd succeeded in doing that somehow. Unfortunately, the one thing he did understand, and fixated on, was my calculation about the number of days we'd be closed.

"Five days for the whole season," Bob said. "It's the third day of the season and you've already lost two—and you're telling me you're going to lose another."

I glared at Sonny. It was time for him to come in with the "good cop" sentiments, reminding Ditzy we were long-term, loyal customers, important to the town, and so on. But Sonny sat slumped in the guest chair.

"I'm sure we can do it, Bob," I reassured the banker.

"Three days, Julia. Your plan says you can lose three days after today. If we go past that, I'll have to go back to the loan committee. I've been clear with you. This was your last chance."

What could I do? I thanked him and said we'd stay in close touch. After saying good-bye, I stared at Sonny who mumbled something that may have been "good-bye," and hung up the phone.

"What the hell was that?" I snapped. "You were supposed to support me."

"What's the use?" Sonny shambled toward the door. "We're done."

"Not on my watch."

Chapter 22

After Sonny left, I called the town offices and set up an appointment for the building inspector to go out to the island in the afternoon with Sonny and me. Then I sat at Dad's desk listening to the tick of his father's mantel clock. Every minute seemed to count down the amount of time we had to save the business. I meant what I'd said to Sonny. I'd sacrificed too much to see it go down. And for such an irrelevant reason. A murder and a fire didn't mean the business wasn't viable. It was just bad luck.

Gus's lecture on Sunday still rang in my ears. He'd told me not to be a victim, not to let my business be pulled under by this mess. But what could I do?

Before the fire, Lieutenant Binder said the murder probably had nothing to do with Morrow Island. What if that was true? What if the fire was a coincidence or even a planned distraction, intended to take the police in the wrong direction?

While the state police investigated the fire at Windsholme and tried to tie it to the murder, I decided to follow up on their original theory—that the body had been left hanging from the staircase to upset Michaela.

But who would want to upset Michaela? And in such a horrible way? Someone who knew her, clearly. Someone who had reason to hate her. Someone very close. They say hate is the flip side of love. There has to be great passion to hate.

Who would feel so passionate about Michaela? Tony was at the top of the list. Lynn, the maid of honor, implied Michaela cared more for Ray than she did for Tony. Could Tony have been jealous of Ray? When we met at the Bellevue to review the wedding costs, there'd been something about Tony I distrusted. Some hidden agenda. But I had no idea what it was. If Ray and Michaela were lovers, that might explain why Ray had gotten so drunk the night before her wedding.

I had to find out more about the wedding party—what they'd done and where they'd been on the night Ray Wilson was murdered.

My eye fell on a box of brochures in the corner of the office. They'd come from the printer just a couple days earlier. I needed to deliver them to the hotels in the area. Hotel guests frequently asked

about lobsters, harbor cruises, and authentic
Maine experiences, and of course, we offered
them all. We wanted the Snowden Family Clambake to be the first thing the desk clerk recom-
mended. In all the craziness, the brochures hadn't
been delivered. I filled a tote bag with them, fig-
uring I could drop them off at the hotels where
Michaela and Tony's wedding party had stayed
and ask a few questions at the same time.

The first place I planned to hit was the Lighthouse Inn. It was an important hotel in the
harbor and the last place Ray Wilson was seen
alive. Chris Durand had told me he watched Ray
walk through the doors to the hotel at a little after
1:00 on the morning he died.

As I walked toward the inn, I passed the entrance to the town dock. I glanced at our ticket
booth where Livvie was talking to a small crowd.
No doubt people who'd been booked for the
clambake who were seeking refunds. I sighed and
kept moving. I was on a mission.

When I got to the Lighthouse, I hit gold.
Clarice Kemp was at the front desk. What luck.
That woman was the biggest gossip in town.
Rumor had it she didn't even need to work. She
probably would have hung around in the lobby
of the Lighthouse with her ears open and her
mouth flapping for free. But for decorum's sake,
she answered the phone and took the occasional
reservation for pay.

"Julia!" she cried, as thrilled to see me no doubt, as I was to see her. Clarice had her sources and I had to be one of the hottest ones in town at the moment.

Clarice had a thin face and a beak nose. She wore her brown hair (Clairol Nice'n Easy 115, I'd been told) in tight waves that framed her face and jaw. It had been the same style since I was a child—or maybe even since she was.

"Clarice!" I returned her enthusiasm. "I just came to drop off these brochures. We hope you'll recommend us to your guests."

Clarice took the pile of brochures I handed her, staring at them dubiously. "But I thought you were closed. The murder? The fire?"

"A couple days at most," I assured her breezily. "The fire damaged only the side porch of Windsholme. Nothing to do with the clambake business." While I was there, I intended to get positive information flowing through the town's channels. Before she could ask anything else, I said, "I hear the Lighthouse has its own connection to the murder. Ray Wilson stayed here the night he was killed."

Clarice settled her elbows on the front desk for a long natter. "He was supposed to." She straightened up and looked from side to side to make sure no one was listening. "But, he didn't. The maid said his luggage was in the room, tux hanging in the closet, but his suitcase was never unpacked, the bed never slept in."

"Really?" *Interesting news.* "I wonder where he could have gone that night?"

"You wonder. We wonder. The state police definitely wonder. They've been here more than once, I can tell you that. The maid, she's a Russian girl on a student visa, you understand."

Oh, I did. By high summer about half the workers in the harbor would be foreign "students."

Clarice continued. "She's terrified."

Another collateral victim of Ray Wilson's killer. "You mentioned Ray's tux and suitcase. Do you happen to know if he had a big camp trunk in his room?"

"A trunk?" Clarice put on her thinking face. It was new information for her. "Why, no. I was here at the front desk when the state police carried everything out. There wasn't any kind of trunk. But they did tow his car out of our parking lot. It could have had a trunk in it. Is the trunk important?" Clarice squinted at me, eager for another murder tidbit.

"Did the police ask about it?" I pressed.

"Uh, no. Not that I heard. You're the first one to mention it."

"Then I'm sure it's not important." I was sure of no such thing. The camp trunk bothered the heck out of me. What could have been in it and where had the trunk gone? "Any theories about where Ray Wilson went that night after he left the hotel?"

"I heard that hunky Chris Durand dropped him at the front door. The night desk guy said this Wilson came in, obviously drunk. While he was in the lobby, trying to remember the way to his room, his cell phone rang. Can you imagine? After 1:00 in the morning?"

I shook my head, indicating that I, indeed, could not imagine such an affront to acceptable behavior among humans as a cell phone call that late at night.

"The night guy said Wilson didn't even answer the phone, just looked at the display and staggered out the side door. The night guy went after him because everything but the lobby door is locked at night, so he was worried Wilson wouldn't be able to get back in the way he went out. But Wilson was nowhere to be seen."

"I wonder what the police think?"

"I don't know. Who could have called Wilson at that hour? It must have been one of the wedding party, right? They were the only ones in town who knew him."

"Right," I confirmed her speculation. "Must have been one of them." There was no point in telling Clarice that Ray Wilson was from Bath. I was after information about the wedding party and didn't want to get Clarice off track. I knew as soon as I left, she would be telling people, "Julia

Snowden says it's one of the wedding party who called Ray Wilson that night."

I, too, thought it must have been. But who?

From the dockside, I carried the lighter tote bag back up the hill toward the Snuggles Inn. The two "maiden ladies" who ran it, Viola and Fiona Snug, were not actually British, though they always seemed so to me. Their parents had moved to Maine from England before the sisters were born, so their father could work as the golf course pro at one of the resorts out on Eastclaw Point. They'd been raised taking tea, wearing jumpers instead of sweaters, and eating pudding instead of dessert. They always had at least one spoiled and happy dog.

Fiona or "Fee" was a plain woman bent over with arthritis, always in a skirt and sensible shoes. She was forever calling out, "Walkies!" and taking the dog, currently a friendly Scottish terrier, for a rigorous tramp up and down the harbor hills. With her bent back, she looked like a question mark bustling along the road.

Viola or "Vee" was something else entirely. In her seventies, she was still glamorous, with a beautiful head of coiffed snow-white hair. Even on days when she didn't plan to leave the house, she wore full makeup, a tailored dress, nylons, and pumps. In the dead of winter, she wore boots with lambs wool cuffs around the ankles and high spiked heels. As she grew older, the boots caused no end of arguments with Fee, who feared Vee would fall and break a hip. The whole town feared Vee would fall and break a hip. But she never did.

When their parents died, the sisters took their inheritance and bought the Victorian ginger-bread house across the street from my parents and created the Snuggles, one of a dozen bed and breakfasts in the harbor. My dad fixed various things around the inn, mowed the lawn, and shov-eled their snow. They, in turn, lay out and cared for the beautiful English gardens at our house. The sisters always felt a special bond with Livvie and me, two sets of sisters, and treated us to tea and scones whenever they got the chance.

"Julia!" Fee cried through the screen door as I made my way down their walk.

"Hello, Fee. I've brought you our new brochures." Though, at their insistence, I'd been calling them by their first names for almost a decade, the names still stuck in my throat. To me the sisters would always be, "The Misses Snug."

Before I knew it, I was sitting in their old-fashioned kitchen, drinking tea, eating scones, and accepting the commiserations of both ladies about the clambake's recent troubles. I knew if I were patient, the conversation would inevitably turn to Ray Wilson. I didn't have to wait long.

"We were shocked, just shocked by the murder of that young man on your island. And the bride and her attendants stayed right here in this house," Fee said.

"Julia, didn't you recommend us to Michaela?" Vee asked, eyes narrowing.

I admitted I had. "Did anything seem unusual to you about Michaela and her bridesmaids?"

"Not at first," Fee answered. "They seemed like ordinary bride and attendants." Busman's Harbor was a popular wedding destination, so the ladies had a strong basis for comparison.

"But then?" I asked.

"But then, they came back from the rehearsal dinner and all hell broke loose." Vee was always the more outspoken.

Fee blushed a little at the swear word, but after more than seventy years together, they'd learned to tolerate each other's foibles. She picked up the thread. "They went out to Crowley's after the rehearsal dinner. It was quite late when they got back. Vee and I were in our bedroom, listening to that nice Jimmy Fallon on the television, waiting for the group to come in."

The ladies had their own bedrooms in the winter, but during the season they stayed together in a little room off the kitchen, so they could rent out all the upstairs rooms to maximize their income. Like most B&Bs in the harbor, they didn't give guests keys, so the ladies had to wait up to lock the door after whomever was the last one in.

"I got up to lock the door when I heard the most terrific row coming from upstairs." Fee leaned over the kitchen table and lowered her voice. It wouldn't do if current guests heard her gossiping about past customers. "It was the bride, Michaela, and the other one, Lynn, the maid of honor."

"What were they fighting about?"

"The maid of honor yelled, 'Leave him be. Why do you care about him so much? He's nothing but trouble.' Then that Michaela shouted, 'How can you be so uncaring? Something was really wrong with him tonight.' Then the other one shouted, 'The same thing that was wrong with him every night not so long ago. He was drunk off his . . .' uh,"—Fee searched for the correct word to substitute for the one the maid of honor had undoubtedly used—"posterior."

"So then what?" I prompted.

"Then Michaela said, 'I don't care. I'm going to find him.' And the other one shouted, 'Are you crazy? Are you trying to sabotage your marriage before it even starts? Stay away from him.' Then that nice Michaela came down the stairs, talking on her cell phone. She said to whoever it was, 'I'm coming over right now.' And she banged open the front door and marched out into the night."

"Goodness. What happened next?"

"I went into the parlor to wait for Michaela to come back. I figured at least then Vee could get some sleep." Vee had to be up extra early because she cooked the Snuggles' wonderful English breakfasts.

"I sat up reading until a little before two," Fee continued. "No sign of Michaela, though I overheard the maid of honor leave her several messages, saying how sorry she was and to please come back."

"What time did Michaela return?"

"I don't know." Fee looked sheepish. "I fell sound asleep in my chair. Vee woke me when she got up to make breakfast."

Vee took up the tale. "When the girls came down in the morning, Michaela was with them. They all seemed to be the best of friends. It was like everything from the night before was forgotten."

Fee's eyes widened. "Imagine, me snoring away in my chair with the door unlocked while a murderer was on the loose."

"Have the police interviewed you?"

"Oh yes, dear. That nice Lieutenant Binder came along with his handsome sergeant. They asked all sorts of questions," Fee said.

"They only came the once." Vee sounded slightly disappointed. "We told him everything."

Binder and Flynn knew from the maid at the Lighthouse Inn Ray hadn't stayed in his room the night he died. They knew from the Snugg sisters Michaela had gone out. I just hoped the cops were paying attention and weren't completely distracted by the fire.

Chapter 23

I stood on the sidewalk outside the Snuggles with my even lighter tote bag of brochures. It seemed pretty obvious to me who had called Ray Wilson when he'd been in the lobby of the Lighthouse Inn and caused him to turn around and go outside again. Clarice had said that Ray merely glanced at the display on his phone while he was in the lobby. He must have called Michaela back once he got outside and then gone somewhere to meet her. But why would a bride go off on a middle-of-the-night rendezvous the day of her wedding?

I was certain Michaela hadn't killed Ray. I didn't believe that a girl from New Jersey who didn't know Busman's Harbor could have taken Ray out to Morrow Island in the dark. Nor did I believe she had the strength, at least by herself, to hang his body from the staircase at Windsholme. Most compelling, she'd been next to me when we discovered the body. Unless she was the best actress I'd ever seen, her distress was genuine.

Before the fire, Binder had theorized that the body was left at Windsholme to upset Michaela, so the police didn't think Michaela killed Ray, either.

If Michaela was responsible for Ray leaving the Lighthouse Inn after the wedding party's celebration at Crowley's, who was responsible for him never going back?

I swung my tote over my shoulder and headed across the footbridge to the other side of the harbor.

Tony had spent the night before his wedding-that-wasn't in the honeymoon suite at the Bellevue Inn. As far as I understood, he and Michaela lived together in New York, but like a lot of couples, they'd observed the traditional separation on the eve of their wedding.

Unfortunately, the desk clerk on duty at the Bellevue was a kid I didn't know. I introduced myself to him and did my usual spiel about the brochures. He raised an eyebrow when I said, "Snowden Family Clambake," so he'd heard about the murder, but just pointed to a rack in the lobby and said, "Put 'em over there."

"Do you work nights or just days?" I asked as conversationally as I could.

"Just days."

"Who works nights?"

"Wally."

Thanks, very helpful. "He around?"

"He. Works. Nights," the desk clerk answered as if I weren't very bright—which perhaps I was not, I realized when I thought about the question.

"I meant, does Wally live on the premises?" Lots of the bigger hotels like the Bellevue had small attic rooms and dormitories where they put up summer help.

"Nooo," the desk clerk answered slowly, so poor dim me could take it in.

"Thanks." What was I doing there anyway? Binder and Flynn would have covered all this ground already.

Outside, I gathered my thoughts. The groom was the obvious person who might have had a motive to kill Ray. I had to find out if Tony had slept in his room the night of the murder.

I walked partway down the footbridge and looked back. The Bellevue was the largest and most popular hotel in Busman's Harbor, the one that was full when the others still had VACANCY signs outside. Nonetheless, it had a slightly ramshackle appearance. Part hotel, part motel, it had been built onto during boom times and left alone during busts. If there had even been architects involved with the various additions, none had paid attention to stylistic or historical continuity.

I knew from long familiarity with the Bellevue's brochures that its honeymoon suite had a distinctive balcony with a gorgeous harbor view. Scanning its helter-skelter facade, I eventually spotted the balcony. It was three stories up on the far right side, away from the dining room and other public areas.

I scouted for an entrance to that part of the building. When I found it, the outside door was unlocked, not an unusual thing in the daytime when guests would be coming and going and the maids would be hard at work cleaning rooms. I climbed the stairs to the third floor, angling down the twisting hallways toward the part of the building where I thought the honeymoon suite must be. Partway there I caught a break. A sign for the honeymoon suite pointed down a long hallway toward the front of the building. There was only one room at the end. Its double doors were open, a maid's cart parked in front of it.

Before I could lose my nerve, I walked up and knocked on the doorjamb. "Hello!"

The maid poked her head out of the bathroom. She had on rubber gloves and held a toilet brush. "Hello?" She was Chinese and spoke with a heavy accent. I had no doubt that, like the Russian girl at the Lighthouse, the maid was on some kind of "educational" exchange—which meant she'd paid a middleman an exorbitant fee for a visa and transportation to the States. For that, despite whatever might have been advertised, she'd gotten a minimum wage job. In the worst cases, and I had heard the Bellevue was worst case, "students" were charged virtually every dime they made for room and board. It really was a scandal. I worried what she was most likely "learning" on her educational exchange was what incredible slobs, not to mention poor tippers, Americans could be.

"I'm thinking of staying here for my honeymoon," I lied. "The guy at the front desk said I could look around."

"Yes," she answered carefully. "Very nice room. You like it?"

I understood that this was an opportunity she probably wasn't getting enough of, a chance to practice her English.

"Beautiful," I said. And it was. A spacious room with expansive views of the harbor islands and the yachts at their moorings, high enough up that it would be absolutely private even with the curtains open. For form's sake, I opened the French doors, stepped out onto the balcony, and took in the view, looking across the harbor at the backside of the Snuggles and my parents' house, solid as a rock, on the top of the hill.

"I heard there was a murder here," I said to the girl when I went back into the room.

"No, no. Not here." She shook her head. "The friend of the, the . . . person who dead stay here."

"A friend of the victim." Might as well help her with her vocabulary. "How interesting. Did the police question you?"

She nodded yes.

That must have been scary for her.

"I tell them everything they ask."

"What did they ask?"

"Did he, the friend, sleep in this room that night?"

"Did he?"

"I think so. His clothes all around. He shave in the sink. I'm certain. But he sleep on top of the bed. Not under covers. There was a . . . a . . ." She struggled to find the word. "Like this." She went to the bed and lay on top of the bedspread. Then she got up and pointed to the slight dent her body made. "See—where he sleep on top."

So Tony had been in the room, at least for a while. But he hadn't had a good night's sleep. Prewedding jitters, or because something had caused him to leave the room before he got into bed? I wondered what Binder and Flynn thought of the maid's answers. A dent in a bedspread and some whiskers in the sink weren't evidence that the groom had slept there through the night, as far as I was concerned.

I pulled a twenty-dollar bill from my wallet,

handed it to the maid, and said I would strongly consider the Bellevue for my honeymoon.

   As I tossed my empty tote bag on my shoulder, my stomach rumbled. Lunchtime . . . actually almost past it. I crossed the footbridge and headed straight to Gus's.

Chapter 24

Tuesday was one of the days I'd been eating lunch at Gus's regularly with Chris Durand. It wasn't something we ever talked about or planned. I was always there Tuesday, Thursday, and Saturday at 1:00 and so was he. It was a little later than most working people in the harbor ate, so by the end of the meal we usually had the place to ourselves.

I'd expected that by the start of clambake season our lunches would have been over, I'd have been spending every day on Morrow Island, and Chris's landscaping and cab businesses would have been going full swing. But that Tuesday, I wasn't on the island, so I was thrilled to see Chris's cab parked outside Gus's door.

Chris was already in "our booth" with his food when I walked in. "Hey, beautiful," he called.

Once again I looked down at my work boots,

sweatshirt, and jeans, and grimaced. "Let me order," I said.

Gus was grilling a burger and had his back to the counter, so I waited. You didn't talk to Gus's back. He had us all trained to wait until he turned around. And he didn't turn around until whatever was on the grill was perfectly cooked and in its little checkered cardboard boat.

"I'm sorry about the fire, Julia," Chris said when I finally sat down. "What did Ditzy say?" Chris had sat across from me and listened to me rant and scheme about our financial situation for months, so leave it to him to cut right to the important question.

"What could he say? We have five down days built into the schedule. We've only had two so far." I said it with far more confidence than I felt.

"Still . . ." Chris let it hang there. We both knew the down days were for bad weather, not for murder. The bad weather would still come.

"How about you? Has Lieutenant Binder let up any?"

"I haven't seen him yet today. Makes a nice change."

"Before the fire, Binder told me he didn't think the murder had anything to do with Morrow Island. He thought the body was put at Windsholme to upset the bride."

"Upset? More like terrorize. But that's good news. I mean for you. Not for her."

"For you, too. Why would you want to hurt a woman you never met? Anyway, with the fire, I'm afraid Binder may be back to thinking Wilson's death has something to do with the island." Talking about the fire reminded me about the cleaned-up playhouse, which reminded me, I wanted to ask Chris—

"Julia Snowden!" Gus shouted, his usual method for letting people know their food was ready. As I walked into the front room to retrieve my lunch, I saw a car pull up behind Chris's cab. An official Maine state police car. Binder and Flynn. *What are they doing here?* If ever I wanted Gus to invoke his "no strangers" rule, it was right then.

Binder and Flynn made their way down the steps and came through the door.

"Christopher Durand," Flynn yelled.

The few other diners in the booths looked around.

"Here." Chris jumped up from our booth.

"We've got a warrant to search your vehicle."

"Sure." Chris fished in his pocket for his keys. "Let me open it for you."

"Not here," Flynn said. "State lab. We want to search it micro-scop-ickly."

"Oh." Chris looked confused. "You want me to drive it there?"

"No. We've got a tow truck coming."

"Sure." Chris stood tall, but the color had drained from behind his tanned face and his hand shook ever so slightly as he gave Flynn his car key.

I could tell by the flicker of his eyelash that Binder hadn't missed the slight tremor, either. I realized both my hands were clenched at my sides. So unfair. First they'd taken away my livelihood by closing down the clambake. Now they were taking Chris's by impounding his cab.

Chapter 25

A tow truck came and took Chris's cab away. Binder and Flynn said they'd drop Chris at the parking spot where he kept the pickup he used for his landscaping business. When they left, I felt a little dizzy. Chris had nothing to do with the fire at Windsholme. He had no reason to want to upset Michaela. He didn't fit into either theory of the case Binder had said they were pursuing. Why would they take his cab?

I wanted to call out to Chris to get a lawyer, but I didn't want to say anything in front of Binder and Flynn. Besides Chris was a grown-up. He'd know what to do.

Gus cleared his throat and I looked over at the counter where my clam roll and fries sat in their cheery paper boats. I shook my head. I couldn't eat anything now. Gus quietly threw them into the trash. "No charge today."

My cell phone beeped. Sonny. "Where are you?

Etienne and I are waiting at the dock with the building inspector."

Building inspector? Man. The most important thing going on in my life and I'd completely forgotten about it.

Sonny, Etienne, Jamie, and a pudgy, middle-aged man I didn't know were waiting on our Boston Whaler when I scurried to the dock.

"At last," Sonny called in a voice that could be heard for blocks. "Glad you could be bothered."

I glared at him and put out my hand to the stranger. "Julia Snowden."

He introduced himself as the Busman's Harbor building inspector.

I turned to Jamie. "You coming, too?"

"Hi, yourself." He smiled politely in the face of my rudeness. "Lieutenant Binder asked me to come along. Still technically a crime scene."

Sonny steered the boat away from the dock. "What kept you?"

"I ate lunch at Gus's." That was an exaggeration, since I hadn't actually eaten anything. "The cops . . . er"—I stole a glance at Jamie—"state police impounded Chris's cab." There was no reason not to tell them. Jamie, for sure, already knew, and the news, including the nugget that I was there when it happened, would be all over the harbor by the time we got back.

"Tough break," Sonny said. "But if anyone knows how to behave when the cops are taking an

interest in you, it's Chris Durand." Sonny and
Etienne shared a laugh about this, and I thought
I saw some amusement in Jamie's eyes, too. Sonny
loved making references to the sketchy part of
Chris's life I never saw, the part that had been in
trouble since high school.

Jamie moved toward the stern and I followed.
"Chris isn't really a suspect, is he?"

"You know I can't tell you that."

Impounding Chris's cab still didn't make sense
to me. "I know the desk clerk at the Lighthouse
Inn saw Ray *after* he got out of Chris's cab," I said
to Jamie. "I know Michaela called Ray from the
Snuggles and left in the middle of the night to
meet him. I know Tony probably didn't sleep in
his bed the night of the murder, either. How does
any of this add up to Chris being involved?"

Jamie looked horrified. "Julia! What the heck
have you been up to?"

"The state police are going to make me lose
my family's business. Am I supposed to just sit
and wait?" I channeled Gus's flinty Maine inde-
pendence.

"The state police didn't murder anyone on
your family's island. If this murder made your financial problems worse, that's on the killer, not
the police. And yes, you are supposed to sit and
wait. That's exactly what you're supposed to do."
Jamie exhaled after he finished his little lecture.

Glancing past him I was relieved to see Morrow Island come into view. When you don't do all the seal-and-lighthouse ogling, it really is a short trip from the harbor.

As we climbed onto our dock, Gabrielle came out of her house. Something passed wordlessly between her and Etienne and he put an arm around her.

"They were here all morning," she said. I understood she meant the arson team. "They took many, many photographs and took away some burned boards."

"Standard procedure, if they suspect arson," the building inspector said. "The boards will be tested for accelerant."

We walked toward Windsholme. In the daylight, the damage to the porch looked worse than it had the night before. The inspector walked around, taking photos and making notes on a form.

"Do you see evidence of accelerant?" I asked.

"Yes," the inspector and Etienne answered simultaneously, and I remembered I was in the presence of not one, but two men who really understood fire.

"It's hard to figure how it could have burned so fast and hot without it," the inspector said. "Even though firefighting is a challenge out here, you people jumped on it right away. This really burned."

Gabrielle headed back to her house, sniffling slightly at the sight of the ruined porch. The rest of us went around to the front of Windsholme. Jamie opened the security device on the big front doors and let us in. The inspector went straight through the great hall to the dining room. Its interior smelled heavily of smoke and at the east end of the room there was water damage to the hand-painted wallpaper. The French doors to the side porch were a charred mess, with half the upper panes gone. But the room was intact.

"Doesn't look bad," the inspector admitted. "I'll have to see the floors above and below to make sure there's nothing structural."

Together, we trooped around the house while he poked and prodded. The inspector focused only on the far left side of the mansion by the porch, so even though there were four floors to view, it didn't take him very long.

"You had some electrical work done here recently, as I recall," the inspector said.

"Two rooms on the main floor," I confirmed. "We were going to use them as dressing rooms for weddings and such." What a dream that seemed like. "Did the electrical work cause the fire?"

The inspector shook his head. "No. Nice job. I inspected it this spring."

A little later, I found myself alone with Etienne

in the top floor hallway while Sonny and Jamie looked over a bedroom with the inspector.

"How'd it go at the station this morning?" I assumed his interview with Binder had gone forward despite the events of the previous night. "It's rough the way Binder's interviewed you so many times. Why won't he take your word that you didn't hear anything that night?"

Etienne hesitated. I thought he wasn't going to answer, but then, keeping his voice low, he said, "You might as well hear this from me. Binder is interested because I was here the night of the murder. But he's also questioning me because, well, because I met Ray Wilson before. Before the day he died."

"What?"

"Shhh." But it was too late. My involuntary shout had attracted Jamie's attention and he moved toward us. With a quick shake of his head, Etienne ended the conversation.

Suddenly, I felt like the wind was knocked out of me. The hallway closed in. I gasped, trying to get some air, but couldn't. I swayed on my feet, dizzy and unable to breathe. The tightness in my chest was so intense, I thought my heart would burst.

Next thing I knew, Jamie was forcing my head down to my knees, commanding, "Breathe slowly, into your hands."

Blood rushed to my head. I thought I might pass out. For the life of me, I couldn't breathe. *Please, please don't let me pass out in front of these guys.*

"Julia, breathe into your hands," Jamie commanded.

I cupped my hands over my mouth and nose and inhaled. Miraculously, air entered my lungs and my heart slowed down. After what felt like an hour, but was probably less than a minute, I stood up unsteadily.

"You okay?" Sonny asked.

"Fine," I lied. I was lightheaded and exhausted. As the adrenaline surge from the panic attack ebbed, it left me without physical resources, weak and trembly. I wanted more than anything in the world to get out of there, but when I tried to move my feet, I found I couldn't. I stood, shivering through a brief, embarrassing discussion about who was going to carry me down the stairs.

"I can walk." I could barely talk, but I figured if I could convince them, I could convince myself. Etienne looped a strong arm under mine. The journey down the grand staircase was excruciatingly slow.

At last, we were back outside and Jamie secured the doors behind us.

"What do you think?" I asked, glad to be outdoors and on firm ground. "Can we open the clambake?"

No one said a word about what had just happened.

"That's really more than one question," the inspector answered. "Since you don't use the mansion in your business, you can open as soon as you tear down what's left of the porch and find a way to secure it so none of your customers have access. As far as I'm concerned, you can open as soon as you get that done. Then it's up to the police."

"So we can reopen as soon as the police give us the go ahead?" I clarified.

"Yes, and as soon as you get rid of that porch and secure the house."

"Do we need a permit to pull the porch down?"

"Lady, this ain't Manhattan."

Despite the physical effects of the panic attack, I felt elated. I just had to convince Binder, and we could open the day after tomorrow.

Chapter 26

Etienne dropped us at the town dock. After our hallway conversation, I'd never gotten him alone again. I was shocked by what he'd told me—that he'd met Ray Wilson while he was alive. How could that have happened? In what way could their lives have possibly intersected? And why hadn't Etienne told me this before? There had been so many opportunities—aboard the *Jacquie II* the day of the murder, Sunday when I'd met him on the town dock, or even the day before at the clambake when he'd told me Binder wanted to interview him again.

When we got to town, I walked alongside Jamie.

He finally realized I was going the same place he was. "You coming to the station?"

"You heard the building inspector. The town isn't my problem. Binder is. I figure it won't hurt to beg."

"Julia, I've made Lieutenant Binder aware of your situation."

"And I appreciate it, but asking directly still has to be the best thing."

Jamie looked concerned. "Are you sure you're up to doing this right now?"

"Yes." And I was. My body felt like I'd run for miles, but otherwise I'd been fine since we'd gotten out of Windsholme.

It wasn't my first panic attack. I'd had them before, though not for months. I thought I'd left them behind in New York. But then again, the last several days had brought nothing but stress. I'd had a pervasive sense of unease about Windsholme since the moment I'd seen Ray Wilson's body hanging from the staircase—and no wonder. That had to explain my panic attack on the top floor.

At the police station, even more law enforcement people were crammed into the cubicles than there'd been just two days before. Arson investigators, I imagined, had joined the bustling team. The civilian at the front desk took me straight into the conference room to see Binder. "Wish me luck," I called to Jamie as I left him.

About half a dozen officers were in the room, though I didn't see Detective Flynn. Binder stood up from behind the table and cleared his throat. "Can you give us a minute?"

The other officers scattered.

"Ms. Snowden." Binder remained standing. At first I thought he was being polite. Then I realized he stood because he wanted to keep the meeting as brief as possible.

"Lieutenant, I've just met with the building inspector and he says I can open as soon as you give the go ahead," I exaggerated slightly.

"Did he now? I want to hear what the arson team tells us about the presence of accelerants in your fire."

"But why? You told me you didn't think the murder had anything to do with Morrow Island."

"And then there was the fire, and now we're rethinking." He stood with his sports jacket open, a pen in his left hand. The very model of reasonableness. His calm detachment probably made him a good cop, but it was making me crazy. Why couldn't he understand how important this was to my family and me? Why didn't he feel the same urgency I did?

"I'm not sure you understand—"

"Ms. Snowden, I do. But I let you start up the clambakes too soon the last time, and now I regret it. We have some great leads. Let us wrap this thing up, then you can open."

I could tell he wasn't going to budge. "Can you at least give us permission to demolish what's left of the porch, so we can open right away when you give us the go ahead?"

"I'll check with the arson investigators and see what I can do."

As I opened the station door to leave, I ran right into Chris Durand coming the other way.

"Julia! I'm so glad to see you."

"What're you doing here?"

He shrugged and stepped back so I could get outside.

"If you're here to plead for your cab, it probably won't get you anywhere. Binder doesn't care if he destroys your income, believe me."

"No, nothing like that."

As we moved outside into the sunlight, I noticed he looked pale and worried. I longed for his usual, "Hey, beautiful."

Chris cocked his head toward the bench on the green across the street from the police station. We walked the short distance to it and sat down. He put his head in his hands and said, "I'm here for another interview."

"What? Why? I don't get this," I fumed. "I know the desk clerk at the Lighthouse saw Ray *after* you dropped him off."

"And then saw him leave again."

So Chris knew that, too.

"Anyway, I'm sure this meeting is about what they found in my cab."

"What could they have found in your cab?"

"For one thing, I'm sure they found that my cab's been cleaned. Very thoroughly. Recently."

"So what? So you keep a clean cab."

"Not that kind of cleaning. And for another, I'm pretty certain they found blood in my cab. Wilson's blood."

It was the second shocking revelation of the day, after Etienne's admission that he'd met Ray Wilson when he was alive. I wasn't sure how much more I could take. But I was also sure, deep in my bones, Chris hadn't murdered anyone. I was as certain of his innocence as I was of my own. "How did Ray's blood get in your cab?" I asked.

"Wilson was really drunk when I took him back to his hotel from Crowley's. He got sick in the back of my cab. I was angry. For one thing, it meant I couldn't pick up any more fares, and the bars were just closing. He'd cost me a bundle. So I drove to the marina, grabbed a bucket and some rags off my boat. It wasn't until I opened up the back door of the cab that I saw his vomit was full of blood. I held my breath and scrubbed. It was really bad, so I took all the seats out and scrubbed some more. Anyway, I'm sure that's what they want to talk to me about."

I flashed on the image of Ray Wilson hanging from the staircase, blood all down the front of his pink polo shirt. "Did you tell the police about the blood when they interviewed you before?"

Chris shook his head. "I never thought it would

go this far. I thought they would catch whoever it was long before they got around to searching my cab. I guess I'll be telling them now. I know it looks bad. I feel like an idiot."

"What happened after Ray was sick?"

"Exactly what I told you the other day. Wilson got out of the cab and went into the Lighthouse Inn. Like a lot of drunks, getting sick seemed to make him feel better."

"Did Ray go into the hotel lobby with his shirt covered in blood?" Surely Clarice Kemp would have mentioned it, if that were the scuttlebutt.

"He had a windbreaker with him. He put it on. He was so drunk, he couldn't zip it up. I got out of the cab and helped him. The zipper stuck, and I caught my finger."

"Are you saying your DNA is on Wilson's jacket?"

Chris nodded. "Could be. Was he wearing the jacket when you, you know . . ."

"When I saw him hanging from the staircase? No. Just a pink polo shirt with blood down the front. No windbreaker."

We sat on the bench for a moment, each absorbed in our own thoughts. It was so wrong that Chris was mixed up in this.

"Julia, I can't believe what a mess this has turned into. I'm scared about what could happen."

Scared? I couldn't imagine Chris scared. Yet there he was, telling me it was so. Him confessing his fear rattled me more than anything else in the conversation.

Chris stood and turned toward the station. "Here goes nothing."

"I think you should get a lawyer."

"A—I can't afford it. B—I didn't kill the guy. I'll just have to trust in the system."

Chapter 27

I sat on the bench a while after Chris left. The conversation had been unlike any we'd ever had. Since March, I'd poured out my emotions to him—my anger at Sonny, my frustration at being home, my fears for the clambake, but it was the first time Chris had ever been open and vulnerable with me. He'd never talked about how he felt, ever.

I was glad I'd been there when he needed me. Elated he'd opened up to me. But I wasn't as trustful of the system as he claimed to be. I pulled out my phone and texted Michaela. r u still bath? Boy, that text looked funny.

She responded immediately. yes at m-i-l help!

So, she was still at her almost mother-in-law's house. I remembered Tony's mother from the non-wedding day. A pinched-faced woman who looked none too happy, though it was impossible for me to say why—Ray's absence, the informal wedding, or some longer-term issue, like displeasure at her son's choice of bride. Anyway, it sounded like Michaela needed rescuing.

I texted back. **coffee?**

yes! when?

25?

done. front n centre.

By which I guessed she meant the Cafe Creme on the corner of Front and Centre Streets in Bath in twenty-five minutes.

A few minutes later, I drove out of Busman's Harbor and headed up the peninsula to Route One. I'd had to borrow my mother's car, which made me feel like a teenager. I really needed to solve my transportation problem. But buying a car would mean I wasn't planning to return to Manhattan any time soon, and with the clambake closed for business, I couldn't let myself even think about that.

As I drove over the bridge into Bath, Maine, I saw the hulking mechanical cranes at the Bath Iron Works shipyard that overhung the natural beauty of the Kennebec River. It was one of my favorite views, visual evidence that Bath was a working town as well as a tourist town. Front Street was historic and inviting, a walkable amalgamation of upscale clothing stores, trendy restaurants, and antique stores, along with funky used bookstores and casual pubs.

Michaela sat in the coffee shop reading a book.

She'd snagged a great seat on a couch in the big front window. I could see why she liked the place. It was New York City–like in its ambiance, though with more room between the tables. My heart went *ping* as I imagined being back in the city at a place just like it.

Michaela greeted me as if we were long lost friends. I wondered if she'd left her mother-in-law's house the minute she got my text. We hadn't been close in New York, but I was probably the closest thing she had a friend in Maine. As she hugged me, I wondered why anyone would want to ruin this woman's wedding day, and in such a horrible way. There was only one person I could think of. Tony. I took a seat in the comfy chair across from her.

"I'm so glad you're still here," I said.

Michaela rolled her eyes. "I'm not. Living with Tony's parents is a nightmare. His dad is great, but as far as his mom is concerned, no one will ever be good enough for her Tony. I knew that when I married—agreed to marry—him, of course. But I hadn't realized I'd be staying at her house for days when I was supposed to be on my honeymoon."

"Michaela, I'm so sorry. For everything."

"It's okay." She sighed. "It's not your fault. It is what it is. Tony and I will stay until after Ray's service at least. His body's been released. Tony is with Ray's parents making the arrangements.

So much time has gone by, they want to have the service as soon as possible. Tomorrow even." Michaela's voice got a little husky as she spoke about Ray. "But enough about my troubles. How are you?"

I filled her in on my news since the weekend. She'd heard about the fire. "I never thought my wedding would bring so much unhappiness to both of us."

The pretty, young barista called out that my cappuccino was ready, along with a refill for Michaela. We sat for a moment enjoying the warm drinks while I gathered my courage to ask the next question. Despite my sympathy for Michaela, saving the clambake had to be my highest priority.

"The clambake is pretty much shut down until this murder gets solved. I know this has been worse for you than for us, but if we're closed for even a few more days, we'll lose the business altogether. So I have to ask, is there anything at all you haven't told Binder that might help him? Is there anything you have told him that he's not following up on?"

Michaela drew her pretty dark brows together. It wasn't where she'd expected the conversation to go.

She didn't say anything, so I prompted her. "I know you and Ray had an argument in Crowley's the night before he was murdered. And I know you called him from the Snuggles and were gone for several hours that night."

Michaela looked into her coffee cup and said nothing.

"Were you and Ray having an affair?" I asked it boldly and baldly. I had to get the question out.

"No! Whatever gave you that idea? It was nothing like that." I saw a flash of the bride aboard the *Jacquie II* who'd grasped my arm so tightly it went numb and demanded we turn the boat around. Michaela was so even-keeled most of the time, but there was a temper burning down deep.

I didn't want to admit her maid of honor had hinted about a relationship with Ray. Or that Binder had said Ray's body was left the way it was to upset her. So I didn't answer her directly, just pushed on. "What did you fight with Ray about, then?"

The anger drained away just as quickly as it erupted, replaced, it seemed, by sadness. "I can't tell you."

"Why can't you tell me? Ray's dead."

"I know, but I made a promise. And nowadays, I keep my promises."

Nowadays? What did that mean? I felt like I was walking a tightrope between her emotional extremes. I tried again. "Where did you go that night? Were you with Tony?"

"Tony!" Her eyes widened in surprise and she sat back in the deep couch.

"Because I don't think he slept—"

It took me a moment to realize she wasn't listening to me. She was staring through the plate glass window at something behind me. By the time I turned around, Tony pushed his way through the front door of the coffee shop.

"Hi, babe. Hi, Julia. This looks like fun. Mind if I join?"

If Michaela said more than two words after that point in the conversation, I don't remember what they were. Tony confirmed that Ray's funeral would be the next afternoon; the gathering afterward would be at Tony's parents' house. Ray's parents just weren't up to hosting. Michaela chewed on her lower lip while Tony talked about his boyhood in Bath and growing up with Ray, how they'd swum in the tidal waters at Popham Beach and played basketball together in high school. Like Michaela, Tony was casually, but expensively dressed. The cashmere sweater tied around his shoulders demonstrated how far he'd come from being a townie in Bath.

When he spoke about Ray, Tony appeared wistful, not angry. Not betrayed. Not guilty, at least as far as I could tell. His hand sought out Michaela's, just as he had when I'd talked to them in the dining room at the Bellevue Inn.

The more Tony talked, the more ridiculous I felt that I'd suspected Tony of murdering Ray out of jealousy. For one thing, Tony seemed absolutely secure in Michaela's love. And for another, though he wasn't broken up and sobbing, his reminiscences about Ray were warm, not tinged by anger in any way.

So Tony wasn't jealous of Ray. But there was something about Tony—the way he took control of the conversation, the way Michaela was so quiet in his presence—that left me uncomfortable. And I still didn't understand Michaela's relationship with Ray. If it wasn't an affair, why did she go out to meet him on her wedding's eve?

I promised them I'd go to Ray's funeral the next day and said my good-byes. I got into my mother's car and headed home, feeling frustrated. What had I been thinking? That I'd out-investigate the state police major crimes unit? All I'd succeeded in doing was wasting the day. I was farther than ever from discovering who'd killed Ray Wilson.

Chapter 28

I shouted to my mom that I was home and ran upstairs to my office. I checked my cell phone to make sure that Binder hadn't called to say we could open. No such luck, not that I expected it after our "chat." I set about confirming with everyone we'd be closed tomorrow, yet again. No one was surprised. Livvie hadn't accepted any reservations. If I'd been able to be more honest with myself, I'd have been more honest with the employees and sent out a "stand down until further notice" type of e-mail. Instead, I was upbeat as possible and stated we were "day-to-day."

That chore behind me, I read a few blogs and generally procrastinated. I was discouraged about everything. The clambake business. The murder investigation. I could hear Mom in the kitchen, cooking us dinner. *God help me.*

My eyes fell on the Sunday *New York Times* I'd been reading earlier, the real estate section still open on the top. I'd never finished going through the paper. I decided to dream about Manhattan apartments a little more.

As I pulled the *Times* to my lap, I noticed a page in the real estate section was dog-eared, just like the one containing Tony and Michaela's wedding announcement had been. I turned to the page. About halfway down in the left-hand column was a story about Tony and Ray.

OFF THE GRID BUT LUXE

Resort developers Tony Poitras and Ray Wilson have found a winning formula for today's overwhelmed consumers. Can't take a break from your smartphone, e-mail, or social media, even on vacation? Poitras and Wilson's resorts force you to slow down and smell the roses. Built on islands, the resorts purposely offer no Internet, cell coverage, or television. You can't feed your addiction because these services just are not available. But unlike most other "off the grid" vacations, these resorts are luxurious. You can't get online, but you can get a massage, a sumptuous meal, and a bottle of Dom Pérignon.

Built from the enormous "summer cottages," hunting lodges, and private hotels of the super rich of another age,

Poitras and Wilson's properties allow guests to live it up old-school, as in old school tie. Customers pay four figures a day at the low end to be whisked in and out via helicopter for an experience one described as a cross between a "luxury spa and an English country house party." Poitras and Wilson have properties in the Finger Lakes of New York, near Mackinaw Island, Michigan, off Vancouver, British Columbia, and in the Caribbean. They are currently on the hunt for more properties.

A chill ran through me. Who the heck was I dealing with? At first, I'd assumed Michaela had approached me about her wedding reception because we'd been acquaintances in New York. Later, I'd learned that wasn't true. Tony had grown up just down the coast and had chosen Morrow Island for their wedding. Now it turned out, Tony and Ray were also in the business of turning islands into resorts. Were they after Morrow Island?

After a truly terrible dinner, I rushed back to my office. I stayed up late into the night, searching the Web for everything I could find out about Ray and Tony. For the most part, the articles confirmed what I'd read in the *Times*. They had started as contractors, then became residential developers, then hit on the idea for luxury resorts in remote places without cell service or Internet. Part of their "winning formula" was to get the properties cheap from cash-strapped owners.

I visited all the Web pages for their resorts and they were, indeed, lovely places, former country homes that Ray and Tony gutted and rebuilt with attention to period detail and an overall sense of cosseting for their guests. Some articles in local papers near the resorts complained about the environmental impact of things like indoor swimming pools on small islands, not to mention the noise of the helicopters coming and going, but for the most part, Ray and Tony seemed to be welcomed as environmentally conscious custodians of places that would otherwise have been lost.

I found much less, nothing in fact, about Quentin Tupper III, the man who'd appeared, left me a newspaper, and then disappeared again. As I'd remembered, tons of Tuppers lived in Maine, particularly on that part of the coast, so there were genealogies galore online and newspaper stories about lots of Tuppers, but not Quentin. I wondered how a grown man who lived in New York City could leave no footprints on the World Wide Web. Had he never run in a road race, sung in a chorus, donated to a charity, or reviewed an online purchase? It seemed so unlikely.

I'd been irritated when I found the dog-eared wedding announcement. I'd thought Quentin Tupper was rubbing my nose in the tragic events that occurred at the Snowden Family Clambake's very first wedding reception. Now, I didn't know what to think. Was he sending me some kind of message?

I vaguely remembered that he lived somewhere in my New York City neighborhood. I wanted to contact him, to ask what he was up to, but there was nothing.

I searched until I fell into bed, exhausted, at two in the morning.

Chapter 29

I woke up the next morning to a gray glow outside my windows. My bedroom usually offered great views of the harbor, but I could barely make out the Snuggles Inn across the street. I climbed back into bed. There was no clambake to run, anyway.

I was awakened a few hours later by my cell phone. "Ms. Snowden, Lieutenant Binder. You're cleared to go ahead and take down the rest of that porch."

"Does that mean we're open for business?" I could barely contain my excitement.

"No. Let's take this one step at a time. I said you could demolish the porch."

"Thank you, thank you, thank you." There followed a series of calls between Sonny and me and radio calls between Sonny and Etienne. We decided Sonny would borrow his dad's lobster boat—his dad hadn't gone out in the fog—

because the big plywood sheets we needed to close off the dining room's French doors wouldn't fit in our Boston Whaler. Etienne would bring the Whaler in, then would return to the island with Sonny and the supplies in his dad's boat. I was responsible for returning the Whaler to the island.

After I hung up, I became aware of the sounds of voices and banging as well as a smell I remembered well from my childhood. Still in a T-shirt and pj bottoms, I descended the back stairs into the kitchen.

Livvie was there with Page, along with Sarah Halsey and her son Tyler. Mom had her back to me, facing the stove. They were all busily engaged in the process of making strawberry rhubarb jam. Rhubarb jam day was a family tradition, and judging by their jumpy, chattering ways, Page and Tyler were pretty excited about it.

"No school?" I asked.

"We got out yes-ter-day." Page sang it rather than said it. Like a lot of Maine kids, she loved foods that turned other children green. She was brought up eating all manner of crustaceans and bi-valves, after all. I'd seen Page and Tyler fight over the last fiddlehead fern in a bowl. But nothing, in my opinion, was stranger than her love of rhubarb, the plant that grew like a weed and tasted, unless mixed with something sweet, like bitter celery.

Rhubarb grew all around our house, and my

mother, combining her skinflint upper-class
Yankee upbringing with her thrifty Maine house-
wife ways, couldn't stand not to use every bit of it.
So on a day she designated in June every year, all
rhubarb not previously used in pie, cake, or com-
pote was cut down and turned into strawberry
rhubarb jam.

I helped myself to coffee and sat on the back
stairs out of the way. I smiled hello to Sarah, remembering how uncomfortable she'd been when
I last spoke to her at the clambake. She smiled
back as she chopped rhubarb stalks.

Livvie and Sarah were close friends. They were
about the same age and had been pregnant at the
same time—too young, in my parents' opinion,
and in mine, truth be told. But while Livvie and
Sonny were obviously deeply in love, Sarah had
arrived in Busman's Harbor alone, taking what
retail work she could get during her pregnancy.
Her mother Marie showed up not long before
Tyler was born and had never left.

They rented an apartment over Gleason's
Hardware store on Main Street. Sarah got her
GED and then her teaching degree, no easy feat
with a baby and a job, especially when the nearest
university was an hour commute each way. She
taught kindergarten in town and worked for us
summers and weekends. My father had hired her
after Tyler was born, and I knew she depended on
her clambake income. Her mother was a lunch

lady, also at Busman's Elementary, and she, too, worked for the clambake in the summers, cooking with Gabrielle. Tyler had grown into a polite, funny boy who was Page's best friend.

Sarah had always been diffident around me, which was something I felt badly about. True, I was her summer boss and a couple years older, but neither should matter. As far as I was concerned, she had nothing to be ashamed of and a lot to be proud of.

As I watched, Sarah continued slicing rhubarb while Livvie cut up strawberries. Page stood at the sink washing another batch of rhubarb while Tyler removed the jam jars and lids from their boxes. Livvie had quietly co-opted the jam making, as she had all the other food preparation chores. My mother was still as much a part of the day as ever, but Livvie was the one who actually determined the amount of each ingredient and cooked the jam.

I shuddered remembering my mother's version—gray, slimy, awful. I died of embarrassment every December when Livvie and I delivered jars of it, festooned with bright red bows, to neighbors for the holidays. Now that Livvie cooked the jam, it was delicious, but I wondered how many of our neighbors still poured it straight down the sink without even tasting it.

As I sat watching, I tried to recall where Sarah

had come from. I remembered when she turned up in town, a pretty girl, her pregnancy already showing. Somewhere along the line, had I heard that Sarah and her mother had moved to Busman's Harbor from Bath?

Bath, where Tony and Ray were from? Maybe Sarah knew them. Maybe that explained her presence at Crowley's the night of the murder. Remembering how she'd freaked out the last time, I wasn't going to ask her anything in front of the kids.

I stood up. "Got to get dressed."

"Where are you off to today?" Mom asked.

"Over to the island. The cops said we're free to clean up."

Sonny and I had minimized our descriptions of the damage from the fire when we'd told Mom about it. Of course, almost every guest had a camera and there were plenty of ugly pictures and even videos of the leaping flames available online, but that was nothing Mom needed to know about.

"That's good, dear. It's foggy." My mother looked pointedly out the kitchen windows and it was true, the fog hadn't burned off yet.

"Maybe you'll see the ghost!" Page crowed. Then she and Tyler collapsed into giggles. "Woo-woo-woo! The ghost! The ghost!"

Like all good Maine mansions, Windsholme had a ghost. Actually, it had three. A stonemason killed during the mansion's construction, a parlor maid who died of a burst appendix during a storm in the 1890s, and my mother's great uncle Hal, who was killed in France during World War I. Why Hal had returned to the island to do his haunting, no one had explained.

"Have you seen the ghost?" I asked Page.

"Of course, silly." Page hadn't lived on Morrow during the summer the way Mom, Livvie, and I had, but she'd spent a lot of time there. Before money got so tight that Livvie had to work in the ticket booth, relegating Page to Mom's care, Page had spent almost every day on the island during the season, running pretty free.

During her spring vacation this year, while Sonny, Chris, and Etienne were cleaning up the island, Page had gone out every day, with Tyler, if I remembered right. I was glad she'd had that time on Morrow, climbing the rocks, exploring the tide pools, building forts in the woods. The island was a special place for a kid. You felt like you knew every inch of it, like you ruled it. I thought of Page in that unbroken chain of children in my family playing on the island, starting with my great-grandfather and his siblings and continuing to my grandmother, my mother, and Livvie and me. I was sick and sad that part of Page's childhood, of all our childhoods, might come to an end while it was my responsibility to save it.

"Page, did the men fix up the playhouse for you and Tyler to use when you were out on the island this spring?" I asked.

"No. It was a mess. But I think they should!"

Chapter 30

It was still foggy when I set out for Morrow half an hour later. I couldn't see much, but I could see enough. I knew the route so well it would be easy to slip into mental autopilot when making the trip, always a dangerous thing on the water. I stuck close to the shoreline and listened to the foghorn, bleating its warning from Dinkums Light.

I came through the mouth of the outer harbor into the Atlantic Ocean. Because of the fog, I stayed close to Westclaw Point. I followed it until I could see Morrow Island. As I came up to the inlet across from our beach, a new house loomed out of the fog. Built of dark gray granite and glass, it seemed thrust up by the boulders on which it stood. The house was massive and sleekly modern, more appropriate to Malibu than coastal Maine. But I didn't hate its looks. The building seemed oddly at home in its environment. I spotted Morrow Island across the water and headed for it.

I was happy to be heading out to the island before Etienne and Sonny. I needed to spend some time alone. Not alone, actually. I assumed Gabrielle would be there, but she usually stayed close to her house or her vegetable garden when she wasn't working.

I pulled up to the dock and called to Gabrielle. I didn't want to scare her. She appeared in a second story window of her house and waved to me. "I'm going up to Windsholme to wait for the guys," I yelled. She gave me a thumbs-up sign that she'd heard and understood.

I stood at the bottom of the lawn looking up at Windsholme. Even with its ruined side porch, the mansion was beautiful, perfectly proportioned, solid and strong. Until the fire when we'd almost lost it, I'd always viewed Windsholme as a burden. I'd never lived there and neither had my mother. It was too expensive to maintain, but even more expensive to demolish. Its plumbing was erratic, its wiring dangerous and shut off in all but the newly rewired rooms. The cost of gutting it, fixing all those things, and carting away all that horse-hair plaster was prohibitive to even think about.

As I walked up the hill, I thought about my great-great grandparents who'd built it. My mother had an ancient photo of them with their five children and servants arranged stiffly on

Windsholme's lawn. For the first time, I found myself wondering what they were like. Was this place a refuge for a happy family? Had they let their children serve them imaginary tea in the playhouse? Or, more likely, was the big house a place where they entertained to impress, their children watched over by nannies, seen but not heard? Why didn't I know the answer?

True to his word, Binder had already sent someone out to remove the security device on Windsholme's doors. I opened them and stepped inside.

I stood stock still on the spot where I'd been when I first saw Ray Wilson's body. I breathed in and out, evenly and deliberately, willing myself to roll back my memory to the great hall before it had been sullied by that sight. The air smelled of its familiar damp, with a new smokiness added. I tried to block out the acrid smell. I wanted to feel the same way about the house as I had before all the terrible things occurred. I knew from experience it was the best way to handle my panic attacks.

When I was recruited out of business school to the venture capital firm, the job was great. And I was pretty good at it. But then the economy turned and instead of helping entrepreneurs grow their companies, my work was all about downgrading projections, laying off staff, and selling assets. Too often, during the worst of the credit crunch, we were closing companies up altogether. My job became more like presiding over a dozen deaths a year. And right after my own father died.

The panic attacks had started then, in the worst of the downturn and always when I was faced with a difficult task, like telling a company board no more money would be coming to keep them afloat or telling a founder he was no longer the right person to lead his own company. I was in my twenties. What business did I have relaying that kind of terrible news to people?

I'd suffered from panic attacks in the anonymous ladies rooms of a dozen start-up companies and in airports on my way to San Jose, Provo, and Boston. My body always reacted badly when my head forced me to do something my heart resisted. The best way to combat the attacks was to get back up on the horse—to go back into the boardrooms, to get on the next plane. I had to do the same thing with Windsholme. Exorcise the demons and make it mine again.

I stood for several minutes in the great hall until I felt I could move on, then started moving through Windsholme's empty rooms. Most of the furniture had been carted off the island and sold at auction during the Depression. The rest, legend had it, had been broken up and burned in the fireplaces on cool summer nights. I thought about that generation, too, my mother's maternal grandparents. They'd been wild partiers in the twenties, but in the 1930s they were the first generation faced with keeping the island in the family. In truth, Morrow probably hadn't been sold because at the time there was no one to buy it. But the taxes had been paid somehow and the town hadn't seized the island.

I roamed through the ground floor. In the two-story kitchen, I climbed the iron spiral staircase to the balcony that ran all the way around its second level. The built-in cabinets once held china, silver, crystal, and table linens within easy reach of the footmen and butler attending to the dinner guests. I moved through the swinging door into the dining room and inspected the hand-painted Asian scenes on the wallpaper, especially in the east end of the room, where it had been damaged by smoke and water. The sight made me sad. I stood for a few minutes, breathing in and out, getting comfortable with the sight.

From there, I walked through the empty office and the billiard room before crossing to the living room and the ladies drawing room. Both opened through French doors onto the front porch.

When I was ready, I went back to the great hall again and climbed the stairs, passing the point where Ray Wilson had hung. I walked methodically from one end of the long upstairs hall to the other, opening each door, making the rooms my own again. In the master bedroom, which was over the dining room, there was more smoke and water damage, but it was limited to the wall adjacent to the side porch roof.

I continued up the curving staircase to the top floor, open to the ceiling, giving drama to the great hall three stories below. The rooms on the top floor were much smaller than those in the rest of the house, with lower ceilings and small dormered windows. It was the territory of the servants.

As I had on the other floors, I opened each door and stood in the doorway or entered the room. At the midpoint of the hallway, across from the open landing, I turned a knob, but the door stuck. It was a perennial problem in a house that was always damp. I put my shoulder against the door and pushed as hard as I could. Nothing.

I felt something whoosh past my feet and jumped a mile. "Le Roi!"

The Maine coon cat sat by the door frame, looking at me, fully aware that he'd scared the bejesus out of me. Morrow was his island. He merely suffered our presence.

"How did you get in here?" I'd closed the front door behind me, and he couldn't have passed through the burned French doors in the dining room.

"Julia? What are you doing?"

I looked over the railing. Gabrielle was in the

great hall below. I must have been so focused, I hadn't heard her enter the house.

"Up here. I can't seem to get one of the doors opened."

Gabrielle ran up the stairs, wiping her hands on her apron. "That happens always. You know—the damp. Etienne just radioed from the town dock. He and Sonny are on their way. They'll need your aid unloading when they get here."

"Sure. Help me open this door?"

Gabrielle shook her head. "Leave it be, Julia." She surprised me by taking me in her arms and giving me a fierce hug, which I returned. When she released me, she said softly, "What do you do here, Julia? Etienne told me what happened yesterday, how you broke down right in this hallway."

"I'm fine. Really I am." How could I explain I was exorcising my fear of a house I'd known all my life? "I'll be right down."

"Okay, but I don't like to leave you." Gabrielle left reluctantly.

When she was gone, I worked my way down the hall to the other end, opening every door. I went back to the door across from the landing and tried it again. It didn't budge.

By the time Sonny and Etienne arrived, the fog had burned off and the island was bathed in sunlight.

Demolishing the porch was a delicate operation. The last bit of roof had to come down without killing us, then the remaining pillars and rails, and finally the last of the burnt decking had to be pried off. The great stone footings would remain, a sort of ghost porch until it could be rebuilt. We aimed to get the area as cleaned up as possible so our guests wouldn't look at Windsholme and ask, "What happened?" That was the last thing we wanted to revisit at every clambake.

Etienne, who actually understood construction, mostly directed. Sonny, of course, argued with him, because Sonny was the greatest living expert on everything. I could sense Etienne losing his patience.

"When we finish this, we should take down as much of that damaged plaster inside as possible so I can haul it out on my dad's boat," Sonny said.

"Let's just get this porch job done so we can open up the clambake," Etienne warned.

"But while we have the boat—"

Etienne lost his temper. "We have enough to do! We only have your father's boat for a few hours."

Both of them looked at me, the tiebreaker. That had been our dynamic all spring. Once again, I had to side with Etienne. I had no way to tell if the porch part of the job would take the rest of our time, but any work required to get the clambake open had to take priority.

"Let's just take care of this porch."

"Figures," Sonny grunted and walked away, hauling some boards toward the fire pit.

I didn't tell Sonny and Etienne about my desensitizing walk through Windsholme. When the time came to nail the plywood over the space where we'd removed the destroyed French doors, I simply went into the house and braced the boards from the inside. Nobody said anything about it.

While Sonny carried another load down to the fire pit, I approached Etienne. "When we were here with the building inspector, you said you'd met Ray Wilson before."

"Yes. He came to the island. He said his best friend was getting married here and he wanted to play a trick, so he needed to take a look around."

"A trick?"

"You can't very well tie old shoes and cans to the groom's car out here, so he said he was looking for something 'more creative.'"

"And you let him look around?" Knowing what I knew about what Ray and Tony did for a living, I had my own suspicions about why Ray wanted to see the island.

"Sure. Why not? You said you wanted to do whatever we could to accommodate these private events people," Etienne reminded me.

I hate having my own words come back at me. But that triggered a happier thought. "How did Ray get to the island?"

Etienne looked at me like I was crazy. "On the freeway."

"No, I mean did he get himself over or did someone bring him?"

"Came by himself."

"Did he rent a boat or borrow it or what?"

Etienne raised his shoulders and turned up his palms, the universal symbol for "who knows?"

Ray could have come out to the island the night of the murder on his own to set up his trick on Tony. If there even was a trick. If it wasn't just a pretense to see the island. But could he have made it, drunk as he was? Chris said he seemed more sober after he threw up.

Even if Ray could have navigated on his own, that didn't answer the question of who might have met him. And killed him. And hung up his body from the staircase.

When the porch was demolished Sonny and I took his dad's lobster boat filled with debris back to the harbor. As soon as we got within cell range, I called and left a message for Binder, thanking him for allowing us take down the porch and begging him to let us open tomorrow. When I ended the call, there was a message from Michaela providing directions to Ray's funeral that afternoon. And urging me to come. Poor Michaela. She was friendless at such a stressful time and stuck with that gargoyle of a mother-in-law.

Chapter 31

After Sonny and I loaded the remains of the porch into his truck so he could make a run to the dump, I hurried home. I was so intent on getting changed for the funeral, I nearly tripped over Fiona Snuggs, who knelt on the winding walk outside my mother's house, pulling weeds. "Sorry, Miss, er, Fee."

"Just tidying up."

When my father died, Sonny had taken over the tasks of mowing the Snugg sisters' lawn and shoveling snow off their walks. The sisters had gone on caring for the gardens at my mother's house, just as they always had. Over the spring, I'd gotten used to finding a seventy-five-year-old woman crouching in our garden. Though it made me feel awkward, I knew Fee would refuse all offers of help. My sister did a little better with her. Instead of asking, Livvie just jumped in. Fee had decided that of the two of us, Livvie was the potential gardener, probably a reasonable perception, and had started mentoring her in the art of flowers and shrubs.

I helped Fiona to her feet.

"I was thinking about our conversation the other day," she said, brushing dirt from her denim skirt. "About the night of the murder. I think I've remembered something more."

I waited.

"I told you that maid of honor called Michaela several times and left messages apologizing for their fight. But I've remembered she called someone else."

"Do you know who?"

"No, but she said something like, 'She's with Ray. Where do you think she is?' And then 'You need to come over here, right now.'"

Tony. It had to be. Add to it the evidence that his bed wasn't slept in that night and who else could it have been? But why would Lynn order Tony to come to the Snuggles? Wouldn't she have sent him out to look for Michaela and Ray?

"Did Lynn leave the inn that night?"

Fee pushed a hand through her short, gray hair. "I don't know. Remember, I fell asleep in the chair."

"So soundly you might not have heard the maid of honor going out or coming in?"

Fee blushed. "Well, I didn't hear Michaela come in, did I? And yet there she was in the morning."

The older woman put a steadying hand on my shoulder and stepped back to admire her handiwork. "Beautiful, isn't it?"

I looked across our front yard, which was dotted with irregularly shaped flowerbeds. In one, bright pink peonies blazed in contrast to cool purple irises. In the shade, astilbe bloomed among the variegated greens of hosta. In the sun, yellow day lilies reached for the sky and red roses climbed the side of the garage. *When had all this bloomed?* I'd been so heads-down busy and obsessively worried about the clambake, I hadn't even noticed.

"It's beautiful, Fee," I said, giving her a little hug.

Now what had I come home for? Oh, yes, I was in a hurry to get to a funeral.

"Julia!" Michaela was at the back of the nondescript, 1960s Catholic Church when I entered for Ray's funeral. She threw her arms around me and hugged tight, confirming my suspicion that she really needed a friend. She led me to one of the very front pews, just behind the couple I took to be Ray's parents. I hadn't known Ray Wilson when he was alive, and I wouldn't have presumed to sit in such a prominent spot if I'd been on my own, but I was there to support Michaela, so I followed her lead. Not long after we settled into our seats, an elderly priest and an adolescent altar girl took their places on the dais and the organ began a slow, sad hymn.

The doors at the back of the church opened and six men entered, standing beside the flower-draped coffin. Tony was at the front right corner as they wheeled Ray Wilson's body slowly down the center aisle. I could tell at a glance Tony's suit was worth more than the total cost of what the other pallbearers wore.

As I stared back up the aisle, following the coffin's progress, I was surprised to see a woman I recognized scuttle into the next-to-last row. Marie Halsey, Sarah's mother. *What is she doing here?* I'd wondered just that morning if she and Sarah were from Bath. Marie's presence seemed to confirm it. I looked around to see if Binder or Flynn or even one of the local Busman's officers was there, but couldn't spot anyone.

The coffin made its slow progression to the front of the church where the pallbearers turned it over to the care of the priest. Some of them genuflected before they made their way to the front pew opposite Ray's parents, though Tony did not. The priest welcomed the mourners and we moved into the funeral mass. A young woman who may have been a cousin read some lines from the Bible. Next to me, Michaela snuffled and wiped her eyes. Beside her, Tony's mother sat with the same disgruntled expression she'd worn the morning of the nonwedding. She looked as if she longed to run up on the altar and explain to the priest what he was doing wrong. Tony's father sighed.

Tony ascended to the lectern to give the eulogy. He removed a folded piece of paper from his suit pocket, spreading it carefully in front of him, though once he started speaking, he never glanced at it. "Ray Wilson was my best friend," he began. "He was my business partner, and my brother." Tony's voice broke slightly.

I felt Michaela quiver beside me as she fought unsuccessfully to hold back her tears. She gripped my hand.

"We found each other in Mrs. Kearney's kindergarten class right here in Bath. Ray came up to me on the first day and announced that we would be best friends and would play together at every recess. How did he know, at five years old, that we'd be able to accomplish so much, good and bad, together?

"On the good side of the ledger, there was the basketball championship we finally brought home for the Shipbuilders in our senior year, the college scholarships we both earned as a result, and the successful business we built together.

"But there was also the trouble we got into. The time we snuck through the woods into the Pick Your Own Strawberries field and ate so many we couldn't run away when the farmer came to yell at us. Or the time we took two lovely ladies down to the beach to watch the sunset and got Ray's car stuck in the sand so badly, his dad had to come rescue us with a tow truck."

The congregation laughed. In front of us, I watched Ray's father pat his mother's back as she wiped away a tear. Her profile turned to me, I caught the hint of a smile. Tony's mom continued to glower.

"Those are just the stories I can repeat here," Tony said. "Everyone saw Ray as the troublemaker. My parents blamed him. *His* parents blamed him. And the truth is, he was the instigator and the talker. The one who thought of the ideas and the one who tried to talk our way out of it when things went terribly wrong. But it took both of us to get into that much trouble, just like it took both of us to build our business. That's why I stand before you, feeling like I've been cut in half, like my own limbs are missing." Tony's voice broke and the congregation quieted.

"Those of you who knew Ray well know his troubles didn't end when we were boys. He had his demons, and he did some things in his life he deeply regretted." Tony words were thick with grief. "That's the greatest shame in all this sadness. Ray tried for so long to be a better man, and at last he was succeeding. He'd cleaned up his life, and far from making him less fun, sobriety made him more fun, more enthusiastic. More eager to embrace life and live it for all it was worth. Ray had just begun what I am sure would have been the very best part of his life."

Sobriety? Ray was drunk the night he was murdered.

At the lectern, Tony continued. "And now, he'll miss it all. I won't be the best man at his wedding. Our children won't play together as we'd dreamed. We won't continue our cutthroat golf games until we're too old to hold a club, as we'd planned." Tony was openly weeping as was almost everyone in the church.

I put my arm around Michaela and hugged her shaking shoulders.

Tony left the lectern and moved down to pat the wooden coffin lid. "I love you, Ray," he whispered.

The priest took the reins and somehow we stumbled through the rest of the mass. When we gave our neighbors the sign of the peace, I turned and looked back at Marie Halsey. She stood alone in the next-to-last pew. Behind her was someone even more surprising—Lynn, the maid of honor. *What is she doing here?* She didn't have a good word to say about Ray when he was alive. *Is she here at last to support Michaela?*

Finally, the mass was over. The priest invited everyone back to Tony's parents' house after the graveside service. The coffin, flanked by the pallbearers, rumbled up the center aisle.

Outside the church, the men from the funeral

parlor loaded the coffin into the hearse. The maid of honor went up to Tony's parents and hugged each of them warmly. It was not the greeting of relative strangers. *There's history there,* I thought.

A few people who weren't going to the cemetery approached Ray's parents. They shook hands, accepted embraces, and were gracious as two people could be in the circumstances . . . until Marie Halsey approached them. When Ray's mother saw Marie coming, she whirled around, turning her back. There was no mistaking Mrs. Wilson's intention. She meant to cut Marie Halsey dead.

And if that wasn't enough of a snub, Tony's mom's voice cut through the noise of the crowd. "I can't believe you would even come here!"

Chapter 32

I stayed through the graveside service and went to the reception at Tony's parents' house. Michaela was largely left alone while Tony and his family played host. Tony's mom served a fussy tea with little sandwiches and cakes, which seemed incongruous given Ray and Tony's high school friends, the fishermen and ironworkers who made up most of the guests.

I sat with Michaela on the deck of the neat ranch house, wondering where Lynn was. Once again, her maid of honor was AWOL when Michaela needed support.

I didn't intend to talk to Michaela about our interrupted conversation of the day before. The funeral had been tough enough for her. So I was surprised that she was the one who brought it up.

"I want to apologize for the way I acted yesterday when we talked about Ray," Michaela said.

"It's nothing," I said and meant it. If anything, I should have been the one to apologize for asking if she'd had an inappropriate relationship with the best man in her wedding party.

"No. I was rude. Overwrought. I'm just so emotional . . . with all that's happened." Michaela spread her gorgeous, long fingers on her knees. "I want to talk about my relationship with Ray. He's dead. Nothing I say will hurt him." Her nails dug into the dark fabric of her skirt. "Before you can understand about Ray, there are some things I need to tell you that you don't know about me."

She paused for so long I wondered if she would go on. But she did. "I started drinking in college, just the normal way normal people do. Except, I didn't know then, I'm not normal. I partied pretty hard, but so did everyone around me. After college, a whole bunch of us moved to Brooklyn, where we made more friends and kept going out. Every night I got drunk and every morning I woke up feeling terrible, but it was my life and I didn't question it." She looked into my eyes, making sure I was getting it.

Nothing I heard surprised me. Most people drank too much in college and some people continued drinking hard into their twenties. That's where I'd first met Michaela years ago, in clubs around Manhattan.

She took a deep breath and went on. "What I didn't notice was, the gang was breaking up. The others started having careers instead of jobs and didn't go out during the week. They had serious relationships and got married and by then they were only going out on holidays and special occasions. But not me. I was still getting drunk every night and working at the same stupid retail job I found when I first went to the city. I'd had dreams of working in the fashion business, but got totally sidetracked.

"I went to the same neighborhood dive, drank my dinner, and stayed out way too late every night. The bar was a comfortable place where 'everybody knew my name.' But one night, I had a moment of clarity. I looked around and realized who 'everybody' was. People who were alone, working in dead-end jobs, if they worked at all, with no friends or sign of any life outside that barroom. I saw a woman about ten years older, who'd been drinking across the bar from me for two years, and it was like looking at my future self. The smudged makeup, the unsteady hands. It was terrifying.

"I left the bar and found a meeting. AA. It's been a huge struggle, but I haven't had a drink in three years. That's where I met Ray. It was his first meeting, too." Michaela smiled at the memory. "I know it's supposed to be anonymous, and that's why I didn't tell you yesterday when we talked. But actually, Ray was quite open about what he'd been through.

"We were drawn to each other immediately. Ray made me laugh. After I'd been sober a year, Ray introduced me to Tony, and that was it. Love at first sight. Since I'd gotten sober, I'd changed jobs . . . from clerk to assistant buyer, something with a future, and I was working my way up in my company. At last, I was ready for a serious relationship. Tony and I have been together ever since that first date." Michaela's features softened, warmed by the memory of meeting Tony for the first time.

"Ray and Tony got more and more successful. Ray was the salesman, in charge of persuading the property owners to sell them the land, and then marketing the resorts to upscale buyers. Tony's the numbers guy and also oversees the planning and construction. Ray had been a college drinker like me, a little wild even as a kid, as you heard today. And then, as an adult, his job reinforced his tendencies. He was always wining and dining people. So it was hard for him to stop drinking. He had a much harder time of it than I did. There were lapses, some ugly scenes. He was a belligerent drunk. People judged him."

Certainly Lynn, the maid of honor, had. How many times and in how many ways had she said to Michaela, "Forget him. He's not worth it."

"But I saw how hard Ray tried," Michaela said. "Before that night in Crowley's, he hadn't had a drink in a year. I was shocked by his behavior.

It was like someone had flipped a switch and brought back the old, crazy, drunk Ray. I was desperately worried about him. Not just because he'd fallen off the wagon, which was bad enough, but also because his years of drinking caused health issues. Drinking could kill him."

The blood in Chris's cab and down the front of Ray's shirt. "Is that what you and Ray fought about at Crowley's? His drinking?"

"Yes. I begged him to stop."

"And why you called him on his cell after you'd gone back to the Snuggles?"

"Yes. I saw where his behavior was headed. I wanted to help."

"You left the Snuggles to meet him? Where did you go?" I felt bad for pressing her, but she'd initiated the conversation.

"Nowhere. We walked along Main Street and talked."

"You were gone from the Snuggles Inn for at least a couple hours. It's hard to believe you and Ray just walked along Main Street all that time. It's four blocks long."

"I don't know what to tell you, Julia. We found a bench outside the hardware store and talked. The last time I saw Ray, he was alive, slightly more sober and headed back to his hotel. I wish I could help. I want Ray's killer arrested, too."

We sat quietly for a moment. Michaela stared through the picture window into the living room.

I followed her gaze. Lynn stood with Tony and his parents, deep in conversation.

"She was Tony's college girlfriend." Michaela answered the question I hadn't asked. "She's had trouble adjusting to the idea of me. And trouble letting Tony go, though they hadn't been a couple for years by the time I came along. Tony was a big jock on campus when they dated, but I don't think Lynn ever imagined he'd make so much money. He's the one that got away."

"But why—?"

Michaela smiled. "When you give up drinking, you give up your drinking companions. I'm still building new friendships. Lynn is important to Tony. Besides, as they say, keep your friends close—"

"And your enemies closer," I finished.

Michaela laughed. "Honestly, I'm fine with her. I really am." She sat back in her deck chair, her posture relaxed.

She was through talking about Ray, but I still had something I needed to know. "That night, when you went to meet Ray, did you run into Tony?"

"Tony? No. He was at the Bellevue."

"No, Michaela, he wasn't. His bed there wasn't slept in. Lynn called him from the Snuggles and asked him to meet her."

Michaela's brown eyes flashed beneath her thick lashes. "What are you implying?" She said it so loudly, the few other people on the deck turned to stare at us. It was the same quick mood change I'd seen in her the last time we'd talked, the fiery temper buried down deep.

"I'm not implying anything. I assumed Tony and Lynn went out looking for you."

"Where did you hear this? Who told you these lies?" Michaela shouted.

Through the picture window I saw people in the house turn their heads. Tony's mother stared at us, openmouthed.

I remembered, much too late, the old adage about killing the messenger. "Michaela—"

"I think you should go," she commanded.

"I'm sorry," I said, and I really was. I slunk off the deck and walked to my car, wishing I could make myself invisible.

Chapter 33

Back in Busman's Harbor, I put my mother's car in her garage and went along to Gus's. It was late in the afternoon. I hadn't eaten anything at Tony's house. I hadn't expected to be leaving so soon.

When I walked through Gus's door, I couldn't help glancing at our booth to see if Chris was there. It was Wednesday, not one of our days and not even lunchtime, so it was a completely unreasonable hope. I realized how much I'd depended on him the last few months. I'd thought Michaela was the one who needed a friend. After she'd dismissed me so abruptly, I realized that maybe I needed one, too.

I wandered to the counter and sat down. The place was almost empty, not unusual for that time

of day. I ordered a burger and fries. Gus turned
to work the grill.

"Well look who's here." Quentin Tupper III
stood beside me. I'd been so absorbed in my own
misery, I hadn't heard him come in. He sat down
on the stool next to me. He wore a rumpled blue
button-down shirt, khaki shorts, and leather boat
shoes, a very different uniform than the few other
men in the restaurant. He looked like he'd gotten
off one of the yachts in the harbor, come to gawk
at the locals.

"You gave me a newspaper," I said rather stupidly. Last night, I'd searched in vain for him on
the Internet and here he was in the flesh.

"I was leaving town. You seemed like you
wanted it."

Yeah, right. He found out where I lived and
came over to deliver a used newspaper that he
could have far more easily thrown away because I
seemed like I wanted it?

"There were two pages with corners turned
down," I said. "The page with Tony and Michaela's
wedding announcement and the page with the
article about Tony and Ray's business. Like you
were calling them to my attention."

He nodded, affirming it had been deliberate.

"Why?"

"I thought you should know."

"You thought I should know?" He was irritat-
ing me.

"I thought you should know about what Wilson and Poitras were really up to. Their plans for your island."

Gus put the burger down in front of me. The fries were still cooking. Gus didn't believe all the items you ordered had to arrive simultaneously.

"Why didn't you just give me the newspaper while we were here? Or for that matter, just tell me Ray and Tony were in the business of building resorts on private islands?"

Tupper shifted on his counter stool. "You didn't tell me your last name. I didn't know who you were until after you left. Then Gus told me. Don't thank me, by the way."

Gus had his back to us as he pulled the potatoes from the fryer. I was never quite sure how much he picked up of the conversations that went on around him while he was working. He didn't suffer fools gladly, and I bet he blocked out most of it. About eighty percent of what he'd overhear would drive him crazy. But I thought I saw him stop for just a second and snap his head to the side very slightly, as if trying to dislodge water from his ear.

"Thank you for what?" I asked Quentin. "For your cryptic messages I might never have found?"

"Suit yourself. Like I said. I just thought you should know." Tupper placed his order with Gus and toddled off toward a booth.

"Bull crackers," Gus said as soon as Tupper was

out of earshot. "I never told him who you were. Couldn't have. He left before you did, remember? And don't let him fool you with that disinterested party routine. He owns that horrible glass monstrosity out on Westclaw Point, right across from your island."

I hadn't heard from Lieutenant Binder all day, so I stopped at the police station. He was in the same conference room where he'd been the day before and was surrounded, if possible, by even more people, paper, and equipment. Once again, he asked everyone to leave when I entered. On his way out, Jamie raised his eyebrows at me in what I took to be a warning not to get into trouble.

"I've come by to see if we can open tomorrow," I said to Binder. "The porch is down and the town will give us permission to reopen. It's all perfectly safe."

Two vertical lines formed over the bridge of his ski-slope nose. "Safe. That's a curious word to use for a place that's been the scene of a murder and an arson fire. It was arson, by the way. We found chemical traces of accelerant on the porch, both the decking and rails."

I wasn't as surprised to hear it as he thought I'd

be. Etienne and the building inspector had thought the same.

"You see how this changes things," Binder said. "We originally thought Wilson's body was left in your mansion to hurt or scare the bride. But it looks a lot more like this might have something to do with your family or your business. Any ideas?"

Something was going on. Tony Poitras and Ray Wilson developed resorts on islands. Quentin Tupper was playing some kind of game with me. There'd been that strange scene with Marie Halsey and Ray's mother at the funeral. I didn't understand any of it. I'd been dead wrong in my hypothesis about Tony being jealous of Ray.

I didn't want to make a fool of myself in front of Binder so I answered straightforwardly, keeping my vague suspicions to myself. "The business doesn't owe any money except to the bank. We haven't fired anyone recently. And I never met Ray Wilson while he was alive. So I don't see a connection."

"Maybe you never did, but Etienne Martineau met Wilson. He's admitted it."

"I know. He told me. Wilson was planning some silly prank on Tony, the groom."

"Is that what Mr. Martineau told you? I'm afraid it's not true. Ray Wilson approached Martineau about buying your island."

What? "That's ridiculous! He never did. I'm sure if he had, Etienne would have told me. Besides, Etienne doesn't own the island. It's not his to sell."

Binder put up a hand. "I hear you, but that's what Martineau told us. I recommend you talk directly to him about it."

My head felt swimmy and Binder sounded like he was far away. Why in the world would Etienne have kept that from me? I pulled myself together enough to ask, "So can we open tomorrow or not?"

"Now that the arson results are in, I want to do one more search of the island with my team. Tomorrow. Then we'll see where we stand."

We'd been closed Sunday, open for one glorious day on Monday, closed again yesterday and today. Three days lost. Now he was telling me we were certain to be closed again tomorrow. Four of the five down days in the business plan gone. I tried one more time. "I'm not sure you understand how urgent it is that we open. Our financial situation is—"

"Ms. Snowden, believe me. I understand your situation quite well. For one thing, Officer Dawes reminds me every day. For another, I've spent plenty of time investigating your finances." He smiled. "If you had any insurance on that old mansion, I'd be looking at you for the arson fire."

Was that a joke? It was a hell of a time for him to develop a sense of humor. I didn't know whether to laugh or freak out. "I want to be on the island tomorrow when you search it," I said with as much force as I could muster.

"Thanks," he said. "I'm sure that will be helpful."

I left police headquarters and fast-walked down to the town dock. Our little ticket kiosk was locked up tight with a sad sign in the window indicating the clambakes were canceled until further notice. I let myself in and raised Etienne on the radio, telling him we needed to talk immediately. He agreed to come in from the island right away.

When he arrived, we sat on a bench overlooking the harbor. The cocktail hour cruises had left, so it was quiet, if not completely private. I could tell Etienne was anxious. It was unlike me to order him around. He was my father's best friend and knew more about the clambake than I did. I wondered if he'd guessed what I wanted to talk to him about.

"I've just come from seeing Lieutenant Binder," I began. "He tells me Ray Wilson approached you about buying our island."

Etienne stared at his boot-clad feet.

"Etienne, what's the deal? Why would Ray

approach you in the first place? And why didn't you tell me?"

"I didn't tell you, because I didn't think it mattered. It was talk, not a real offer. I could tell he was feeling me out. I figured if he had a real offer, he would present it to you and your mother. I thought he was just trying to get an idea of what kind of offer your family might look on with favor."

Etienne's Québécois accent was more pronounced when he was stressed, but what he was saying made sense. I'd worked with a lot of great salesmen during my time in venture capital and they all made sure the "influencers" were on their side before they approached the "decision-makers." Certainly, Etienne was the first person I would have consulted if someone approached me about buying Morrow Island. My mother, who actually owned it, would have relied on him, too. On him and on me, if she could even face the emotional trauma of selling Morrow.

"Did he mention a figure?" I almost hated to ask.

"Six million dollars."

Wow. That would be enough to pay off the bank, save my mother's house in the harbor, provide her a tidy sum to live on, with money left over to send Page to boarding school when the time came. Livvie and Sonny could invest in a business, and I could do . . . whatever I wanted.

Etienne took my hands in his huge, calloused ones. "I did not encourage these conversations to hurt you, Julia. I believe in you. I believe you will be able to save the clambake. But what if you can't? I thought I would keep the offer warm for you. Keep the channels of communication open. For your mother. Especially after Sonny turned Wilson down flat."

Wait. Sonny did what?

Chapter 34

Sonny was in my office working at the computer. I walked in and shut the door. Over the last few months, we'd tried, not always successfully, to keep our frequent disagreements about the business away from the rest of the family.

"Sonny, we need to talk."

"Okay, just let me finish—"

I pulled the plug on the computer. "You're done."

"What the hell—?"

Blood pulsed in my ears while questions rushed out of me like a torrent. "Why didn't you tell me you'd met Ray Wilson before the morning of the wedding? And that he'd offered to buy the island? And since you haven't been honest with me, have you, at least, been honest with the police and told them you met him? Are you freaking insane?"

"Julia, take a breath before you have a heart attack. And give me a minute to explain."

I pulled my phone out of my pocket and started the stopwatch function. "Start now."

"Very funny. Okay. Calm down. I didn't tell you, and I didn't tell the cops I'd met Ray Wilson before because I didn't know I had. He wasn't in great shape the morning of the wedding, if you remember. I took a quick glance at the body after you discovered it, but I didn't recognize that the person hanging there was him. I didn't remember his name, either."

"Some guy offers you six million dollars for our debt-ridden property and you don't remember his name?" I was so angry my voice was up in dog-whistle range by the end of the sentence. Sonny lost some of his ruddy color at the mention of the price.

"We never got to numbers, okay? I told him right up front the island wasn't for sale. Because it wasn't. That's what your father used to tell everyone who asked. 'We're keeping it in the family.'"

That stopped me. "Dad had offers for the island?"

"The island, the business, especially during the boom. He always said no."

"Times are different now."

"Really?" Suddenly Sonny was the one doing

the shouting. "What are you going to do? Take the money and leave, Julia? Leave just like you always do?"

I came back at him just as loud. "That's the second time you've said that, Sonny. I don't appreciate it."

"Because it's true. You were gone. Livvie and I were here. Your dad got cancer, and we were here. Livvie bought your parents' groceries, cooked their meals, ferried your dad to all his treatments. With a kid, Julia. A little kid. And where were you? I ran his business as best I could so all of us would have something to live on and to keep that damn island your mother loves so much in the family. And where were you?"

"Just shut up, Sonny. I'm here now and I've given up my whole life to be here."

"I get it. I get that you want to sell the island and hightail it out of here back to your New York City life—"

"What? Sell the island?" Page was in the doorway, lip quivering. Neither of us had heard her open the door. "Grandma said to call you for dinner." Then she turned and bolted down the back stairs.

"Now look what you've done!" Sonny started to go after her, but I grabbed his shoulder.

"You better tell Lieutenant Binder all of this," I

hissed. "Because Etienne's already told him Ray Wilson approached you about selling the island."

"What does Etienne have to do with this?"

"Ray talked to him about purchasing the island, too."

"What? I never knew that."

"Doesn't feel so good, does it—being kept in the dark about things that are important?"

Chapter 35

Dinner was a quiet affair. Sonny's and my fight was the elephant in the room. No one wanted to talk about it, but no one wanted to talk about anything else, either. Page stared at her plate like she couldn't bear to look at me. I wanted to reassure her, but I didn't want to touch the topic of selling Morrow Island in front of my mother.

After about ten minutes of nothing but the sound of forks scraping across plates, casting around desperately for any neutral topic, I said, "I ran into Quentin Tupper III at Gus's today."

"That's nice, dear," Mom said. "His parents are lovely people."

"He owns that new house on Westclaw Point, across from the island." All four of them looked at me like, why was I bringing this up? Of course they knew about Tupper's house. I was the only one who didn't know about it, the one who'd been away, as Sonny had just reminded me. "Where does his money come from, anyway? Family?"

"Oh, no. There are far too many Tuppers for him to have inherited a lot of money from family," Mom answered. She was something of an expert on the topic of inheritance. The only reason our family had held onto Morrow Island was because Mom was the only child of an only child.

"Quentin Tupper invented some kind of window when he was in college," Sonny said with the authority of one who knows. "He hasn't had to work a day since. He gets paid a royalty for every one that's sold."

Some kind of window? What kind could it be? I cast my mind over all the potential investments I'd looked at while I was working at the venture capital firm. Solar? Insulated? Self-cleaning?

"Isn't that nice," Mom proclaimed. "Imagine. Windows. What did you talk to him about, dear? Do you think you'll see him again? Maybe you'll be going out?"

Oh, great. I'd thought this was a neutral topic. I knew the reason for my mother's enthusiasm. Someone to go out with might keep me happy enough to stay in the harbor and run the clambake business. Of course, she didn't yet know there might soon be no clambake business for me to run.

"Mom, he's like fifty years old," Livvie protested.

"I don't think he's that—" I started to say.

"I don't think Quentin Tupper, er, dates women," Sonny interrupted.

Page got that about twenty seconds before Mom said, "Oh."

Funny, I hadn't felt that vibe at all.

With that, the subject of Quentin Tupper III was mercifully retired. We ate the rest of the meal in silence.

Livvie had saved some of the rhubarb and strawberries back from the jam-making session and baked one of her delicious rhubarb sour cream coffee cakes. It's delicious smell still lingered in the house, but no one had the heart for dessert. As soon as the meal was over, Sonny gathered up his little family and took them home.

I helped my mother with the dishes. She asked if I wanted to watch TV with her. The only set in the house was in the tiny sitting room off her bedroom.

I said, "No thanks," and went to my office. But there was nothing to do there. No clambake to run. We'd been closed for three days and wouldn't be open tomorrow. I expected I'd be hearing from Bob Ditzy in the morning.

On that depressing note, the walls began to

close in. Even though I was tired, I had to get out of the house. I headed out for a drink.

Crowley's was an expensive tourist bar, but it masqueraded as a dive—to give visitors a sense they'd had a real Maine experience. It was cavernous, as you'd expect a wharf-side warehouse to be, with a big open ceiling, exposed beams, and rough planks on the floor. The place had a decent crowd—Thursday night building up to the weekend. No live music on a weeknight, but most of the tables were full.

Chris wasn't working as a bouncer. I admit I was disappointed. I'd come to the bar as much because I hoped he'd be there as for the drink. He'd heard all the details of my epic battles with Sonny. I needed to talk about this latest one, to unload. But no Chris. Plus, I worried about how his meeting with Binder had gone. I hoped he was okay.

Out of the corner of my eye I saw someone wave from the far end of the bar. Jamie. *Jamie?*

Even though Jamie and I were exactly the same age, for some reason, in my mind, he was still back in junior high, back in the years when we spent the most time together. It never occurred to me that I'd run into him in a bar. But why not? I squeezed through the crowd and climbed onto the stool next to him. I'm too short for barstools.

My feet didn't reach the footrest and dangled on either side of me.

Jamie ordered me a mojito. "Tough day?" he asked.

"You don't know the half of it. Or maybe you do."

At least he had the grace to laugh.

"Seriously, can you work your magic and get Binder to let us open? I think the bank's going to call tomorrow and shut us down for good."

"The lieutenant knows your situation," Jamie said in a warning tone.

"So help me out. Is this case anywhere near being solved?"

"You tell me. You're the one playing detective."

Okay. What the heck. "I know Michaela called Ray the night of the murder and I know she left the Snuggles to meet him. I know the maid of honor called Tony and his bed wasn't slept in that night. I know Ray was a recovering alcoholic who hadn't had a drink in a long time, but he did that night. He was sick in Chris's cab, which is why Chris cleaned it. There was blood in his vomit." I took a breath. "How am I doing so far?"

Jamie raised his eyebrows. "Not bad. I'm impressed."

Why not go for broke? "I know Ray had talked to Etienne about buying Morrow Island. I know the fire on the island was arson, though I can't for the

life of me figure out what it has to do with us." I
didn't say anything about seeing Sarah's mother
at Ray's funeral. I figured the cops might not
know about that. I also didn't mention Ray's
approach to Sonny. Etienne had told Binder
about it, but I thought it was up to Sonny to come
clean. I swiveled to face Jamie. "So now, it's your
turn. You tell me something."

"Oh, no. That's not going to work."

"C'mon, I know you're dying to."

Jamie looked up at the ceiling like he was
trying to figure out what was safe to tell me. I was
surprised he even considered it, but he was a few
drinks ahead of me. "Okay. How about this? Ray
Wilson had major drugs in his system when he
died. Someone drugged him."

"Get out. What kind of drugs?"

"That, I am not going to tell you.'"

I wasn't going to let him get off the hook so
easily. "So he was drugged and then hung him
from the staircase? Are the drugs what killed him?"

"He had drugs in his body. He was dead when
he was hung. That's all I'm going to say." Jamie
shifted his body away from me like he was afraid
he'd said too much.

"And the police are sure he didn't take the
drugs himself?"

Jamie was silent.

"C'mon," I prodded. "You can't leave me hanging."

"Geez, Julia."

"No pun intended. Believe me. How do you know he didn't take the drugs himself?"

"There were no drugs on him or in his hotel room. And the levels in his blood were high, way too high . . . and doubly dangerous when mixed with alcohol. He wouldn't have taken that much and had so much to drink unless he was trying to kill himself."

"You're sure he didn't kill himself?"

Jamie burst out laughing. "And then hung himself from the stairway at Windsholme after he was dead? You are one cheap drunk. That's your first mojito."

Oh, right. I guess that scenario was unlikely. I finished my drink and signaled to the bartender for another round. "How long before he died was he drugged?"

"Several hours."

"He was drinking right here in this bar several hours before he died." I started to get excited. Who had been in Crowley's that night? Michaela, Tony, the maid of honor. The entire wedding party, in fact. And Sarah Halsey.

And Chris Durand.

Damn.

The bartender arrived with mojitos for both of us.

Jamie and I closed down Crowley's. After he told me about the drugs in Ray Wilson's system, we moved on and talked about everything except the murder—our days at Busman's Elementary, our high school and college summers working at the clambake. When I asked why he became a cop, he answered, "to help people." Then he asked why I became a venture capitalist, and I answered "same reason," which four mojitos in, we found hilarious. I laughed until I cried.

He insisted on paying for my drinks, which I protested, and on walking me home, which I didn't, because I felt awfully wobbly. On my front porch he kissed me. Between one thing and another, it had been a while since I'd been kissed, but I was certain that's what it was. A gentlemanly graze of the lips.

He mumbled, "G'night," and took off down the block like a rocket.

Chapter 36

By morning, the whole night seemed like one terrible idea after another. Going to Crowley's, sitting with Jamie, the mojitos, the walk, the kiss. *Argh.* The harder I worked at forgetting the whole thing, the more I remembered.

The persistent buzzing of my cell phone finally got me out of bed. The display read, BOB DITZY. I didn't answer. I figured there was a limit to the terrible news he could leave in a phone message. Four days closed, one to go. He'd said if we were closed today, he'd have to inform his loan committee.

There was also a message from Lieutenant Binder saying his team would do "one last" search of the island this afternoon and I was welcome to come along. They'd meet me at 1:00 on the town dock. That, at least, was welcome news. If we were cleared to open the clambake by 4:00 or so, I had time to call my suppliers and at least let the hotels in the area know we were back in business, so they could send their guests in our direction.

That left the whole morning open with too much time to think. About everything. The murder. The loan. The fire. The kiss.

It's not that I didn't like Jamie. He'd been a friend all my life. I just didn't think of him *that way*. And besides, I liked Chris.

I could freak out about the business or freak out about Jamie, but neither seemed productive. Or, I could go see Sarah Halsey. As far as I knew, Binder hadn't had anyone at Ray Wilson's funeral to observe the strange scene between Sarah's and Ray's mothers. Even if he did have someone there, a state cop might not have recognized Marie Halsey. I decided to visit Sarah.

I'd never been to Sarah's apartment over Gleason's Hardware on Main Street. When her mother opened the door, I was shocked by how tiny the place was. It's not unusual in resort areas for housing to be too expensive for teachers, firefighters, and cops to live in the town they serve. Sarah had managed to find a place in town by making a major sacrifice on space. The door opened into the living room, which was currently decorated with several hundred strewn Legos. Tyler waved when I walked in, then returned to his building project. Right off the living room, I could see a bedroom with two twin beds. I guessed those belonged to Tyler and his grandmother. Sarah probably slept on the uncomfortable-looking pullout sofa in the living room.

Sarah came out of the bathroom. There was no way in that tiny apartment she hadn't heard me come in.

"I need to talk to you. It's about Ray Wilson."

Sarah nodded toward Tyler and gave me a warning look. "Tyler, I'm going outside to talk to Miss Snowden for a minute. Stay with Grammie. I'll be right out front." She led me out onto the sidewalk in front of Gleason's and gestured toward an outdoor bench.

"I saw your mother at Ray's funeral," I said when we'd sat down.

"She told me. I knew you'd wonder why she was there."

"Sarah, can you help me save the clambake? Please tell me what you know about Ray."

Sarah sat on the bench and stared off at our little town—the library, the post office, Small's Ice Cream across the street. "I want to help you. I really do. Not just to save my job, but because your family's been so good to me. Your dad hired me to work at the clambake when Tyler was only six weeks old. Remember, I used to take him out to the island every day and your mom would watch him and Page? I don't know what I would have done without your family."

"Then tell me about you and Ray Wilson."

Sarah blushed deeply and took a deep breath. "I was sixteen, working for the summer in the Penny Candy Store in Bath."

I nodded to show I knew the place.

"Ray came in with Tony and a bunch of his other friends. He was just out of college, working and taking his summer vacation in Bath, visiting his family and old friends." She hesitated. "What can I say? I was his summer fling."

"You were nine years younger than he was!"

"I told him I was twenty. It was all so glamorous. He took me sailing. We went out every night. We walked right into bars when I was on his arm. I got drunk for the first time. He was the handsome, sophisticated older guy who'd been away to college and lived in New York. My life wasn't like yours and Livvie's. I didn't go away to boarding school. I'd never been outside of Maine. I fell hard."

I felt badly for her. The poor kid. It was easy to see what had happened. "And then?"

"His vacation ended. He went back to New York. I went back to my life, except for one thing."

"You were pregnant." I remembered seeing Sarah and my sister when I came home from college for Christmas, still looking like kids, with skinny legs and big tummies.

"Now you know the whole story. Ray Wilson was Tyler's dad." Sarah let out a long breath.

"Does Livvie know?"

"I told her the same thing I told everyone else. Tyler's dad was 'some jerk.' And he was."

"But I still don't understand why Mrs. Wilson cut your mother down at the funeral. I would think for Tyler's sake, Ray's parents would try to get along with your family."

"So you saw that. Mom was so embarrassed." Sarah balled her fists. She seemed to be marshaling her courage to go on.

"You said you'd do anything to help the clambake," I reminded her.

"And I meant it. This is just hard for me." If possible, her blush deepened. "The truth is, I never told Ray about Tyler. In those two weeks we were together, on some level, I understood that Ray drank too much. Not like his friends, getting a little wild on vacation. In my heart, I knew what the problem was. My dad was a drunk. So when I found out I was pregnant, I didn't want to put my kid through what I'd been through." She swallowed. "After Tyler was born, I did get in touch with Ray a couple times. I wanted to tell him. But each time I met him, he was drunk. So I never did."

She stopped again and I waited. I knew there

was more she wanted to tell me. I just had to be patient.

"A couple years ago during one of Ray's attempts to sober up, he came to see me."

"Ray Wilson came here to Busman's Harbor?"

"Walked right up and knocked on my door. It's not like we're hiding or anything. Tyler answered and it took about thirty seconds for Ray to put it together. All he did was ask Tyler how old he was. Maybe Ray suspected. Maybe there'd been rumors. Ray was furious, as you can imagine. It's a big thing to keep from somebody. That's why Ray's mother acted the way she did at his funeral."

Everything she'd told me made sense . . . except I still couldn't figure out why she'd been at Crowley's the night of the murder. It couldn't have been a coincidence. I would have thought she'd want to avoid Ray, not seek him out. "Why did you go to Crowley's that night, Sarah?"

"I wanted to talk to him, but he was drunk again. Then he got into a huge fight with the bride. So I went home." The blush dropped away and she turned pale and shaky. "I'm so sorry for any trouble I caused your family, Julia. Ray was my problem and I thought I had it handled. I never would have imagined everything that's happened since."

"I'm sorry, too, Sarah, but you haven't caused us any trouble. Whoever killed Ray did that." I realized I was saying to her exactly what Jamie had said to me. "Have the police questioned you?"

She nodded. "Originally because I was in Crowley's that night."

"And you've told them everything you've told me?"

She nodded. "Swear to God."

Chapter 37

I still had a lot of time to kill before I went out to Morrow Island with Binder in the afternoon, so I borrowed my mom's car and headed to Quentin Tupper's house on Westclaw Point. Bob Ditzy had rung my cell phone two more times, but hadn't left a second message, which I figured was all to the good.

Twenty minutes later, almost at the end of the point, I turned down Tupper's driveway, which was really just a double track. I was amused to see what I took to be his car parked out back—a mint-condition, antique wooden-sided estate wagon. I imagined Quentin driving up Route 95 from New York City in it. Quite a sight.

I walked around the property to the ocean side and climbed the steps to his deck, calling "hello," loudly. I imagined unexpected visitors, or even strange cars, were rare that far down the point. The house was massive, a three-story wall of dark gray granite, with huge windows all along the front looking out to the wild North Atlantic.

Windows? Wasn't that how Sonny said Tupper made his fortune? I leaned on the deck rail. A long dock ran from the property out to a sleek sailboat moored in deep water. Forty-footer, I guessed. A single-hand, high-tech, carbon-fiber racing boat. Custom-made, with all the bells and whistles.

Despite the luxurious look of the house, the deck was sparsely furnished with a standard-issue picnic table and two worn Adirondack chairs. At the end of the deck next to the railing was a telescope, trained right on Morrow Island. I couldn't resist. I looked into it.

Across the water, I saw our little beach surrounded by great slabs of rust-colored rock. Beyond the rock, the hill rose up, covered on the backside of the island with a dense growth of scrub oak and pine. Rising above all that, I could see the slate roof, chimneys, and fourth floor dormers of Windsholme.

I turned the telescope to look at the inlet just down the coast from Tupper's property where the tide had deposited all the inflatable toys Livvie and I had lost when we were little. If Ray Wilson went to the island at low tide and left a boat on the beach to be washed out, that was where it would have turned up. But I didn't see a boat or anything else.

"Beautiful, isn't it?" That man was always sneaking up on me.

"I was just thinking the same thing," I said.

"I've seen humpback whales breach right out there between your property and mine. Magnificent creatures."

"I've seen them, too." *From our island.* "Your house is beautiful . . . to go with the beautiful setting."

"Thanks. I love it here."

"Did you design the windows?"

"What?"

"My brother-in-law told me that you invented some kind of window."

Quentin threw his head back and laughed. "Is that what they're saying around town? Not windows, *Windows . . . with a capital W.*"

Oh my God, he invented Windows? No, of course he didn't.

Quentin motioned toward the two Adirondack chairs on the deck and we sat down. "I was a classics major. The kinds of language skills classics majors develop are perfect for computer programming. I dabbled in that, too and while I was still at college I developed a tiny piece of code that makes almost every computer program you use run minutely faster. Whenever someone buys a certain operating system or application that runs on it, I get a few fractions of a penny."

My God. I tried to figure out how much money that would be. Hundreds of millions was the best I could come up with. "Are you still a computer programmer?"

"Nope. Never really was. Just hit it lucky with a few lines of code."

"So what do you do now?"

He sat in the Adirondack chair, looking comfortable and at home with himself. "Nothing."

"Nothing? No one does nothing." My work in venture capital had given me a pretty clear idea of what the very rich do. They sit on the boards of nonprofits, they take up expensive hobbies, they dabble in politics. Sometimes they even invest in small companies where they drive the management crazy with suggestions because having once made a lot of money doing one thing, they think they know everything about everything. I was overly familiar with that kind of rich person. But someone who did nothing? That was outside my experience. Yet I remembered, I'd found not a single trace of Quentin Tupper on the Web.

"It's a challenge to do nothing, believe me. I've had to cultivate it carefully. All around are entanglements. Say one word at a meeting of your condo board and the next thing you know, you're on a committee—or worse yet, running the thing. Attend a charity event or give a little money to your alma mater, and you end up calling all your friends to put the squeeze on them. It is very, very difficult to do nothing, but through hard work and attention to detail, I've accomplished it."

"You sail." I pointed to the beautiful boat moored at his dock.

"I do. It's part of my overall do-nothing plan. I walk out to the end of my dock and sail away. I never plan ahead. I don't race. I never give parties on my boat. I buy whatever supplies I need at the next port. "

Very soon, if the clambake failed, I'd probably be doing nothing myself, though that had never been part of any plan. Doing nothing without Quentin's resources didn't seem like much fun at all.

"You arrived in Busman's Harbor the morning of Ray Wilson's murder," I said. "The paper you gave me had a front section and a sports section from the early Sunday edition, as well as the parts of the paper only New York metro readers get. For you to be sitting at Gus's by 7:00 AM on Sunday when we first met, you must have left New York in the wee hours. That seems like an odd thing for a man who has no appointments or obligations."

"I answer to no one. I come and go as I please."

He was starting to annoy me again. "Really, Quentin. Why did you give me that paper?"

Quentin smiled, trying to diffuse my irritation. "My family has owned this land for eight generations. Did you know that? It was never any good for farming. There was almost nothing on it before I built this house, just a little fishing shack my ancestors used to enforce their traditional

claim to lobstering in these waters. But this isn't
the first home I've built. I had a gorgeous place in
the Hamptons. Peaceful, convenient to New York.
But then some jerk movie producer bought the
place across the bay from me and put in a helipad. It was like living in Fallujah. Helicopters
coming and going at all hours."

I squinted at him, wondering *what in the world
does this have to do with me?*

He continued. "Tony Poitras and Ray Wilson
have been looking at property in Maine for a while.
Your island isn't the first one they scouted. But they
have very specific requirements. They need town
water and power like you have. They need to be out
of cell range for all carriers and likely to remain
so. They need a flat spot for a helipad and they
need a property with a single owner. They don't
share their islands with others. When you start ap-
plying the criteria, the number of target properties gets pretty small. And one of them is right
across the water from me. Yours."

I knew Ray and Tony had considered buying
our island. Ray had approached Etienne and
Sonny. But now I understood better why they
were interested in Morrow specifically. "So you
thought you'd warn me?"

"When I saw that article in the real estate section of the *Times*, and the announcement saying
Tony Poitras's wedding was on Morrow Island, I

figured it wasn't a coincidence. I got in my car that night and drove to Busman's Harbor. When I got to Gus's to have breakfast, I heard about Wilson's murder. I honestly didn't know who you were when I met you. But when I found out, I wanted to tip you off about what Tony and Ray were really looking for on your island." He'd been speaking so rapidly he ran out of breath. He exhaled, blowing a rush of air out through his lips. "That's it. That's all. I swear. Just trying to help a neighbor out."

"Why didn't you just talk to me?"

"I was headed back to New York. I didn't want to leave a message with your brother-in-law. I thought it was better to give you the facts I had in hand rather than my speculation."

There wasn't much more to say. I thanked him for his explanation as he walked me to my car. When I started the engine, he put his head in my window. "Stay strong, buddy. Stay strong. Fight the bank. Solve the murder. A fancy resort with a helipad is the last thing I need across from my land."

I pulled out of his driveway, trying to remember. Had I said anything about the bank?

When I got back to town, I walked to Gus's. If he wasn't too busy, I could fit in a quick lunch before I went out to the island with Binder and his people. I glanced at my cell phone as I walked. No new calls from Bob the Banker. A relief.

At Gus's, I looked for Chris. I longed to see him. So much had happened since we'd talked outside the police station. But he wasn't there, even though it was Thursday, one of our days. It had been a rough twenty-four hours for me—the fight with Michaela, the fight with Sonny, the calls from the bank. My head was spinning after my conversations with Quentin and Sarah. I couldn't make heads or tails of anything. I really needed to talk to someone. To talk to Chris.

I wandered over to the counter and sat down. The place was medium crowded. And to their credit, nobody asked me anything about the murder or fire. I silently blessed the Mainers' credo of "mind your own damn business."

"You're lookin' a might droopy," Gus said when he came to take my order.

"Oh, Gus." Tears sprang to my eyes. I hadn't realized until that moment how much I wanted to see Chris. Needed to talk to him. I was overwhelmed by everything I was dealing with. I was alone. One tear escaped from the corner of my eye and rolled down my cheek before I blinked it away.

"There, there. There's no crying at Gus's place."

That seemed like a new rule, and like all Gus's

rules, it seemed arbitrary and unenforceable, but somehow Gus got everyone to tow the line. "What's troubling you?"

What was troubling me? Was he kidding? I took a quick spin through my life looking for any single area that was "fine," and came up empty.

When Gus realized I wasn't going to answer, he continued. "Murder? Arson? Bankruptcy? Is that all? *Nil carborundum illegitimi*, Julia. Don't let the bastards grind you down. Your family business is too important to this town."

Murder. Arson. Bankruptcy. *Plus, I kissed the wrong boy when I was drunk.* I started to tear up again. I stared at the menu scrawled on the blackboard. I'd memorized it when I was six and Gus hadn't added or subtracted an item since.

He turned away with a frustrated sigh. Before I knew it, he'd put a double-sized piece of his wife's three-berry pie and a cup of coffee in front of me. "Pie solves most things."

He went off to attend to other customers while I drowned my sorrows in the flakey, buttery crust. I closed my eyes and rolled the tangy blue, black, and raspberry filling across my tongue, hoping to hit every taste bud. Pie. Gus might have something there. I definitely felt a little better.

I hadn't allowed myself think about the six million dollars Ray Wilson had mentioned to Etienne. I took just a moment to fantasize about it and about my life with no debt, no family responsibilities, no obligations. I felt a wonderful sense of freedom, like I was floating.

My cell phone chirped. Sonny. *Great.* I answered.

"You on your way, Your Highness? We're all waiting for you down at the dock."

Chapter 38

I ran over the hill and down the other side toward the town dock. Was this the new me? A person perpetually late to important appointments?

On the stern of the harbormaster's boat stood three state cops I didn't recognize, along with Detective Flynn and Lieutenant Binder, who was staring with annoyance at his watch. And Sonny, who I hadn't seen since the tense dinner following our fight last night. And Jamie, who I hadn't seen since he kissed me at 1:00 that morning.

I scrambled aboard. All the ship required was Robert Forman Ditzy and it would have in its tiny stern every man on the planet I did not wish to see at that moment. Binder nodded to the harbormaster and we were off.

The Boston Whaler was tied up at our dock, which meant Etienne and Gabrielle were on the island. I hoped Binder had the courtesy to let them know we were coming. I knew how skittish having strangers on the island made Gabrielle, and all of us showing up without notice was sure to increase her nervousness. As soon as we tied up, Etienne came bounding out of their house. I could tell by his look of surprise that Binder hadn't told him about this last search. Gabrielle followed Etienne closely, as if using him as a shield.

Binder assigned each of the three state cops to search a third of the island. He asked Sonny, Jamie, and Etienne pair up with one of the officers. Etienne hemmed and hawed like he didn't want to accept his assignment. I thought he might be uneasy about leaving Gabrielle alone while there were cops looking under every rock on the island. I understood. Even though I liked Binder and had never found him to be anything but professional and fair, I too, felt the violation. Finally, reluctantly, Etienne agreed to go. He kissed Gabrielle on her forehead and urged her toward the house. Binder gave a nod to Flynn who silently joined Etienne's party.

Binder turned to me and said, "I'd like you to come with me." Together we walked up the great lawn toward Windsholme. At the top of the hill, he veered off and took the path through the woods to the playhouse. He pushed open its Dutch door and we stepped inside.

It was as neat as it had been the last time I was

there. We walked through to the bedroom where the blanket was still neatly folded on the mattress on the bottom bunk. Chris's initials, carved into the board that supported the top bunk, screamed at me as though they were etched in neon. But Binder didn't comment on them.

We returned to the front room. "Nice place to spend your childhood," Binder said in a neutral tone.

"If you mean the island, yes it was. If you mean, specifically, this playhouse, I wouldn't know. During my childhood, we spent the summer in the house where Etienne and Gabrielle live now, and they spent their summers here. With their son." Even as I said it, I suspected Binder already knew.

"Did the playhouse look like this the last time you saw it?"

"If you mean cleaned up, yes, it did. On the day we had the first—the only—clambake of the season, I came over here to look around. It looked exactly as it does now."

"Which surprised you." It was a statement, not a question.

"It did. When I went off to college, my parents decided to stay on the mainland during the summer. My sister was on the swim team at the Y." Funny, I'd almost forgotten that. "And between practices and meets it just wasn't practical to live on the island anymore. So Etienne, Gabrielle and Jean-Jacques moved into the house by the dock, and the playhouse was abandoned. The last time I came here, before this summer, it was in really rough shape."

"What did you think when you saw it all fixed up?"

"I assumed Sonny, Chris, and Etienne fixed it up when they were out here this spring getting ready to open the clambake. My niece and her little friend were with the men during school vacation. I assumed the guys had fixed this place up for them."

"But that's not what happened?"

"I guess not. My niece and her friend said they didn't play here." No point in mentioning the boy who was on the island this spring was Ray Wilson's son.

"Who do you think cleaned it up?"

"I don't know." And I didn't. But the whole conversation had caused a knot in my stomach. What had happened there? Was a stranger living on my island? That was the first time it had occurred to me. A murdering stranger actually *living* on my island.

"C'mon," Binder said. "I want to go through the big house."

When we reached Windsholme, he took a moment to inspect the work we'd done demolishing the side porch then we climbed the front steps and opened the doors. He held the door open and I went through it, grateful I'd taken my desensitizing walk the day before. He led me to the dining room, inspecting the fire damage, and then moved through the butler's pantry. On the balcony of the two-story kitchen, he gave a low whistle. "This place is amazing."

"I guess so." For most of my life, I'd seen this kitchen as something impractical and unusable, with a huge, wood-burning stove and a pump in the soapstone sink for drawing water. In the corner was an ancient propane-powered refrigerator, long disconnected, from back in the days before the island had electricity.

We continued through each room on the main floor. Everything was as it had been the day before. In the great hall, Binder paused. I was sure he was remembering, as I was, Ray Wilson's body hanging from the banister.

On the floor that housed the bedrooms, Binder opened every door. He was relaxed and chatty, asking me questions about my ancestors, most of which I couldn't answer.

"Did you ever find the boat?" I asked.

"What boat?"

"The one Ray used to get here."

"No," Binder admitted. His hand felt along the wallpaper in the master bedroom where it had been discolored by the smoke.

"So you think Ray came out with his killer, who took the boat when he left?"

Binder grunted, noncommittal.

"What about the camp trunk?"

He stopped. "What trunk?"

It seemed like an honest question. Maybe the cops didn't know about the trunk.

"Tony told me Ray Wilson had a big camp trunk in his car when he left New York, and I wondered if you found it. I know it wasn't in his room at the Lighthouse Inn."

"How'd you know that?"

"I have my sources."

Binder grimaced. "Very funny. But thanks, I hadn't heard about this trunk."

We climbed to the top floor. Windsholme never really got hot. Its thick stone walls and the ocean air created a state of permanent cool, but on the fourth floor the air was stuffier than I remembered even from the day before. Binder started at the end of the hallway closest to the porch fire, methodically opening each door. He'd stand for a moment in the doorway, looking thoughtful, but he didn't enter the rooms.

"Did you find the windbreaker?"

He was losing his patience. "What windbreaker?"

"After Ray puked on himself in Chris's cab he put his jacket on to cover the mess. He wore it when he went into the Lighthouse that night. But when I saw him here the next day, he didn't have it on. Just a pink polo shirt."

I thought for a moment the lieutenant would

deny knowing about the windbreaker, too. But he said, "No. We haven't found Wilson's jacket."

We were at the door of the room across from the landing. Binder turned the knob and pushed, but it wouldn't budge, just like the day before.

"It's so damp here," I apologized. "Things are always sticking."

"Why do you keep all the doors closed, anyway?"

"In case birds get in. Confines all the damage to one room."

He grunted, put his shoulder to the door, and shoved hard. It made a loud creaking sound and bowed in the middle, but didn't open. Then he put a foot on the door and leaned in. I thought about reminding him it was an antique, but he'd seen the state of the rest of the place, so I kept quiet. Besides, it was in my best interest that he see everything he wanted. I was just hoping for those magic words *You can open the clambake tomorrow.*

He knelt down and stared at something by the keyhole. "I think this is locked."

Locked? As long as I could remember, nothing in the interior of Windsholme had been locked. There was simply nothing to take. "Was it locked when you searched here after Wilson's body was found?"

"No," Binder answered. "Are there keys?"

"Butler's pantry," I answered, but he was busy

jimmying the door with a long, slim tool. We heard an old lock grind, and the door swung open.

Inside the little room, a mattress was on an iron bedstead. The bed was made with white sheets and covered in an old wool blanket. And on the bed was an entire man's wardrobe—T-shirts, cargo pants, boxers, and socks—folded with military precision.

I started to shake and gasp for air. Binder reached for his radio and called his officers to come.

Chapter 39

"Do you think Jean-Jacques is back?" Sonny was the one who actually said it, though all three of us were thinking it. He and I sat on the dock, our feet dangling over the side and Jamie lounged against a post. I'd avoided a full-blown panic attack, but still felt drained. We were waiting for Binder and Flynn, who were at Gabrielle and Etienne's house, interviewing them again. Binder had sent the rest of his team back to Busman's Harbor with the harbormaster.

"Could Jean-Jacques have been living here?" Jamie asked. "Right along?"

"No way," Sonny and I answered simultaneously. For once, something on which we agreed. There was no way Jean-Jacques had been living on the island for six years.

"Was the playhouse fixed up when you were out here cleaning up in the spring?" I asked Sonny.

He shook his head. "I'm sure it wasn't."

"That's what the kids said, too."

"You asked the kids about it? How long have you known?" He seemed aggravated and accusatory.

I took a deep breath before I answered. "On the day of the first clambake, I discovered the playhouse had been cleaned. I thought it was something you, Chris, and Etienne had done to keep the kids occupied this spring."

"Nope. Way too busy for that."

I flashed him the best smile I could muster. *Yes, Sonny. I got it. You work hard, too.* "Page said she saw the ghost—or one of the ghosts. Could she have seen Jean-Jacques?"

Sonny started to say no, but then rolled his big shoulders. The day had already been full of surprises.

"We all saw the ghosts when we were kids," Jamie said. "We talked about them all the time. Remember the ghost stories around the fire after the guests were gone?"

When we'd lived out on the island in the summers, sometimes as an extra special treat, after the dinner guests left, Etienne and my father would build us a little fire and we'd roast marshmallows. Usually, it was Livvie and Jean-Jacques and I, but sometimes Jamie stayed over. It was Jamie's first mention of a personal, shared memory all day. Neither of us had even breathed a hint about the kiss. What was there to say?

"What will happen to Jean-Jacques if they find him?" I asked.

He wasn't on the island. Binder and his men had searched every square inch of it, quizzing Sonny and me about hidden rooms in Windsholme, island caves, or forgotten outbuildings. Morrow Island was only thirteen acres and there was a limited number of places to hide. If it was Jean-Jacques who occupied the room in Windsholme, and he wasn't on the island, that meant he had a way to get on and off. Binder's team had again searched for signs of a boat and found nothing.

"He's a deserter, right?" Jamie answered. "He'll have to go back. I imagine there'll be some kind of hearing. He'll go to prison."

I hadn't seen Jean-Jacques in six years and only sporadically for seven years before that, but he was a part of my childhood and my heart ached at the thought of him in prison. I felt terrible for Etienne and Gabrielle. "But he didn't desert troops in the field. He walked away when he was on leave, after he'd already done two tours."

Jamie shrugged. "Maybe there's some kind of leniency in those situations. Who knows?"

Binder finally emerged from the house, followed by a drawn and gray Etienne. We piled into the Whaler for the trip to the harbor. I wanted desperately to talk to Binder, but not in front of Etienne. The poor man was in enough pain. I walked to the helm and stood silently by his side all the way to the harbor, hoping my posture conveyed my support. I doubted any greater demonstration would be welcome.

Etienne dropped us at the town dock and left again without saying a word. I checked my cell phone. Three more calls from Bob Ditzy, and he'd started leaving messages. It was well past six o'clock. No point in calling him at the bank at that hour, so why listen to the messages?

"Can we open tomorrow?" I asked Binder.

He looked at me like I was crazy. "There appears to be a fugitive living on your island. No, you cannot open tomorrow."

"He's not there. You didn't find him. Besides, isn't he a problem for the military?"

"Not if he killed Ray Wilson, he isn't."

Chapter 40

At the top of the street we split up. Binder and Jamie headed toward the police station, Sonny and I trudged up the hill to Mom's house. Both of us were so down, it was almost impossible to speak. In twenty-four hours, we would be the people who lost the Snowden Family Clambake.

Livvie's minivan was in the driveway. So was another car I didn't recognize—a sporty red BMW with the top down.

Tony Poitras got up from the porch swing when he heard us come up the front steps. "Your mom said I could wait here."

Sonny shook Tony's hand, mumbled something, and went inside.

I was glad he left us to talk privately. "What brings you here?" It had to be something important. He'd driven for twenty-five minutes and then waited who knows how long.

"You ratted me out." His tone was light, teasing,

but with an edge. "You told Michaela I wasn't in my room the night Ray . . . that night."

"I'm sorry. I didn't mean to upset her. I had no idea she'd get so mad."

He pulled his perfect brows together. "I want to assure you, what happened that night was totally innocent."

"I'm not the one you need to tell."

"I've already talked to Michaela. Now I'm talking to you."

We sat across from one another in my mother's big wicker chairs. It was that time in the early evening when the wind died and everything was still. I heard the hum of a lawn mower from some far-off yard. Other than that, the town was silent.

"I wasn't feeling great the night of the rehearsal dinner," Tony started. "I don't know if it was prewedding jitters, or too much to eat or what, but I left Crowley's early. Michaela was dancing with her girlfriends and having a great time. I didn't want to be a stick in the mud."

"Was Ray drunk when you left?"

"No. I didn't see him take a drink except for seltzer water. He'd been sober for a year. I wasn't worried about it."

"Did you see Sarah Halsey while you were at Crowley's?"

"So you know about that? The answer is I glimpsed her coming in as I was leaving. I don't think she saw me. Frankly, it just made me even happier I'd decided to leave. I didn't want to see her."

"Why not?"

Tony's jaw tightened. "Because she made a chump out of my friend. She'd lied to him, never told him he had a kid. And when he'd sobered up, she tried to keep his son away from him. Ray had a hundred reasons to get sober, but the only one that worked was knowing he had a son. Wanting to spend time with the boy. He tried to work things out with Sarah for more than a year, but she just stonewalled him. He had just told her he planned to sue for visitation. Now he's dead. His son never even knew him. The whole thing is a terrible waste." Tony pinched his nose between his thumb and forefinger.

Ray threatened to sue Sarah for visitation? Why had she kept that information back, when she'd told me so much? I needed time to think. "Can I get you something to drink?"

"Sure. I'll have a beer, if you've got one."

I took a Sea Dog from the fridge and poured an ice water for myself. I'd already done one dumb thing due to drinking in the last twenty-four hours. I needed to be sharp for this conversation.

I handed Tony the beer and sat down. "You were explaining why you didn't sleep in your bed the night before you were supposed to be married. I know the maid of honor called you."

"Michaela was out wandering the streets at 2:00 in the morning, meeting up with a drunk man. Lynn was frantic with worry. So she called me. And I went out to look for Michaela."

"But you didn't find her."

"No. Instead of walking from my hotel to the other side of the harbor, I got in my car. I thought it would be more efficient to drive around look-ing for Michaela than to do it on foot. I drove for a while, but didn't find either Michaela or Ray. I thought she might be back at the B&B by then, so I pulled up in front and called Lynn on her cell. No Michaela. But Lynn came right outside and got in my car to talk."

"Oh, Tony." According to Fee Snuggs, Lynn hadn't asked Tony to look for Michaela. She'd asked him to come to the B&B. Tony had given Lynn exactly what she wanted.

He put up a hand. "*Nothing* happened. Well, almost nothing. I was out of my mind with worry. It was the night before my wedding and my wife-to-be was missing. She'd gone off to meet my best friend. Lynn pointed out that maybe Michaela didn't have her priorities straight in terms of the attention and consideration she gave me versus Ray. There was some frustration on my part. Some venting. But that's it. Nothing happened between Lynn and me." He hesitated. "Even though that might have been what Lynn wanted."

"If nothing happened, then why didn't you tell Michaela?"

"Lynn is a sensitive topic where Michaela is concerned. I didn't think she'd want to know that I spent part of the night before our wedding—"

"With an old girlfriend," I finished.

"But I did tell Lieutenant Binder. I've been completely honest with the cops about where I was that night."

"After you left Lynn, where did you go? There was still plenty of time for you to go back to your hotel and get a few hours sleep. But you didn't."

Tony exhaled loudly as if he'd gotten through the worst of what he had to tell. "I sent Lynn back inside before anything could happen between us. I turned my car around in your driveway, right here. I was going to take one more trip around town before I turned in. I was still worried about Michaela. And Ray. I headed down toward the Lighthouse Inn. I thought maybe they'd gone back to his room. Just for a place to talk. But I never made it. That guy who works for you at the clambake and his wife were walking up from the town dock. I almost hit them. She was in a terrible state. Disheveled and raving. Something about her son. I recognized the guy's name as soon as he introduced himself, Etienne Martineau. Ray had been talking to him about a business deal."

Yeah, about buying my family's island. But I didn't

say it. I didn't want to get Tony off track. I was amazed to hear that Etienne and Gabrielle had been on the mainland that night. It contradicted everything Etienne had let me believe. He said he would have heard anyone coming onto our island, *but he wasn't there.*

"Etienne said his wife was having some difficulties, which was obvious. There was a prescription waiting for her at the twenty-four-hour pharmacy up on Route One. He asked me to drive them there. I wanted to say no, I had my own troubles, but anyone could see the poor guy had his hands full. He told me he didn't feel he could leave his wife on the island alone.

"So I loaded them into my car. She sat in front and he squeezed into the back. And that's it. By the time we got up to the pharmacy and I dropped them back at your dock, it was almost three A.M. I called Lynn. She answered on the first ring and said Michaela was back at the B&B sound asleep. I went back to the Bellevue. I was terrified of sleeping through the wake-up call and missing my own wedding, so I only half dozed on my bed."

"You never got under the covers."

"Okay, now I have to know who your sources are." He smiled, trying to get the conversation back to a lighter tone, but I couldn't get there.

I tried to figure out how his story fit and what

it meant. "What do you think was in Ray's camp trunk?"

He laughed. "I told you. I'm sure it was for some sophomoric prank at my wedding. Some best man high jinx. I loved Ray, but he had a highly questionable sense of humor."

"Etienne said Ray came to the island a few weeks ago to scout it out for a prank. Do you think Ray went out to Morrow Island the night of his murder to set up a joke?"

"And what? Ran into some mad man?"

I didn't respond, but that was exactly what I thought. A mad man in the form of Jean-Jacques. But I wasn't going to tell Tony. It was time to tackle the second subject I had to discuss with him. "The prank wasn't the only reason Ray went to Morrow Island the first time." I kept my voice steady. All business.

"True." Tony took a long draw on the beer. "He was looking at Morrow Island for our company."

"Did he like what he saw?"

"He did." Tony's voice was even, too. Professional. "Losing Ray is a huge setback to my business. But I still want your island. I'll give you one point five million dollars for it."

"That's a quarter of the amount Ray mentioned to Etienne!" One and a half million was exactly the amount we owed the bank. Did Tony know that?

"Those were just feelers. Ray and I had never

agreed on a specific amount. And now, it seems your business is in distress."

There was no point in denying it. "The business was in distress when Ray talked to Etienne and Sonny, too."

"Yes, but back then, those guys believed you were going to save it. You were their great hope." Tony shifted back into his chair. "But it didn't work out that way. Instead, you structured a deal with the bank that's going to put you out of business before the season's even really started."

He didn't just know the amount we owed the bank, he knew the terms. He knew about the five closed days. He'd been talking to Bob Ditzy. If he didn't get the island from my family, he'd get it from the bank.

My cheeks burned with embarrassment and shame. What Tony said was true. It wasn't my fault there'd been a murder and a fire on Morrow Island. But it was entirely my fault that the bank was in a position to shut us down just a week into the season. What had I been thinking? What a stupid, stupid deal I'd constructed.

"It's not my island to sell," I said unnecessarily. Tony had done his homework well. I was sure he knew my mother owned Morrow Island.

"I'm confident your mother will do whatever you advise. You're the financial whiz in the family. The offer's firm. You have until midnight tomorrow to decide. Then the offer goes away and I move on."

My dreams of being the hero and saving the business were in tatters. My brief fantasy of selling the island for six million dollars and having money for Page, Livvie, and Mom was gone, too. But the money Tony was offering was enough to pay off all the debt and save my mother's house. If we sold off the *Jacquie II* and some smaller assets, it would provide a comfortable life for my mother. I had to tell my family about Tony's offer.

Chapter 41

Dinner was quiet again that night. Mom, Livvie, Sonny, and I had a lot to discuss, but not in front of Page, and not while eating.

After we finished, I cleared the table while Livvie washed the dishes. I came up behind her at the sink and gave her a hug. "We need to talk."

"I know. Sonny told me we're closed again tomorrow. That's the fifth day."

While I'd stayed on the porch with Tony Poitras, Sonny had rushed in and told Livvie all his troubles. I longed for that. For someone to tell my troubles to who would always be on my side. For months now, that person had been Chris. I missed him in a way I felt physically.

"Jamie kissed me last night."

"Julia!" Livvie turned from the sink and put her soapy arms around my neck. "That's wonderful. It's what we've been hoping for."

"We?"

"Sonny and me, silly. And Mom. And Page. He's perfect. And he's loved you all his life."

He has? "But I like Chris," I whispered.

Livvie turned back to the sink. "Chris comes with baggage," she said barely audibly above the rush of water. "Besides, you've been having lunch with him all these months. Don't you think if something were going to happen, it would have by now?"

Livvie gave Page a piece of leftover rhubarb coffee cake and parked her in front of the television. Then she and I joined Mom and Sonny on the front porch.

Mom looked up and saw the three of us looking serious. She put a hand to her chest and said, "Oh, no. What is it?"

I sat on the wicker ottoman at her knee, so I could look directly at her. Livvie and Sonny stood behind me. I realized as I proceeded through the story, talking first about the five closed days and the probability the bank would call the loan, that we'd made a mistake trying to shield my mother from the recent issues with the business. She was doing her best to keep up, but the effect of the murder and the fire was a lot to take in.

"But how can it be over before the season's even begun?" she asked.

Red-faced, I explained about the business plan and the structure of our agreement with the bank.

"So the island and the business aren't gone yet?"

"Technically, no." I hadn't even told them about the messages on my phone from Bob Ditzy. I noticed Mom focused on losing Morrow Island and the Snowden Family Clambake. She hadn't said a word about her own house.

"What could save us?"

"If we're closed tomorrow, which we're certain to be, the bank will undoubtedly call the loan. I suppose if someone were arrested for the murder and the fire, then we'd be in a better position with the bank, because we could guarantee when we'd reopen. I've tried to explain to Bob Ditzy that if our revenues are higher than the plan I've given him, we can survive a few more closed days and still pay what we've agreed by the end of the summer. I'm not sure he's heard me, and all this day-to-day uncertainty—not knowing when we'll open again—isn't helping."

"So we can still save it, if someone's arrested tomorrow?"

"Oh, Mom." Tears sprang to my eyes. I couldn't stand the hopeful tone in her voice. If I lost control and started crying, I thought we all would. I swallowed hard and continued. "I just had a conversation with Tony Poitras. He's offered to buy the island for one and a half million dollars." Behind me, I heard Sonny's sharp intake of breath. The last figure he'd heard—from me—was six million.

"We're not selling Morrow Island," my mother said.

"Mom, I think you have to consider this deal. It would pay off our debt and save this house. After we sold the *Jacquie II*, you'd have some income to live on. It's an opening offer. Maybe we can do better. And maybe we can't. Tony knows if he waits, he can buy it from the bank. The alternative is that you're penniless. No house. No income from the business or any other source. Just Social Security. That's it. You haven't set foot on Morrow Island since Dad got sick. I'm not sure how much you'll miss the island, but I know you'll miss this house."

Mom gave her head a little shake. "I don't understand. Wasn't Tony the groom at that wedding for your friend?"

I could see her working hard to take all it in.

Livvie moved to the chair next to her and took her hand. "He is, Mom. But he also develops resorts on private islands."

"I think you'd better tell me everything."

I told her everything I knew about the night before the wedding and what had happened since. Livvie listened quietly while I explained that Ray Wilson was Tyler Halsey's father and, at least according to Tony, Ray had told Sarah he planned to sue for visitation. Sarah was Livvie's friend, but it appeared she hadn't known any of it.

Sonny knew some things I didn't. I'd forgotten he was a buddy with Jamie's colleague, Officer Howland. Sonny told us the drug found in Ray's system was Rophynol, or roofies, the date rape drug.

When we got to the day's events, I paused, trying to collect myself. The best thing was just to say it. "Sonny and I think Jean-Jacques is back and staying at least part-time on Morrow Island."

Mom's eyes widened.

I explained about the cleaned-up playhouse and the room in Windsholme with the neatly folded clothing.

"But he wasn't on the island today?"

"No. He knows the island better than the police do, but if he'd been there today, they would've found him."

"And if we sell the island to this man Tony, he'll build a resort on it?"

"Yes." *Where is she going with this?*

"Don't you see? That can't happen. If the island is no longer ours, if Etienne and Gabrielle no longer live there, how will Jean-Jacques find his way home to them again? We can't lose the island as long as there's any chance he will come back there."

"Mom, I just told you that Jean-Jacques may be a murderer and an arsonist."

"It doesn't matter. Gabrielle can't lose him again. She's not a strong person, emotionally. It will kill her. Promise me, you'll do whatever you can. Promise me you'll try."

Chapter 42

We stayed up talking late into the night, reminiscing about life on Morrow Island. I won't say it was like a wake exactly, because I think each of us, in our own way, held onto the faintest bit of hope. It was more like a conversation carried on at the bedside of a very ill patient. When they left, Sonny wrapped Page in a blanket and carried her out of the house fireman style. I laughed, but also felt a pang. It wasn't so long ago that she'd been a baby in his arms.

I said good night to my mother, gave her a hug, then went to my office and read everything I could about Rophynol on the Web. I knew about date rape drugs. I came of age in the era of their use. But now that I knew what drug had been in Ray's system, I needed to understand it in detail—how long it took to work, its impact on the user, and its side effects.

At sometime after 1:00, I went to bed, but not

to sleep. I had a short list of things I could do in the morning. Even though I wasn't sure if any of them would change things for the better, I felt they had to be done.

I left the house early, before Bob Ditzy could call. It was the fifth closed day for the clambake. The last hurrah. I didn't have much time. I had two goals for the day. The first was to figure out who had killed Ray Wilson. If Binder made an arrest, at least I could guarantee the bank the clambake would be open, which would help to convince them not to call the loan. If Plan A failed, my fallback was to negotiate the best possible deal for the sale of Morrow Island to provide for my mother.

At the Halsey's apartment, Sarah, Tyler, and her mother were crowded around the breakfast bar that served as the only eating surface.

"We need to talk," I said to Sarah. "Let's go out."

I hustled her to Gus's place, neither of us saying a word on the way. I was sure she could tell I was in no mood for chitchat. When we got inside, I put her in a booth and bought coffees.

"Tony told me Ray was threatening to sue you for visitation. Now, why don't you tell me what really happened the night he was murdered."

Sarah put her coffee cup down and stared at the tabletop. Her chin quivered and fat tears fell on its worn surface. There were deep circles under her eyes and she was even paler than usual. "Again, I can't tell you how sorry I am that your business and family have been dragged into this, Julia. After all your father did to help me. And Livvie, who was my first girlfriend in Busman's Harbor."

Sarah broke down, cradled her head in her arms, and wept. I gave her some time to compose herself, handing her napkins from the dispenser on the table so she would wipe her eyes and blow her nose. I glanced around anxiously for Gus, having just been informed the day before about the "no crying at Gus's" rule. Luckily, he was busy at the grill in the other room.

When Sarah pulled herself together, she spoke. "I was determined to keep Ray away from my son. I went to Crowley's that night to convince him that Tyler couldn't handle visitation—and neither could Ray. But I couldn't talk to him, because he was drunk. Again."

"I heard that Ray had been sober for a year."

"It doesn't matter. His behavior that night proved he shouldn't be allowed to spend any time with Tyler."

"And now he won't have the chance."

She broke down again.

I waited while she regained control. "But Crowley's wasn't the end of it that night, was it?"

"No. What I told you was true. Ray and I never

actually got to talk at Crowley's. It was noisy and crowded. He was dancing with the women from the wedding and obviously drinking. He and Michaela got into a huge argument. He was yelling, and so was she. Then the lights came up and it was closing time."

"Then what happened?"

"Nothing. I went home."

"But you didn't stay there." When she hesitated again, I reminded her, "Sarah, you said you'd do anything to help."

When she still didn't say anything, I got up from the booth and poured each of us another cup of coffee. By the time I sat back down, she seemed calmer, more determined to go on. I felt terrible about pushing her, but when it was all over, I had to know in my heart that I'd done everything I could to save the Snowden Family Clambake.

"Ray called me. Right after he got back to his hotel. He was furious and demanded we talk. He yelled and swore at me over the phone. I was scared to death he'd show up at my apartment, so I agreed to meet him."

Ray called Sarah that night? He certainly was busy with that cell phone, considering he was so drunk he couldn't even do up his jacket zipper. Sometimes speed dial was a curse. "Where did you meet him?"

"I told him to meet me at Gleason's Hardware downstairs from my apartment. The owners gave us a key in case there was any kind of a problem with the building. It was the only place I could think of. I felt safer knowing my mother was right upstairs. Ray showed up at the door to Gleason's and I let him in. He was angry with me and wouldn't stop shouting about how I'd deceived him and kept Tyler from him. How I'd ruined his life and was in the process of ruining Tyler's.

"We stood in one of the aisles, screaming at one another. Then I looked around and started to get scared. The place was full of pitchforks, hammers, all kinds of potential weapons. What had I been thinking, inviting a drunk, crazy man in there?"

She looked at me, big-eyed while she thought about her own stupidity. I shrugged, trying to convey it was the kind of mistake anyone could make in those circumstances. But really, how often does a situation like that occur?

"I'd just started to panic when there was a knock at Gleason's front door. At first we didn't hear it because we were yelling, but then the person was just pounding the heck out of the door. Ray let her in. It was Michaela. She shouted at me, too, about this awful thing I'd done to Ray. But she also gave him the business. She said no one would trust him with a child if he were actively drinking. She told me he'd been sober for a year and his behavior wasn't typical. She pleaded with me to let Ray have some kind of regular time with Tyler. She said missing out on Tyler's childhood was the biggest regret of Ray's life."

Sarah looked at me as if to assess how I was reacting to all this. Honestly, I didn't know what to think. I understood Sarah's impulse to protect Tyler. And Ray's desire to know his son. And Michaela's loyalty to her friend. What a mess.

"Then Michaela started to cry, and Ray shut up. He told her he was okay and everything was going to be fine. And that was the last time I saw Ray. Honestly. He and Michaela walked out of Gleason's into the night."

"You told all this to the cops?"

"I swear."

We sat silently for a moment, while I decided on my next step. What I wanted to say was what I absolutely believed, based on what everyone had told me about Ray's behavior that night and on the Web research I'd done.

"I think you put Rophynol in Ray's drink." Sarah was the only one at Crowley's who had anything to gain from Ray's public bad behavior.

"What? Why on earth would I do that?" She blushed crimson, but I noticed she didn't deny it.

"So the whole town would see Ray staggering like a drunk. I don't think you meant to hurt him, at least not physically. I think the drug lowered Ray's inhibitions so far that he lost his willpower and took a drink. And once someone with Ray's poor impulse control took one drink, he was bound to take another. His health was fragile, compromised by years of drinking. I know you didn't kill him, but if you're the one who drugged him, tell Lieutenant Binder it was you. Get a lawyer and turn yourself in. Today."

"I can't." Sarah wept. "What will happen to Tyler?"

What, indeed? I thought about Sarah's original deception, keeping Tyler's existence secret from Ray, and all that had radiated out from it, including Ray's death, Michaela and Tony's canceled wedding, and the loss of our family's business and Morrow Island. I wanted to get the issue of the Rophynol cleared up for the police so they could move on and arrest Ray's real killer.

I knew Sarah to be a good person, but I believed she'd do anything to protect her child. I was sure she was the one who'd drugged Ray and set in motion the events, whatever they were, that led to his death. But I still didn't know how he'd ended up hanging on Morrow Island.

"If you don't tell Lieutenant Binder what you did, I'm going to."

"Julia, please."

"I'll do anything to help you. I will. But you have to tell Binder the truth. Get a lawyer and admit what you did."

Sarah sat in the booth, tears cascading down her cheeks. "I'll think about it. Please, don't go to Binder yet."

Chapter 43

As soon as I left Sarah, I texted Michaela. **where r u?**

   leave 4 NYC today. Meet good-bye?

   where?

   front n centre 25

The coffee shop in Bath in twenty-five minutes. *Good.* **k**

I asked my mother for her car and lit out for Bath. I got to the coffee shop first and claimed a corner table where we wouldn't be overheard. All the coffee with Sarah at Gus's and my near sleepless night had given me the shakes. I ordered a lemonade. I was nervous about seeing Michaela. Things had ended so badly the last time we'd been together.

She strolled in a minute later and greeted me warmly. "We're going back to the city right after lunch. The cars are all packed. I just wanted to say good-bye. And apologize for my behavior after

Ray's funeral. You didn't deserve it." She paused. "I think you realize you're not the person I was angry with. I'm so sorry. We didn't know each other well before last weekend, but you've been a terrific friend to me through all of this."

"No, I'm the one who's sorry. I should never have sprung it on you that Tony left the Bellevue that night, especially on the day of Ray's funeral. I assumed you knew. You and Tony had been interviewed by the police several times."

Michaela shook her head. "But never together. We were never interviewed together." She smiled. "It doesn't matter now. He's told me what happened, and I know he told you. Everything is good between Tony and me. At least our relationship wasn't destroyed by this awful mess. You've been a true friend."

"Thanks. I think of you as a friend, too." I meant what I said, but I also recognized the opening I'd wanted. "I need your help."

Michaela fixed me with an intense, level gaze. "I'll do whatever I can."

"If you really want to help, tell me exactly what happened the night Ray was murdered. The truth this time. All of it."

Michaela pulled her head back and raised a perfectly shaped brow. "I've told you everything."

"Not quite. You told me you met Ray and spent hours walking along Main Street. You didn't tell me you'd found him at Gleason's Hardware store with Sarah Halsey."

Michaela's shoulders slumped. "Sarah must have told you."

I nodded yes, and Michaela continued. "I just didn't see any reason to bring that poor girl further into all this. She thinks I only saw Ray's side of their argument, but that's not true. I understood her reluctance to allow Ray visitation with her nine-year-old. Nobody understands better than I do how self-centered and untrustworthy drunks can be."

"So what did really happen?" My time had all but run out. I had to know.

"I called Ray as soon as I got back to the Snuggles. At first, he didn't pick up, but then he called me back and said he was going to meet Sarah at the hardware store. That didn't seem like a good idea at all, given his condition. I ran over there, hoping I could catch him before he went inside, but it was too late. The two of them were already in there, arguing themselves in circles at the top of their lungs. The town was so quiet, I could hear them from outside.

"I banged on the door to get their attention and Ray let me in. You could feel the tension in the room. He was never a happy drunk. Drinking made him angry and hostile and the last couple years, one of the things that made him angriest was the situation with his son. I tried to reason with both of them and got nowhere. Finally, it was all too much for me. It was the night before my wedding and I was in a dark hardware store trying to reason with two people who were never going to see the other's perspective. I started to cry."

"And that brought Ray around?" Everyone had described him as an immature, practical joker. But it was also clear from all my conversations he was a loyal friend. He wouldn't have wanted to hurt Michaela on her wedding day, of all days.

"It did. Ray finally remembered we were in Busman's Harbor for my wedding to his best friend, not for him and his drama." She wiped a tear from the corner of her eye with the coffee house napkin, then muttered, sadly and affectionately, "Freakin' Ray."

"Then what happened?"

"Nothing. Ray and I left. I walked him back toward his hotel. He'd thrown up earlier and sobered up some, but he was still pretty drunk. I wanted to make sure he got back to his room. At the corner of the parking lot for the Lighthouse Inn, he told me to go on, he had to get something from his car. I said I'd wait and walk him to his room, but he resisted. I didn't want to start another argument. He was in a much mellower place so I figured he could make it the last fifty feet to the front door." Michaela put her elbows on the table and rubbed her temples. "If only I had seen him all the way back to his room, none of this might have happened."

"And you've told all of this to Lieutenant Binder?"

"All of it. Just the way I told you. Oh, and one more thing. One that Binder strangely seemed the most interested in. When Ray and I came out of the hardware store, that cab driver, the one who was in the bar, was standing across the street under a street lamp. He followed us to the hotel."

"Followed you?" *Chris, what on earth were you doing?*

"The streets were deserted. The cab driver followed Ray and me as we walked toward the Lighthouse Inn. A little later, when I looked out my window at the Snuggles, I saw him there, too."

I didn't think Michaela noticed my reaction to that devastating bit of news, or perhaps she saw but didn't understand. We stood and she hugged me with her great long arms. "Tony said he hopes you're seriously considering his offer," she said to the top of my head. "It's good until midnight."

So she knew about that.

Chapter 44

Chris was across from Gleason's Hardware the night of Ray's murder?

From the beginning, there'd been a swirl of suspicion around Chris. At first, because he'd supposedly been the last person in the harbor to see Ray Wilson. Then there was the blood. And finally Chris's presence outside the hardware store.

Making everything worse was, it was the first time I was certain Chris had lied to me. He'd told me he'd gone straight back to the marina and cleaned his cab.

Maybe Michaela was lying. But why would she? Seeing Chris outside Gleason's was such a bizarre and specific thing to say.

My cell phone rang as I reached Mom's car in the public parking lot in Bath. I knew who it was before I looked at the display. Ditzy. I pressed IGNORE and wished I could do just that. A quick look at my list of recent calls showed that the last nine were from him. And he'd left four messages. Feeling like I was climbing onto the scaffold for my own execution, I dialed him back.

"Julia Snowden," he answered. "Glad you're alive. I was beginning to worry."

I made a noise that I hoped he'd take as a response. He did.

"As you're aware, the situation with your loan has become very serious, indeed. You're closed for a fifth day today. That means I have no choice but to recommend to my superiors that we call your loan. Failure to pay it in full within twenty-four hours will mean forfeiture of your business and your property which you used as collateral."

Even though I'd been expecting this, it hit me with such force I couldn't move. I sat in my mother's twelve-year-old Buick in a public parking lot and willed myself to breathe.

"Bob, as I've explained before, the five closed days are just one of many variables in the business plan. For example, if we were to exceed my very conservative revenue projections, we could absorb several more closed days and still make the agreed upon loan payments over the summer." Actually, my revenue projections hadn't been conservative at all, but I was fighting for my family's property and livelihood.

"This loan has already been renegotiated twice. I don't see my superiors going for a third time."

"Please, Bob. You know we're an important

local business, part of what makes Busman's Harbor a tourist destination. Shutting us down at the start of the summer season will be a blow to the entire community."

He was silent for a moment, and I thought I had him at least reconsidering.

"I have a pretty good source in the police department," Bob said.

Of course he did. Everyone in town must be friends with at least one blabbermouth cop.

"I understand there may be a fugitive hiding on Morrow Island. I don't think you'll be allowed to open until he's captured and until arrests have been made for the murder and arson. If you knew when you were going to open, I could argue with the loan committee on your behalf, but as things stand—"

"Give me until tomorrow, Bob. Please. Just give me until tomorrow. If someone's arrested, I'll give you a new business plan. If I can't do that, give me the time to find a buyer."

"You think between now and tomorrow you can find a full-price buyer for your properties?" He sounded surprised. Evidently Tony hadn't told Bob he was also talking directly to us.

"I'm certain of it." Not full price perhaps, but enough to pay off the loan.

He whistled. "Tell you what. It's Friday and already late afternoon in Europe. No one will probably answer the telephone at HQ anyway.

You have the weekend. Either the police make an arrest and you bring me a new business plan by first thing Monday morning or you bring me a confirmed offer from a potential buyer."

"Thank you. You won't regret it."

And he wouldn't regret it, though I feared very much that I would.

I bumped down the barely paved road toward Quentin Tupper's house on Westclaw Point and turned into his driveway. No sign of his wooden-sided estate wagon. *Oh, no. What if he's gone back to New York?* I had no way to reach him there.

I sat in my car writing a note on the back of an oil change receipt when Quentin pulled his car up behind me. *Thank goodness.*

"Ho, there!" he called.

I jumped out of Mom's car. I didn't have time for pleasantries. "I think you should invest in my business."

Quentin's eyebrows flew up toward his sandy hairline. He put his hand on my upper arm and said gently, "I've explained. I don't get involved."

"Then if you don't want a part of my business, you should buy Morrow Island." If I couldn't save the business, I could at least get two buyers bidding against each other for the island and negotiate the best deal for my mother.

"I think you'd better come inside." He led me

into the sleek interior of his house, sat me down at his glass dining table, and brought me an ice water without my asking. "Julia, I have no interest in anyone owning Morrow Island but you and your family."

"But what if we can't hold onto it? I'm doing everything I can, but I've run out of time. Do you want Tony Poitras to build a resort over there with helicopters coming and going or do you want peace and quiet?"

"How much has Tony offered you?"

"I'd rather you just make an offer." I wasn't going to tell him Tony's lowball number.

"Well, I'm not going to buy your island, so it won't hurt you to tell me how much Tony bid."

"One point five million. That's a quarter of the amount Ray Wilson mentioned to one of my employees less than a month ago."

Quentin folded his arms across his chest. "So if you sell to Tony now, instead of letting the bank take it, you can protect some of your assets?"

"My mother's house in the harbor. And the *Jacquie II*." I took a big swig of the ice water, but my throat was still parched. I couldn't take my eyes off Quentin. This had to work. What would he do?

"Am I correct in believing that you don't care who gets the island, you just want a higher bid to go back to Poitras with?"

"Yes," I admitted. If we lost the island, what did I care who got it?

"I won't be your shill, Julia."

My heart sunk.

"But you do have leverage. Remember what I told you. Tony needs very specific things. He needs to be out of cell range, yet close enough to civilization he can get his helicopters to the island easily. He needs water, electricity, and waste disposal. Given all the regulations about building on these islands, he probably needs an existing structure with a footprint big enough to create his resort. And he needs to be sole owner of the island. There are thousands of islands in Maine, but once you apply all those criteria, his choices are much more limited. Use that knowledge and go back to him with a strong counteroffer. I know you can do it."

The weight of the responsibility bore down on me physically. I heard what Quentin said, but I was still in a very weak position. Tony knew I was out of time. "You're going to end up with a fancy resort across the water from you." I stood to go.

Quentin got up, too, picking his car keys off the table. He'd have to move his antique Woodie so I could get out. "I'll take that chance. Good luck."

I certainly needed it.

Chapter 45

I drove back to the harbor, put Mom's car in her garage, and walked down to our ticket kiosk to raise Etienne on the radio. Tony told me he'd seen Etienne and Gabrielle in the harbor on the night of the murder. What were they doing here? And much more important, why had Etienne lied repeatedly about their whereabouts that night?

Etienne's voice was weary when he answered. "Could you come out to the island? I don't want to leave her." I knew he meant Gabrielle. I assured him that I understood and would be out as soon as I could.

The problem was I didn't have a way to get there. I thought about who could take me. Sonny's dad would surely be out lobstering as would most of the working lobster- and fishermen in the harbor. I made a mental inventory of everyone I knew who might lend me a boat and kept coming back to one. On the one hand, he was the last person I wanted to see. On the other, I really needed to face up to him. Chris.

I headed over to the marina.

Neither his cab nor his landscaping truck were in the parking lot, but that didn't surprise me. During the part of the year when he lived on his boat he had to rent space for his vehicles a fair walk away. For all I knew, the state police still had the cab.

"Ahoy!" I stood on the dock and tried to hale Chris. I'd never been on the *Dark Lady* and it would be impolite to board without an invitation. "Ahoy!"

Chris emerged on deck looking disheveled. And by disheveled, I meant dreamy. His shirt was off, his feet were bare, and he wore only a pair of dress pants.

I registered that. Pants, not jeans.

He had a sexy two-day growth of beard.

"Oh, hi. This isn't a great time." He held up his razor to indicate he'd been about to shave, but I had a feeling he wasn't referring to a simple grooming task.

"That's okay. This won't take long." I jumped onto the *Dark Lady*, uninvited.

"Okay." Chris seemed surprised by my boldness.

Frankly, so was I. "I need to borrow your dinghy."

He looked relieved, like—was that all I wanted? "Where're you headed?"

"Morrow. I need to talk to Etienne and he can't come to town right now."

"That's a long way to go in my dinghy."

He was right. It was barely more than a rubber raft, but it had a hard bottom and an outboard motor. I knew it would get me there.

Chris handed me the key to unlock the little boat from the dock. "All set? 'Cause I'm kinda in the middle of something."

"You said you would help me keep the clambake open any way you could."

He nodded. "Yes, of course."

"But then you didn't tell me you were outside Gleason's Hardware the morning Ray Wilson was killed." I tried to keep the hurt, anger, and accusation out of my voice.

Chris gestured for me to take a seat on the banquette in the stern. He sat just around the corner, so close our knees were practically touching. Between my anger at him, my fear about where this conversation might be going, and his nearness to me, my heart beat so hard I was afraid he could see it thumping in my chest.

"So you know," he said.

"Michaela told me. She told Binder, too."

Chris stared down at his bare, tanned feet. "Lieutenant Binder and I have had several conversations about my movements that night. I'm certain we'll have many more."

"Why were you outside Gleason's?"

Chris still didn't look up at me. "I dropped Wilson at the Lighthouse Inn, just like I told you. As soon as he got out, I opened up my cab to inspect where he'd been sick. I was still in the Lighthouse parking lot when he came stumbling back out the side door of the inn. He started yelling into his cell phone, sounding demented. He hurried up toward Main Street.

"I followed him. At first I was afraid he'd hurt himself. He was in no condition to be wandering around town at almost one-thirty in the morning. But then, as he continued screaming into the phone, I started to be afraid he'd hurt someone else."

Chris finally looked into my eyes. He was so close that if I moved my knee a fraction of an inch, we'd touch. Hurt and angry as I was with him, I still longed to cross that chasm.

"If you've talked to Michaela, you know what happened next," Chris went on, seemingly unaware of my heart rate or my desire to touch him. "Wilson charged up the street toward Sarah Halsey's apartment. I waited outside. A couple minutes later, Sarah came down the stairs and let them both into Gleason's. I was still worried. Obviously they had private business. I didn't want to interrupt, but they were in a place filled with all kinds of potentially dangerous weapons and he sounded like he was off his rocker. So I waited to see what would happen. Then the bride came along and banged on the front door of Gleason's. Ray let her in and the three of them were yelling at one another. It was so loud, I could hear it from across the street. Not words, mind you. But noise."

So far, everything he'd told me agreed 100 percent with what Michaela and Sarah had said. "Michaela said you followed her and Ray back to the Lighthouse. And later, when she looked out the window of her room at the Snuggles, you were there, across the street."

"Wilson had calmed down by the time they left Gleason's. Michaela seemed to have the situation under control, but I didn't want to take the chance. I followed them to the Lighthouse. They split up in the parking lot and he went to get something out of his car. I followed Michaela to the Snuggles to make sure she got back okay. There was no one around and I didn't like the idea of her walking alone. Then I went back to get my cab. Wilson was nowhere to be seen. His car was there, and I assumed he'd gone inside."

Chris caught the look on my face and grimaced. "I know, bad assumption. Anyway, then I drove over here, got cleaning supplies, and cleaned up the blood and the puke, just like I told you."

But I still didn't understand why he hadn't explained all that in the first place. Especially since he had told me about the blood in the cab. "Why would you hide this from me? I thought we were in this together."

"I'm sorry. I didn't want to make things worse for you by telling you anymore about that night."

Worse for me? I was already in it up to my neck.

Chris took my hands in his. "This really isn't a good time. I have something I have to take care of. But there's one more thing I want to say. This is a small town. It's been a long time since you've lived here. Sometimes when two people are seen together a lot, people misunderstand the nature of the relationship. Town gossip says there's more than there is. I don't want you to be caught up in that."

Just like that, he broke my heart.

Chapter 46

Somehow I stumbled my way off the *Dark Lady* and unlocked the dinghy. Chris's message was clear. Town gossips thought there was something between him and me. And they were wrong. There was nothing between us.

I sat in the little boat and took a deep breath, trying to steady myself and calm my racing mind. My pulse slowed just enough for me to start the motor and head out into the harbor.

The boat was small and the ride bumpy. Once I got out beyond the mouth of the harbor, I had to fight for control, but from there the trip was short and soon I pulled up to our dock.

"Etienne! Gabrielle! I'm here." I tied up the dinghy and continued to call out. Etienne knew I was coming. Why didn't he come out to greet me?

I knocked on the screen door of their house. The sound echoed throughout the place. No answering call. No sign of anyone at all. The door was unlocked which was typical when Etienne and Gabrielle were on the island alone. Clambake guests had been known to wander into the house, use the facilities, and otherwise make themselves at home, so the door was usually secured when customers were on the island, but otherwise there was little point. At least, it had seemed that way until I'd opened the doors to Windsholme and found Ray Wilson's body hanging from the staircase. Could it have been just one week ago?

"Hello!" I walked through the empty house. Gabrielle kept an immaculate home, but there were signs of life interrupted. Her knitting sat next to her chair, a business magazine, its spine splayed open, was next to Etienne's. I left the house, annoyed and worried. Etienne knew I was coming.

The next place to check was the pavilion and commercial kitchen. We weren't open for business today, probably never would be again, but I had faith in Etienne and Gabrielle's ability to keep busy—cleaning, fixing, improving. Neither of them were built for sitting still, and I imagined the forced idleness must have been driving them crazy. I called around the kitchen and dining area, but found no indication they were there or had been.

A breeze came in across the ocean as I walked out toward the lawn and I realized how preternaturally still the island seemed. How quiet. I walked over to Gabrielle's vegetable garden, which was brimming with bright green lettuce and peas hanging from their vines, needing to be picked. But no Gabrielle. No Etienne.

I hurried back to the playing fields and looked up at Windsholme. A shadow crossed a fourth floor window, the one in the center where Lieutenant Binder and I had found the clothing. Was it someone, or merely the reflection of the sun dancing on the wavy, old glass? That was the explanation behind most of the ghost sightings on Morrow Island.

"Etienne, I'm here!" I yelled up the lawn. If he was inside Windsholme, I wanted him to come out to greet me. But nothing happened.

I walked slowly toward the big front porch. "Etienne! Etienne!" I steeled myself to open the front doors, remembering that last time I'd been in the house just the day before. I'd walked through its entirety with Binder and felt completely safe . . . until we found the room with the neatly folded clothes. Then my family's property had again become alien. I reached for the doorknob and started to turn it.

"Julia!"

I jumped a mile. "Geez, Etienne. You scared me to death."

He'd come around the side of Windsholme, but there was no need to ask where he'd been. He was wearing swim trunks and carrying a beach towel. His chest was bare, revealing his slight potbelly and powerful shoulders. Water dripped steadily from his trunks onto the grass.

"We need to talk." How many times, in how many ways had I said that to someone over the last six days?

"Indeed."

He climbed the porch and we each sat in one of the wooden rockers.

"Where's Gabrielle?" I asked.

"She stayed down at the beach."

"I thought you said you didn't want her to be alone."

"I meant I didn't want to leave her on the island by herself. She's a bit fragile right now."

I turned to face him and took his great paw in my much smaller hands. "Etienne, is Jean-Jacques back?"

He looked away and dabbed his forehead with the towel. "I do not know. I have not seen him. I have only seen evidence of his comings and goings. Gabrielle is convinced he's been here."

I thought about Gabrielle's increasingly nervous disposition. "How long has this been going on?"

"She discovered the playhouse had been fixed up shortly after we finished the spring cleaning. It looked occupied, I think you'll agree. She kept going over to investigate, insisting she'd seen smoke from the chimney. But then we'd get there and find no one, just charred wood in the fireplace."

"Why didn't you tell me?"

"You had so many worries. So much responsibility."

"Oh, Etienne."

He gave me a small, sad smile. "We all have our burdens."

"What about the room with the clothes in Windsholme? Did you know about that?"

He nodded, moving the rocker a little as he did. "Yes, I knew. Once the clambake started there would be people all over the island—and in summer no further need of the fireplace at the playhouse. By then, the electricians who'd done that rewiring for you were gone. Gabrielle is convinced Jean-Jacques moved into Windsholme after the first police search because the mansion was quieter and more private."

That made sense. Inasmuch as any of it made sense. I switched subjects. "You were on the mainland the night of Ray Wilson's murder."

Etienne sighed. His face settled into its familiar outlines, but I could tell he was exhausted. "This has all been very stressful for Gabby. She's been so anxious her doctor prescribed some medication for her nerves. That night she couldn't sleep. With the wedding here in the morning, she was terrified someone would stumble upon Jean-Jacques. And we had run out of her medication."

That alone told me how stressed and distracted Etienne's little household was. When you lived on an island, you became an expert planner, an obsessive list maker. You never ran out of staples or medication.

"Gabrielle was so agitated that night. Neither of us had slept one wink, and with the wedding the next day, I decided we had to go across to the pharmacy."

"Etienne, why didn't you call our house? I could have picked up the prescription and met you at the dock, at least."

"You had a big day the next day, too."

His reluctance to ask for help cut me to the quick. Our families were intertwined in business and friendship. I would have helped him, if only he'd asked.

"If you know we were in town that night, you probably know the rest," he said. "I asked that Tony Poitras for a ride to the pharmacy. He was cruising by the dock. I had no idea he was the groom until we got to chatting on the car ride."

"Did you know he was Ray Wilson's partner?"

"No, it never came up. Gabrielle was obviously in distress and I think we both wanted to get the errand over with as quickly as possible."

Now I was the one who sighed. I turned away so

he couldn't see the tears in my eyes. "Etienne, I wish you had trusted me more."

"It's funny. I wanted to say exactly that to you."

"You wish *I* had trusted *you* more?" I had trusted him with my business, my family's livelihood, and our island every single day.

"Your father compensated me well, and gave me a third of the clambake's profits every year."

I knew that from my study of the books, and if the clambake was ever profitable again, I intended to continue that tradition.

"My expenses have been low," Etienne said. "Neither Gabrielle nor I have extravagant tastes."

I nodded. I knew he and Gabrielle to be frugal Mainers.

"The long and the short of it is, we have plenty of money. I want to help you with the clambake, become your business partner. I should have said something earlier. I guess I was hurt that you never asked, never even considered bringing Gabby and me into the business. Into the family."

"Etienne, I'm so sorry. I never thought—"

"No. You never did. Now I am tired of waiting to be asked. I am offering."

"I'm afraid it's not that simple. Unless something dramatic happens, First Busman's Bank will call our loan on Monday. With an infusion of cash like I think you're offering, we could try to restructure the debt, but honestly, I don't know if it's still possible. If there was an arrest for the murder, it would help with the bank because we could guarantee we'd be open. But we owe a million and a half dollars. If we can't fully pay off that debt, your help may not matter."

"I can handle that amount—the million and a half."

Was this a bad joke? How could Etienne possibly have that kind of money? But then, as I thought about it, the idea seemed more plausible. The bonuses my father had given him during the boom years were healthy. Etienne and Gabrielle had next to no living expenses—the summer rental paid for their house, they'd had no college expenses for Jean-Jacques.

"But I do have some conditions," Etienne continued. "One, I want to be a partner. For that kind of money, I'd expect to own a third of the business. I don't want an interest in the properties, those belong to your family. But I do want to be a formal partner in the business."

The amount he was offering, a million and a half dollars for a third of the business, was more than fair. I was completely comfortable with what he proposed. My father had always treated him like he was an owner anyway. I indicated that he should go on.

"Two—no more work on Windsholme. Leave it as it is. It's the only part of your plan I never agreed with. Three—you stay, at least for the rest of the summer."

Those also were easy. There'd be no money for further improvements to Windsholme even with the cash from Etienne. And I'd always planned to stay for the whole summer, as long as there was a business to run.

"Four—Sonny goes. He's out of the business."

I sat stunned. "Sonny has worked at the clambake since he was a teenager. I don't think he ever meant to harm the business. He's family. I can't throw him out."

"Wake up, Julia. Sonny is a know-it-all who won't listen to advice from anyone. Or take direction. He's stubborn and aggressive. He's impossible for you to work with. Or me to work with. If I am part owner, he has to go." Etienne's voice was insistent. I didn't doubt he meant what he said.

What could I say? My mother had begged me to find a way to keep the island in the family and this was that way. Quite probably the only way. My stomach hurt just to think about it. Etienne had asked me to destroy my family in order to save it, but if we took his deal, the property would still belong to my mother, would pass to Livvie and me, and ultimately, to Page and my children. "I'll think about it. And talk to my family."

Etienne stared down the lawn at his house and the dock, my borrowed dinghy bouncing on the waves. "Good."

I had one more thing to ask. "Do you think

Jean-Jacques killed Ray Wilson and set fire to the porch?"

Etienne shook his head. "I am certain he did not. My boy is not a killer. That was why he could not go back to Iraq. He is incapable of killing anyone."

I left the island in the little outboard. The skies were gray by then and a steady wind had come up. I fought the current and small swells all the way back through the harbor. Large, ploppy raindrops fell just as I got back to Chris's boat slip. No one was around. I was beyond grateful I didn't have to see him.

My phone buzzed to let me know I had a text. Binder. **Please come by headquarters ASAP. Development in case you need to know about.**

I locked up the little boat, put the key in my pocket, and lit out for the police station. Had there been an arrest? Was it possible my luck had turned?

Chapter 47

Binder looked up from his chair at the conference table. "You got here faster than I expected."

"I am absolutely desperate for good news." I remained standing, too excited to sit down.

"Well, I'm not sure if this qualifies or not. Sarah Halsey has been arrested for the murder of Ray Wilson. She's here at the station."

Now I needed a chair. "Murder. I don't understand." Just moments ago, I'd been so happy there'd been an arrest. I thought about Tyler growing up without his mother. I was afraid I'd be sick all over Binder's conference table. "But Sarah didn't kill Ray. She just wanted to show he would be a terrible father and shouldn't get visitation. Her own father was an alcoholic—"

Binder's eyebrows rose. "Ms. Snowden, I'm not sure what you know about the facts in this case. For example, did you know that Ray Wilson died leaving a considerable amount of money to his son, Tyler Halsey, and as Tyler's legal guardian, Ms. Halsey would have had unfettered access to all the money to do as she pleased?"

Sarah hadn't told me that. It was amazing how many half-truths I'd been told in the past week. Still, the Sarah Halsey I knew was a hardworking, grounded mother and teacher with strong moral values. I couldn't imagine her risking prison and losing her son for money. I tried again. "Sarah didn't realize Ray would start drinking again after all this time and that the combination of the drugs and alcohol would kill him. If anything, it was an accident."

"The Rophynol Ms. Halsey gave the victim didn't kill him. He died of a broken neck."

"A broken neck?" Why arrest Sarah for murder if the drugs weren't what killed Ray?

"His neck was broken before his body was hung up at Windsholme."

I was reeling, not sure I comprehended everything Binder said. "But if his neck was broken, then Sarah didn't kill him. And she couldn't possibly have taken him out to Morrow Island and hung his body from the staircase. That would require someone much stronger."

"We don't think he was dead when he arrived on the island. We believe Ms. Halsey doped him up so that he'd be easier to manipulate. He went to the island willingly, where he was killed and hung."

"Still, there is no way she could have strung him up."

"Alone. She couldn't possibly have killed him and hung him from the staircase *alone*. Ms. Halsey has also been charged with conspiracy. Her accomplice is meeting with his attorney right now, making arrangements to surrender. He'll be charged later this afternoon. I think you know him. Christopher Durand."

I stumbled out of Binder's conference room with tears in my eyes and the telltale tightness in my chest that preceded a panic attack—and rammed straight into Jamie in the drab corridor. He took one look and hustled me into something that looked like a supply closet. He switched on the single overhead bulb. The shelves that lined the closet closed in on me and I swayed a little.

"Breathe, Julia, breathe."

I had a vivid image of standing on the top floor of Windsholme with Jamie forcing my head to my knees. The last thing I wanted was a repeat of that. I steadied myself and did as he commanded, closing my eyes and breathing in and out through my open mouth, while I still could. It worked. My heart rate slowed.

"I see you've heard about Sarah."

"Oh Jamie, I can't believe it. Can't you talk some sense into Binder?"

"It's a pretty ironclad case. She came in and admitted she drugged him. And you have to agree, she had a powerful motive."

I felt horrible guilt for forcing Sarah to tell the police about the Rophynol. At the time, I just wanted her to clear up that bit of the puzzle, to remove the drugging from the list of things Binder's team was investigating. I never imagined it would turn into an arrest. "Sarah wouldn't deliberately kill anyone, much less for money," I insisted.

Jamie put a steadying hand on my arm. "One thing I've learned in my short time on this job. You don't know people as well as you think you do."

I wasn't buying it. "But she couldn't have gotten Ray Wilson out to the island in the middle of the night even if he was drugged. And she certainly couldn't have hung him from the staircase."

"She didn't. We believe Chris Durand did that. As her accomplice."

"But why? Why would Chris do something like that for Sarah?"

Jamie looked away. "I've told you too much already. Don't ask me anymore." His voice had a wary edge to it. I knew I was treading on dangerous ground.

"Please, Jamie. Please, please tell me. As a friend."

"As a friend, Julia! As a friend!" The edge exploded into fury. Jamie shouted so loudly I was afraid people in the corridor could hear us. "Are we friends? I'm not sure we are. Did you even call me when you got back into town? No, I found out from your mother. We never saw each other until this case started. I'm not sure you ever would have spoken to me if there hadn't been a murder on your precious island."

Even in the dim light, I could tell he was red in the face and just spitting with anger.

Jamie's voice turned deadly quiet. "Why do you think Chris helped her? Chris Durand is a grown man. With a grown man's needs. Do you think those needs are met by having lunch with you at Gus's three times a week? Of course they're not. He and Sarah have had something going on almost since she got to town. Everybody knows that, Julia, and you would too, *except you haven't been here.*"

With that, Jamie banged out the door, which slammed behind him, leaving me standing in the janitor's closet, shaken to the core.

Outside the police station, a pelting rain driven by wind stung my face and arms. I ran all the way to Mom's house, but was still wet to the skin when I arrived. Sonny's truck was in the driveway, along with Livvie's minivan.

Sonny.

The root of all my problems. The reason we

were in this mess. Blood surged to my face, I was so angry.

He was in my office, behind my desk when I came squishing into the room in my sopping wet clothes.

"What happened to you? You're soaked."

"What happened to me? What happened to me? After my dad died, my idiot brother-in-law persuaded my mother to take out a loan she couldn't afford and then he ran my family's business into the ground, that's what happened to me! And then I gave up my job and my apartment and came here and my life turned to total crap. That's what happened to me."

Sonny stood up behind the desk, "Julia—"

But I wasn't done. "Despite that . . . despite all that, there was a solution right under my nose the whole time. Etienne has the money. He's willing to buy a third of the business. Not the properties, just the business. It would keep the island in the family for my mother and your daughter. But that's not going to work, and do you know why? Because he won't give us the money if you're involved with the business. Because you're such an unpleasant, know-it-all jerk!" I was breathing heavily by the time I finished, and Sonny was, too, clenching and unclenching his fists. I could tell he was about to explode.

"All I ever did was work like a dog for your father," he yelled. "Every day of my life since I

turned nineteen. You may not like what I did, but
I've done my best. I loved the guy and I miss him.
I miss him, too, Julia. I miss him every single day."
Sonny's voice caught and I thought he might cry,
something I'd never, ever seen him do in all the
years we'd known each other.

I was at a loss on how to react. But it turned out
I didn't need to.

The study door flew open and Livvie stood
there, looking pale. "What's going on?"

"What's going on is, Julia's got an offer from
Etienne to save the business."

"Oh—"

"But I'm out. The deal happens only if I walk
away."

"What? Julia, no! That's unfair and ridiculous.
Sonny's worked his ass off at the clambake for ten
years. The last five without Dad. You can't just
throw him out!"

I could have said a lot of things. That Sonny
had worked his ass off driving the business into
the ground. That I hadn't set the conditions, Etienne had. That I could think of no other way to
keep Morrow Island in the family. But Sonny
spoke instead.

"Babe, you don't look too good. What's wrong?"

Livvie's voice, hot with anger just seconds
before, quavered as she said, "Marie Halsey just
called. Sarah turned herself in to the police.
They're charging her with Ray Wilson's murder."

Sonny came out from behind the desk like a shot and took Livvie in his arms. "I am so sorry, babe."

"I don't understand," Livvie said. "How could she have murdered him? How could she have hung him from that staircase?"

I cleared my throat. "They think Chris Durand helped her."

Livvie leaned against Sonny for support. "Oh, no."

Sonny hugged her tight. "Chris Durand. Still spreading trouble wherever he goes."

"They think he helped her because he and Sarah are lovers. Why didn't you tell me?" I demanded of Livvie.

"They—" Livvie started to deny it. But then she saw the look on my face and decided not to lie. "You had a harmless crush. I didn't see how it could hurt anyone. I did warn you he came with baggage."

A harmless crush? My eyes stung with the idea that my baby sister had seen me like a schoolgirl. The way she would see Page in just a couple years. She'd begged me to upend my life and return to town to save the business. Then she'd patronized and lied to me and sided with her husband at every turn. It was all too much for me.

I tried to squeeze past where she and Sonny stood in the doorway. "Get out of my way."

"Where are you going now?"

"To New York City to meet with Tony Poitras and negotiate the sale of Morrow Island. I've had as much of this as I can take. I'm out."

I pushed into the hallway and sped down the backstairs. Behind me I could hear Sonny yelling. *"Leave, Julia! Leave like you always do!"*

Chapter 48

I ran through the driving rain to the garage and backed my mother's car out, my heart pumping with fury. I couldn't abide this. I couldn't abide it one more minute. Family. Responsibility. The endless arguments with Sonny. No home of my own. No privacy, and as I'd just been made savagely aware, no social life. Not a single thing that was mine.

The only way out was Tony Poitras. I'd exhausted every other avenue I could think of. If I could speak to him in person, perhaps I could get a better deal for my mother. I could use the information Quentin Tupper had given me to strengthen my negotiating position. That was the only thing left to salvage. I had just enough time to get to New York to see Tony before the deadline on the offer expired.

The stop sign at the bottom of the hill on Main Street had been there all my life. My school bus had stopped there every day. My mother had stopped there every time she took Livvie and me to the grocery store. When my dad taught me to drive, we'd gone down the hill and stopped at that corner dozens of times.

But somehow, with my windshield wipers working at top speed in the gloom of the day, rehearsing my speech to Tony in my head, somehow, I drove right through it, and . . .

Bam!

A pickup truck flew out of nowhere on my right and crashed into my car, causing it to slip into a spin. The airbag punched me in the chest, took my breath away, and slapped my hands from the steering wheel. I closed my eyes, helpless, as the world continued to turn.

When I opened my eyes, I was on the opposite corner, facing backwards. My chest stung and I moved my arms gingerly, anxious to see if they worked. Still in sopping wet clothes, I honestly couldn't tell if I'd peed my pants.

A dark green pickup sat in the intersection, its front end caved in, hood open like a hungry maw. The poor driver, a kid of not more than nineteen or twenty, was already out of the cab and running toward me.

"Oh my God! Are you all right?"

I shook my hands out and took a deep breath. "I think so."

"I didn't see you. I'm so sorry!"

For a moment, I thought he might cry.

"It was all my fault," I said. And it was. All of it.

It was Officer Howland, Sonny's friend, who came to the scene, adding to my humiliation, if that was even possible. At least it wasn't Jamie. I explained that I'd run the stop sign, that the kid was in the right. The side of my mother's Buick was unrecognizable as anything resembling a motor vehicle. We started the ritual exchange of information.

Howland explained that we'd have quite a wait for tow trucks. It was a Friday evening in the summer season and raining. After he'd filled out some paperwork, he and the kid pushed the disabled truck out of the intersection. I leaned against the driver's side door of my mother's car in the rain and watched.

When who should drive up in his ancient Ford pickup, sitting straight up in his seat and peering over the steering wheel? Gus. Would the horrors of this day never end?

He pulled up behind Howland's cruiser and got out, spoke briefly to Howland, and then crossed the street toward me. "You're drenched."

I looked down at the clothes clinging to my body, the sweatshirt, jeans, and work boots I'd been in all day. I was so sick of these clothes. "I was wet when I left my house," I said stupidly.

Gus didn't ask what that meant. He only said, "Howland says the tow trucks will still be awhile. You wait in my truck."

I shook my head. The last thing I wanted was to be in a confined space with Gus.

But he was having none of it. "I've got the heater running. C'mon. You'll catch your death."

I finally agreed. Not because I was afraid I'd catch my death, but because I was afraid he would. Nobody except maybe Mrs. Gus knew how old he was, but he wore only a thin jacket against the rain. On top of all my oh-so-many disastrous activities that day, I didn't want to be responsible for killing a town icon.

We crossed the street and I got in his truck. He turned up the heater.

"You want to tell me what happened?"

"No." I stared at my lap, fearful of looking anywhere else. But it was useless to fight it. Tears slid down my nose and soon I was telling Gus everything. About the call from Ditzy and Tony's offer and Etienne's offer with its terrible condition. I told him about how I'd screwed up the business plan and doomed the Snowden Family Clambake before the season even started. I confessed about my epic battles with Sonny and how Livvie was on his side. I even told him about Quentin Tupper's refusal to bid on our property and that Jean-Jacques might be back.

Gus listened to it all with a nod of his head.

There might be no crying in Gus's restaurant, but there was plenty of crying in Gus's truck that evening. I told him about Sarah and Chris's arrests. I even told about the kiss from Jamie and the terrible mistake I had made, misunderstanding Chris's friendship and thinking it meant more.

In the end, I pulled myself to a shuddering stop and told Gus the only way out I could see was to sell the island to Tony. At least then I could salvage something for my mother.

Gus didn't say anything for a long time. Then he turned to me and said, "Are you sure you want to do that? You have something more than a business there."

"Please, Gus," I cried. "I just can't hear about how much I owe the town or our employees right now."

"I don't mean that. I meant you have more than a business. You have a family."

Then he got out of the truck and left me alone.

Chapter 49

I cried for quite a while in Gus's truck. The heater steamed up the windows and it was like my own private cave where I could wallow in self-pity and remorse.

My family. I wasn't just leaving a business, I was leaving my family. It had taken a long time for me to see it, but I knew in my heart that everything Sonny had said was true. At some point over the last ten years, my irresponsible, rebellious younger sister had become the mature one. She'd become the one who went over almost every night to make sure my grieving mother ate dinner. She took care of Page and took care of my parents. I was the one who was absent. I had stayed away.

Sonny was the one who had given up his life for the Snowden Family Clambake, not me. Whatever dreams he might have had he'd let go of long ago, laboring for my father every day and night. He'd spent the money he'd borrowed on the same things I would have, repairs to the dock and buildings, getting our ticket sales online. All things that were necessary. All things my father would have done had he lived. Sonny had just gotten caught in a terrible economy.

It hurt me to think that I hadn't recognized Sonny's grief. Of course he missed my father, a man he had spent almost every single day with since he was a teenager. Who'd shaped him as much as anyone and taught him how to be a man and a father, and how to run a business. I'd spent so much time since Dad's death worrying— Was Mom okay? Was Page okay? Was Livvie okay? Was I okay? I had never even thought about Sonny, who in the last ten years had spent more time with my father than anyone, except Mom.

And now, what was I doing? Where would I go when this was over and the business was sold? Back to New York City?

Venture capital had been great fun when I started. I was good at it—good at helping my bosses pick winners, good at nurturing the baby businesses we backed. But I was always working. I spent my life in airports. My apartment was like a closet where I stored my stuff. My business school friends had drifted away after too many turned-down invitations, too many get-togethers canceled at the last moment. Every time a rela-tionship with a guy seemed like it might turn into something, I was off on another trip—which was probably why I'd gotten things so wrong about Chris.

What he'd seen as a casual friendship, I'd turned into so much more. I'd never been to his house. We'd never been on a date, or even seen each other outside of Gus's. We'd never kissed, and that moment on his boat when he'd taken my hands in his and told me I'd misunderstood our relationship was the first time he'd ever touched me. What a total fool I was.

The night before Livvie had called me to come home and save the clambake, I'd been in an airport, as usual. I was exhausted from the travel and the time zones and the stress. With an hour between flights, I'd gone to the gate before my second flight started boarding, sat directly across from the counter, and thought I'd just close my eyes.

I woke up hours later. My plane was gone. In fact, all the planes were gone. The area of the terminal where I sat was half in darkness. Half a football field away, a cleaner polished the floor with a machine. He was the only other human I could see.

I grabbed the phone to check the time. It was after midnight. On my birthday. No one had missed me. Not a living soul on the earth knew where I was, and I knew then that I had to change my life. But I didn't have a clue how or to what.

Livvie's call came the next day.

Until that very moment sitting in Gus's truck, I thought I'd come home to rescue them. Instead, without even intending it, they had rescued me.

The tow truck finally came and took Mom's car away. Gus dropped me at home. Livvie and Sonny's vehicles were still in the driveway. It seemed like every light in the house was on.

You haven't lived until you've had to tell your mother you borrowed her car without permission and wrecked it. When you are thirty years old. Mom took one look at my splotchy, red-nosed face and took me in her arms. I thought I was all cried out, but apparently, I wasn't.

We gathered on the comfy furniture on the porch while the rain pelted down outside the screens. Sonny apologized to me, and I apologized to him. Livvie hugged me and said she was sorry, she knew I'd worked hard and done my best. I said I knew she and Sonny had done the same. I was sorry about all the harsh words Page had overheard over the long, rough spring, but I was glad she was there to see the grown-ups in her life at last behaving like grown-ups.

Though everything seemed changed to me, in fact nothing was. The clambake was still closed. The bank still planned to call our loan. The deadline still loomed on Tony's offer. Etienne's conditions still stood. Chris and Sarah were still in jail. Ray Wilson was still dead.

Sonny cleared his throat. "Livvie and I have talked it over, and we think you should take Etienne's offer. I'll bow out and find some other work."

"No. I won't do that."

"It's the only way to save the island. You said so yourself."

"But it's not our way. This is the Snowden *Family* Clambake. This is about our family." I stood. "I need to get out of these wet clothes. Then I'll go out to the island and convince Etienne to change the terms of his offer. He can still have a third of the business. But Sonny stays."

"I'll go with you," Sonny volunteered.

"No. I don't think you can be there for this particular discussion. I need to go alone. And I need to do it now, so we know where Etienne stands before Tony's offer expires."

Chapter 50

The rain stopped as I ran to the marina to collect Chris's dinghy, but the sky was still steel gray and the clouds hung low. I jumped into the boat, grateful I hadn't returned the key, and started the motor. The lightweight boat hesitated, fighting the current as I headed out to sea.

Before I reached the outer harbor I was wet to the skin. Changing my clothes had been a completely ridiculous exercise. My teeth ached from the boat rising up and slamming down with the chop. I shivered as the force of the wind hit my wet clothes. Maine water was always cold.

At the mouth of the harbor, I briefly considered turning back. The waves would be even higher once I hit the open ocean, and I was already tired from fighting the tiller. But I had to know if Etienne was in or out before Tony's offer expired. I wasn't sure whether Tony was bluffing,

but with so much on the line I didn't want to
test it.

I thought I had good leverage with Etienne. I
would explain, calmly, that he had a choice. He
could accept Sonny as a part of the package and
own a third of the Snowden Family Clambake. Or
my family could accept Tony's offer, which meant
the island would no longer be ours and Etienne
and Gabrielle would have to move away.

I was glad to see the island up ahead. Perhaps
gladder than I've ever been. I tied up the little
boat behind the Whaler. Its presence meant Etienne and Gabrielle were home.

The dinghy's little motor would have been
hard to hear over the rhythmic crash of the waves
against the rocks, so I called from the dock, not
wanting to take them by surprise. "Hello! It's
Julia!" The door to their house was closed and,
in spite of the gloomy day, no lights shone. A
drenched Le Roi ran up beside me and scratched
at the door, meowing. He wanted to get inside, too.

I knocked and called a couple times. I turned
the knob and pushed. It was locked. *Strange.*
Through the window in the door, in the fading
light, I could see into Gabrielle's kitchen. It had
been ransacked. Pots strewn across the floor,
drawers of flatware emptied on the spotless
linoleum. The shelves of her china cupboard
stood empty, the shards of her dishes on the floor.

The scene in the kitchen panicked me. Had

the mad man who'd killed Ray returned to the island? I was sure Sarah and Chris weren't killers. Was it Jean-Jacques?

I banged on the door again hard and shouted, but there was no sign of Etienne or Gabrielle.

I returned to the dock, at a loss as to what to do next. Despite the long June days, night was going to fall soon. It would be a cloudy night, with no moon to guide me home. Something was terribly wrong.

I looked up at Windsholme. It stood silent as it always did. But it seemed like there was an eerie light in the center window on the top floor, the room where Binder and I had discovered the neatly folded clothes. But there wasn't any working electricity in that part of the mansion, only in the two rooms on the first floor I'd had newly wired.

I took off up the hill. As I ran, I considered the alternatives. My cell phone? Useless. The radio? Locked in Etienne and Gabrielle's house. I reached the front porch of Windsholme and threw open the double doors.

I considered for a moment what I might be rushing into. Jean-Jacques most likely . . . in the room he used when he was on the island . . . with some sort of lantern. Was he dangerous? He was a fugitive, someone who'd lived outside society for six years. What would happen if I cornered him?

I had to consider Etienne and Gabrielle. By the look of things at their house, there'd been a terrible struggle. What if Jean-Jacques was holding them, harming them? I had to help. *No one is coming*, I thought. *There's no one to do anything but me.*

I started up the staircase, my heart pounding like the waves on the rocks outside. Not a panic attack, the product of an overactive mind, but real panic. I stood on the landing, breathing carefully, willing myself not to run away.

I climbed to the top floor and paused again, trying to stay in control. From where I stood, I could see the door across from the landing was ajar, light escaping onto the hallway floor. From inside the room came a terrible keening. Gabrielle! What was happening to her?

Keeping flat against the hallway wall, I slid forward in the shadows. I didn't think Jean-Jacques would hear me over the racket his mother was making. About the only thing on my side was the element of surprise. I rushed past the partially opened door to the other side of the hall and peered in.

Gabrielle sat on the floor in the center of the room surrounded by a circle of lit candles. She cradled a grown man in her arms and moaned. *"Mon p'tit chou, mon p'tit chou, mon p'tit chou."*

She'd called Jean-Jacques by that endearment when he was young and he'd hated it. But now, far from fighting her, far from the evidence of confrontation and mayhem I'd seen at their house, he was lying in her arms and allowing her to comfort him.

I took the chance of peering around the door frame, so I could see the other side of the room. What I saw made me clasp my hand to my mouth to keep from crying out. Etienne was tied to the bed, a gag in his mouth and a terrified expression in his eyes. He saw me in the candlelight and raised his great eyebrows at me, showing me the whites of his eyes.

I looked back at Gabrielle holding Jean-Jacques's inert body. He was a big man the last time I'd seen him and it looked as though his wandering years hadn't changed that. I pumped up and down on my knees a couple times and got ready to spring.

My God, what was I doing? Was I crazy? I couldn't go through with it. But then I remembered. No one was coming. It was all down to me. I crouched down again.

"Kee-yah!" It was a weird, cartoony karate yell, but I figured noise would help me. I grabbed Jean-Jacques by the shirt and he flew from Gabrielle's lap.

Flew? Jean-Jacques weighed next to nothing.

In the confusion, it took several seconds for me to realize it wasn't Jean-Jacques at all, but a dummy dressed in clothes like the ones Binder and I had seen in the room. The moment I realized this, Gabrielle's wiry arm closed across my neck and she dragged me to my feet, screaming in French at the top of her lungs. *"Tu as tué. Tu as tué!"*

"What?" My French wasn't good but I got the gist, *you killed him.* "Gabrielle, it's me. Julia. Let go. It's okay."

I slithered around to face her, her arm still around my neck. My back was to the doorway. Gabrielle let go, then put both hands on my clavicle and pushed. I thought I might go over backwards. I shouted, "No! Gabrielle! No!" and took a giant step back to regain my footing. She came after me again, and before I knew it, we were out in the hallway. I kept backing up in the face of her shoving, trying to fight her off without hurting her.

I screamed in English. "I didn't hurt Jean-Jacques, Gabrielle! I would never hurt him. Please believe me. You and Etienne are like my own parents. Please!"

My backside hit the railing of the open balcony just as Etienne let out a sound so loud I heard it despite his gag. I looked back toward the doorway and saw flames. When I'd tossed the dummy into the air, it must have landed on the candles. Its clothes were a ball of fire and soon flames would reach the bed where Etienne was tied.

"Gabrielle, Gabrielle, let me go! We have to save Etienne!"

But the face that looked back at me didn't care or comprehend. She was mad. She threw herself against me, bending me back over the rail. It came to me in an instant. Something like this had happened to Ray. It was how he broke his neck!

I screamed at her and pushed back with all my might, but physics was on her side. I felt sure I would topple over the railing. Smoke poured out of the room and swirled above us, collecting in the high, coffered ceiling. I pleaded, "No, Gabrielle, no. Please, please. It's Julia."

But she didn't stop.

I couldn't straighten up, so I grabbed Gabrielle and pulled her toward me, just as she moved forward for a vicious shove. I thought for a split second that both of us would go over the balcony, but her momentum carried her forward and she sailed by me, over the railing, screaming as she went down. There was a sickening thud in the hallway below.

I was so shocked I couldn't move. Then, I looked over the rail and in the dim light made out Gabrielle's broken body below.

Etienne was shouting against the gag. I ran to the door. The room was almost fully engulfed in flame. The window had exploded open, feeding oxygen to the fire. Flames licked toward the bedding. I had to get Etienne out.

I ran into the room, then retreated, coughing and sputtering. *No one is coming, no one is coming, no one is coming.* There was only one person who could save Etienne. I went in again, crawling toward the bed on my belly, breathing the freshest air in the room.

Etienne strained frantically.

"Keep still," I hissed. I didn't think I was going to get another chance. His arms were secured to the headboard by two short lengths of rope. Once I got him to lie still, the knots were easy to untie, despite my shaking hands. I didn't even untie the gag. I put his arm around my shoulders and the flames chased us from the room.

At the bottom of the stairs, he stared at Gabrielle's body. He made a mewling sound around the gag.

I pulled him from the house and fought to keep him outside. "You can't go back in! Too dangerous." Above us, flames leaped out of the fourth floor windows toward the night sky.

"The radio!" I yelled. "Etienne, we have to get back to your house." I undid the gag as he fought me off.

"Non, non, non." He ran back into Windsholme.

I stood there for a moment, too shocked to move. *No one is coming.*

I charged through the door and was greeted with such a whirl of smoke I nearly ran out. *No one is coming.* I called to Etienne, but in the roar of the fire, I couldn't even hear myself. I knew he'd gone to the bottom of the staircase where Gabrielle's body lay. I fell to my knees and crawled toward the spot.

A loud crack sounded above and a long, flaming span of the banister careened down, nearly hitting me. I wanted to call out, but knew I had to conserve my breath. I crawled on in the dark and the noise, waving an arm in front of me with each movement. Just when I thought I would have to turn back, I hit something. Etienne's strong calf. I pulled on his pants leg, shouting, "We have to go!"

With Gabrielle in his arms, he took a step toward me.

For a moment, I feared I'd gotten turned around in the fire and wouldn't be able to find the door. I decided I had to back out on my knees, exactly as I'd come in. I pulled on Etienne's ankle. Step this way, step this way. Slowly, so slowly, we moved back across the room. Etienne coughed continuously in the smoke-filled air. The moment my foot hit the threshold of the doorway, he staggered to a stop.

"We have to go!" I screamed. "We have to go out. Now." I pulled myself up, hugging Etienne and the still body of Gabrielle. The stairs burned around us, flames leaping. I gasped, even the few feet I gained by standing made it more difficult to breathe. I put my arms around his waist and pulled him the last few steps out the door.

Outside, breathing heavily, I moved behind

Etienne, pushing him down the steps and then down the lawn away from the burning building. Finally, when we were at the midpoint between the house and the pavilion, he laid Gabrielle gently in the grass and we turned and looked back.

The inside of Windsholme was an inferno. The stone walls that had protected the house from the porch fire now had the opposite effect. Inside, the flames built and roared as if they were in a giant, stone oven. As Etienne and I stood and watched, flames leaped out the windows toward the wooden gables and up into the roof.

"Is Jean-Jacques somewhere in there?" I asked Etienne.

He shook his head. "He never was. He never has been."

A noise like a freight train barreling through the night sounded as a third of Windsholme's roof caved in. Slates fell into the house and flames shot thirty feet into the sky.

Etienne fell over the broken body of his wife and wept.

I heard a shout behind me. It was Quentin Tupper, running up the lawn. "I saw the flames," he panted. "From my house. The Coast Guard's on its way."

And soon they all were there. The Coast Guard, the Busman's Harbor Fire Department, the harbormaster, along with Lieutenant Binder and Detective Flynn.

Chapter 51

When it was almost dawn, after we'd been questioned separately for hours, they loaded Etienne and me onto a Coast Guard ship. We sat together in the stern, both of us covered in soot. My eyes still blinked from the irritation.

Lieutenant Binder went off to attend to something, calling to Detective Flynn who'd been watching us. I had the feeling Binder left Etienne and me alone on purpose. It wasn't like either of us could go anywhere, and there was so much to be said.

"Etienne, what happened?" I had to know. I wouldn't be able to make sense of anything that had happened to us until I did.

Even through the grime, I could see his sadness. "Gabby did not do well with . . . with what happened with Jean-Jacques. You have noticed this?"

"Yes," I said.

"No one has understood how badly it has gone

for her. I talked to your father about it, back when it began. But soon, he was sick with cancer and had troubles of his own. Gabby just got worse." Etienne was another person who was missing my father. His best friend, his confidant.

"But I don't understand—"

"This spring, someone cleaned up the playhouse. I don't know who it was. I thought perhaps Sonny had done it for the kids, but he said no when I asked him. Gabrielle took this as a sign Jean-Jacques was back. She became convinced he was living here on the island." Etienne's voice caught.

I attempted to imagine what he was going through at that moment, but could not.

"I tried to reason with her. I took her everywhere on the island. But wherever we were, she claimed Jean-Jacques was somewhere else. Gabby left food in the playhouse. She went into town and purchased the clothes you saw, which she lovingly washed and folded." Etienne paused, then regained control. "I didn't know what to do. I talked to her doctors. They prescribed medications. They said it was an obsession, but I knew it was something else. I believed she really saw and heard him."

When Etienne saw the puzzled look on my face, he added, "In her mind, Julia. It was all in her disturbed mind."

"Oh, Etienne." I felt terrible about what he had

been coping with. And how I hadn't known. Because I hadn't been there. And then, even after I returned, I hadn't taken the time to see.

We stared silently back up the hill to Windsholme for a moment. The fire had almost died, but not completely.

"At some point, she became convinced he'd moved from the playhouse to Windsholme," he continued. "She was worried to death about the work you had done there, the electrical work and so on. And the fact that you encouraged the bride to fix herself up in the house. Gabrielle believed if you could save the clambake, you were going to start using Windsholme as a part of it, and Jean-Jacques would have no place to go.

"She also worried about the island, if the clambake failed you would have to sell. I tried to keep the financial worries away from her, but she was always here on the island. She overheard a lot. Things you said. Things Sonny said."

I'd never thought about the effect all our discussions that spring had on Gabrielle. I was careful around my mother, and around Page, but I never had been around Gabrielle. She must have been scared to death. "And then Ray came and said he and Tony wanted to buy it."

Etienne closed his eyes, remembering. "Yes. He said he wanted to scout the island to set up a prank on his buddy the groom. I invited him into our house. I had no idea who he was or where the conversation would go. Right in front of Gabrielle, he talked about buying the island. She panicked, as I knew she would. But I was able to convince her you'd never sell."

I nodded. "And then Ray arrived on the island on the night of his death to set up his trick on Tony."

"He came out while Gabby and I were still in the harbor. When she saw the little boat tied up at the dock, you can imagine how excited she was. 'He's here! He's here!' she yelled. She ran straight up the lawn. Wilson had left the mansion door wide open."

"He had the dummy in the camp trunk." I had only just worked that out.

"Yes, and he was about to hang it from the landing. I suppose it was meant to be funny."

A "you're doomed" sort of message for Tony. Not funny at all. But those who'd hated Ray Wilson, and even those who'd loved him, had talked about his adolescent, frat-boy sense of humor. Ray Wilson had brought the rope he was hung with to the island as a joke.

"Gabrielle attacked him," I said.

Etienne nodded that was true. "It was the last thing Wilson expected. A crazed woman running at him. She was furious, convinced he planned to hurt Jean-Jacques."

I began to realize what had happened. Ray's reaction times would have been slowed as a result of the alcohol and the drugs Sarah gave him, making it difficult to put up much of a fight.

"Before he knew what happened, before *I* knew what happened, she pushed him over the railing."

"He broke his neck."

Etienne nodded sadly.

"But why, Etienne, why did you hang him from the staircase?"

"Gabby insisted. And I did think it might accomplish what she wanted. It would get you to stop renovating Windsholme and convince Wilson's partner to stay away from the island. I wanted to go on as before."

Instead, the effect had been the opposite.

"I was trying to do the best I could, to keep Gabby together. I knew she was mad. Maybe I became a little mad as well."

"What did you do with the camp trunk—and the boat?"

"I filled the trunk with rocks, put Wilson's jacket in it, towed his little boat out into the ocean, and sunk it all. I recognized the boat. He'd stolen it from one of the yachts by the town dock. I knew the owner wouldn't miss it for months."

"And the porch fire?"

"Gabby. By that point she was desperate for everyone to go away. She did not mean to hurt Windsholme. Not as long as she thought Jean-Jacques was living there. She knew the mansion wouldn't burn."

"But tonight, how did you end up tied up?"

"We'd been keeping vigil, waiting for Jean-Jacques every night this week. We hadn't slept in days. I tried to refuse to let her go to Windsholme tonight. You saw what she did to our kitchen. Going to the mansion was the only way to calm her. I must have dozed off on the bed as we waited. I was so exhausted. Gabby had been paranoid for days that I would try to scare Jean-Jacques off, or turn him in. I think she tied me to the bed in order to make sure I wouldn't interfere."

Etienne put his head in his hands and wept. "She was completely mad at the end, Julia. Please forgive her."

Chapter 52

Three weeks later, I waited on Morrow Island to greet our special guests as they disembarked from the *Jacquie II*. It was a beautiful evening for a clambake.

Livvie and Sonny had moved out to the island for the summer. Page could have the same island childhood Livvie and I had, and our mother before us. Sonny took over Etienne's job as the bake master, which meant he and I had different spheres, different responsibilities, which cut down a lot of arguments. We'd both been reminded recently how critical our health was, physical and mental, and how important family was. It taught us to compromise when the situation called for it. Livvie loved being on the island and tended Gabrielle's vegetable garden every day.

Page adopted Le Roi. When she hugged him to her chest, his back legs fell below her knees. He was obviously annoyed, but let her do it, anyway.

He was still the king of the island. The human beings came and went, but he remained.

We reopened the clambake with Quentin Tupper as our "very silent" partner. He continued to resist, protesting that investing in the clambake sounded, "too much like work." I finally convinced him he didn't need to be involved at all and buying a third of the business was hugely preferable to having a resort, complete with helicopter pad, across from his property. So far he'd been next to invisible, which was the way he wanted it. I actually would've liked having a partner to talk to about the big decisions.

One of the biggest decisions was what to do about Windsholme. In the end, with the building inspector's blessing, we erected a chain-link fence around its perimeter and left the mansion as it was. It looked awful, and sometimes I thought we should have sold the property to Tony Poitras and let him build one of his beautiful resorts on the ruins. But then I looked around and saw the happy families at the clambake, most of them people who could never enjoy Morrow Island if it was a high-end resort, and I knew we had done the right thing. In the fall, when the clambake closed for the season, we would decide what to do about the building.

Marie Halsey brought Tyler out to the island with her almost every day to play with Page. The kids had a little moneymaking enterprise where they sold shells and sea glass to the guests. Sarah's lawyer thought he could negotiate the charge against her down to something called criminal misadventure. She didn't kill Ray, though she may have been a party to impairing his judgment to the point where he went out to a little island in a big ocean in the middle of the night. She'd probably only get probation. The plea deal would clear the way for Tyler to inherit Ray's money with Sarah remaining as his legal guardian.

A rumor floated around that Sarah had told the cops who'd sold her the Rophynol.

"Gee, I wonder who that could have been?" Sonny said.

I knew he meant Chris. I wasn't naive. Chris worked as a bouncer, owned a cab and a boat. An almost perfect setup for a drug dealer. There had always been rumors about him. But I didn't think it was him. If Sarah had informed on Chris, why was he still walking around? Not that I'd seen him, but I would've heard if he'd been arrested.

Binder must have believed Etienne's story and my account of what happened the night Windsholme burned. He persuaded the prosecutor to charge Etienne with misuse of a cadaver for hanging up Ray's body, the least serious offense available. Etienne would pay a fine, but nothing worse. He was staying with us until it all got straightened out. He came to Morrow Island one last time, to scatter Gabrielle's ashes off the little beach. Afterwards, he said he'd never set foot on Morrow Island again. My heart broke for him.

We'd invited everyone we knew in town out to the island for a clambake. It seemed like the best way to show people we were back in business and it was safe to recommend us. I stood on the dock, welcoming Mr. and Mrs. Gus, Fee and Vee Snuggs, Clarice Kemp, Quentin Tupper, and even Bob Ditzy. Bygones needed to be bygones. I'd invited the Chinese maid from the Bellevue and the Russian girl from the Lighthouse Inn. And Lieutenant Binder, Detective Flynn, Jamie, Officer Howland, and anyone who had helped us along the way. I'd seen Jamie around town a few times. We'd each gone out of our way to be polite. Neither of us had said a word about the kiss or the fight.

When the *Jacquie II* emptied out and the crowd moved up the lawn, I stood for a moment, hoping.

Even with Livvie and Sonny living there, my mother still hadn't come out to the island. I finally understood why she hadn't returned in the five years since my father died. I thought the island represented her happiest childhood home, and the place where she met my father. She didn't want to color those memories with her grief. And now, she had the grief of Gabrielle to deal with, as well. It was my hope, and Livvie's, with Page as a lure, my mother would someday return to the island. But not today.

I knew my mother wasn't coming, but someone else was missing.

I hadn't run into Chris around town. It didn't strike me as odd, necessarily. The season was in full swing and I'd always known our lunches together would end then. Besides, as he'd told me on that awful day when he was arrested for something he didn't do, I'd misunderstood our relationship. One thing I was sure of, though. He'd been the one who cleaned up the playhouse. Everyone else denied it. I shuddered thinking about how two small acts, Chris cleaning the playhouse and me having a couple rooms in Windsholme rewired, had hastened Gabrielle's descent into madness.

Finally, Captain George came down the gangplank. He crooked his arm at the elbow and cocked his thumb back toward the cabin. "There's someone onboard who wants to see you."

My mother! She'd come after all. She probably needed my moral support to step onto the island. I scurried onto the boat, calling, "Mom?"

But it wasn't my mother. When I entered the *Jacquie II*'s cabin, Chris stood in the center of the deck. In spite of everything, my heart soared. But I knew better than to have any expectations. He had plainly told me not to.

"I know it's a busy night for you," he said, "but I wanted to see you. To explain some things." He paused. "Sarah Halsey and I have been friends a long time."

My cheeks burned with embarrassment. "You don't owe me any explanations," I managed to say. In fact, he'd already explained. He'd told me I misunderstood.

"I think I do." He moved so close I could smell him, that intoxicating scent of a man who's washed off the sweat, but who smells of hard, physical work. The scent of all the men who were truly important in my life.

"Sarah was alone when she came here. Pregnant. She worked at the T-shirt store on Main Street before she attended that birthing class where she met Livvie. Before your dad gave her a job. I met her then and started watching out for her."

I wanted to protest again that he didn't need to tell me, mostly because I didn't want to hear.

"There was something between Sarah and me after Tyler was born, but it's been over for years. When I was involved with her, Tyler became important to me. He still is. My relationship with Sarah these days is all about him. Only about Tyler. His dad was a roaring drunk and I do whatever I can to take up some of the slack."

Chris took both of my hands and pulled me closer to him. "That's all it is, Julia. That's all it ever was. It's a small town. That's what I meant when I said people misunderstood. They misunderstood my relationship with Sarah." He paused and put a hand under my chin. "I think, also, some people misunderstand my relationship with you."

He pulled me to him. "You're the one I've wanted, all along." And then he kissed me, hard.

Recipes

Snowden Family Clam Chowder

The Snowden Family Clambake Company serves traditional New England Clam Chowder by the gallon. This recipe has been adapted for home use by Bill Carito, but will be just as yummy.

¼ pound thick-cut bacon, chopped
1 large onion (approximately ¾ pound), chopped
2 large potatoes (approximately 1 pound), cubed
2 bottles clam juice
½ Tablespoon chopped fresh thyme
1 pint shucked and minced or chopped clams with their juices reserved (4 cans)
1½ cups whole milk
1½ cups half and half
Salt and pepper to taste

Using medium heat, cook the bacon in the soup pot until crispy.

Add the onion and cook 5 minutes.

Add the potato cubes and cook 2 minutes.

Add the bottled clam juice, reserved juices from the clams, and thyme leaves, and bring to a boil. Turn down the heat and simmer for 10–15 minutes until the potatoes are tender. While the potatoes are simmering, combine the milk and half and half and gently warm in a saucepan (or microwave) to just past lukewarm.

Add the milk, half and half, and the clams to the pot when the potatoes are tender. Bring to a gentle simmer (do not boil) and cook an additional 10 minutes.

Salt and pepper to taste.

Serve with crackers or crusty bread.

Snowden Family Blueberry Grunt

Most Maine families have multiple recipes for blueberry desserts—duffs, grunts, slumps, crunches, crisps, pies, and coffee cakes. Throughout New England and the eastern provinces of Canada, it's possible to get into a quite lively discussion about which is which. Whatever you call them, these desserts are delicious. Here's the one the Snowden family serves at the clambake. This recipe was adapted for home use by the late Maine author A. Carmen Clark.

½ cup water
1 quart blueberries
⅔ cup sugar

Topping

1½ cups flour
2 Tablespoons butter
2 teaspoons baking powder
½ teaspoon salt
¼ cup sugar
½ cup milk

Preheat the oven to 400 degrees.
Grease a deep baking dish or casserole and into this put the berries, sugar, and water.

Place in the oven for 20 minutes while mixing the dough.

Blend the butter into the flour. Add other ingredients and mix in with a fork, making the dough.

Spoon the dough over the hot berries.

Bake for 20 additional minutes.

Livvie's Lobster Mac and Cheese

Livvie is the real cook in the Snowden family and her lobster mac and cheese is delicious. The sharp taste of the cheese with the sweetness of the lobster meat, and the textures—springy noodles, toothsome lobster, and crunchy panko breadcrumbs—cannot be beat. Livvie uses local cheeses that can only be purchased in Maine, but simple substitutions are supplied.

1 pound elbow macaroni
2 Tablespoons butter
2 Tablespoons flour
1½ cup milk
⅛ teaspoon grated nutmeg
½ pound grated Hahn's End Eleanor
 Buttercup cheese (or substitute Fontina
 or Monterey Jack)
½ pound grated Hahn's End Olde
 Shiretown cheese (or substitute cheddar)
1 pound cooked lobster meat
 (approximately four lobsters)
½ cup snipped chives

Topping

1 cup panko bread crumbs
2 Tablespoons butter
¼ cup Parmesan cheese

Preheat the oven to 450 degrees.

Grease a 9x13 baking dish with butter.

Boil water and cook pasta for approximately five minutes until just barely al dente. Drain well and return the pasta to the pan. Set aside.

Heat the milk to lukewarm (one minute on high power in the microwave).

Over medium heat, melt the butter in a 2–3 quart saucepan. Whisk in the flour, stirring constantly for two minutes. Remove from the heat and add milk slowly, stirring constantly to prevent lumps.

Add the nutmeg, salt, and pepper to taste.

Return the pan to the heat and bring the liquid to a boil, stirring constantly. Reduce the heat and gently simmer for 4–5 minutes, stirring occasionally until the sauce thickens. Pour over the cooked macaroni.

Add cheeses, lobster, and chives and gently stir together until combined. Turn the mixture into the baking dish.

Melt the butter and mix with the bread crumbs until fully coated.

Stir in the Parmesan cheese.

Spoon over the top of the pasta.

Bake for 20–25 minutes. The top should be golden.

Gus's Clam Hash

Gus doesn't let anyone into his restaurant unless he knows them, or someone he does know vouches for them. That means you may never be able to taste Gus's delicious clam hash. But if you follow this recipe, you'll get very, very close!

2 large Maine potatoes
1 large yellow onion
2 cans minced clams (Gus uses 1 cup of
    freshly minced clams, but if you buy a
    good brand of canned, it will be almost
    as good.)
Salt
Pepper
2 Tablespoons heavy cream
2 strips bacon
1 Tablespoon butter

Prick the potatoes with a fork and microwave on high for 5 minutes or until they can be easily pierced with a fork.

Cut onion in eighths, then put in a food processor and pulse 10 times.

Peel the cooled potatoes and chop them into large cubes.

Put the cubed potatoes in the food processor with the onions and pulse to combine.

Add salt and pepper.

Add the drained clams and cream. Pulse to combine.

In a frying pan, cook the bacon until crispy, then remove and set aside.

Add the butter to the bacon fat in the frying pan.

Add the hash from the food processor and press down into the frying pan.

Cook for 5–6 minutes on medium heat until the bottom begins to brown.

Turn and cook the other side.

Keep flipping to add more crust as desired.

Top with crumbled bacon.

Gabrielle's Tourtière

Every French Canadian family has a treasured recipe for these famous meat pies, which are often served on holidays. This is Gabrielle's recipe. It is Julia's favorite meal.

Pie Crust

3½ cups flour
2 teaspoon kosher salt
1½ cups shortening or lard
1 egg, beaten lightly with a fork
1 Tablespoon apple cider vinegar
¼ to ½ cup ice water, as needed
1 Tablespoon milk (to brush over finished pie before baking)

In a food processor, using the metal blade, pulse the flour and salt to combine.

Add the shortening and pulse until reaching the consistency of corn meal.

Add the egg, vinegar, and ¼ cup ice water. Pulse, adding additional ice water, if necessary, until ingredients barely come together in a dough ball.

Turn out onto a cutting board and pat together evenly into a large oblong.

Divide into four pieces. You will need two for the tourtière. You can freeze the other two for later use.

Refrigerate.

Remove from the fridge ten minutes before using.

Filling

2 pounds pork shoulder in 1–2 inch chunks
1 large onion chopped
1 teaspoon kosher salt
2 cups homemade chicken stock, or low-
   sodium canned stock
3–4 cups diced potatoes
1 teaspoon cinnamon
1½ teaspoon ground cloves

Preheat oven to 400 degrees.

In a food processor, using the metal blade, pulse pork to a rough chop (10–20 pulses).

Combine the pork, onion, salt, and stock in a saucepan. Bring to a boil, then simmer gently, stirring often, for 4 hours until all the liquid evaporates.

Put the potatoes in a saucepan and cover with water. Bring to a boil and cook 3–5 minutes until just tender.

Put the cooked potatoes and pork in the food processor. Add spices, and pulse 4–5 times to combine.

Roll out one crust between two pieces of wax or parchment paper and place it in a 9-inch pie plate, then spoon in the filling.

Roll out a second crust and top the filling with it.

Brush the second crust with milk, and make holes with a fork.

Bake for thirty minutes.

Livvie's Strawberry Rhubarb Sour Cream Coffee Cake

Strawberry rhubarb jam day is a big day in the Snowden house and part of the tradition is Livvie making her Strawberry Rhubarb Sour Cream Coffee Cake for the family to enjoy later that day.

Cake

2 cups flour
1 teaspoon baking powder
1 teaspoon baking soda
½ teaspoon salt
1 cup sugar
¼ pound unsalted butter, room temperature
2 eggs
½ pint sour cream
1 teaspoon vanilla extract
2 ½ to 3 cups strawberries, halved, then sliced
2 ½ to 3 cups fresh rhubarb, cut into ½ inch pieces

Topping

½ cup sugar
⅓ cup flour

2 teaspoons cinnamon
½ stick unsalted butter, room temperature

Preheat oven to 350 degrees.

Grease a 9x13 baking dish with butter.

Measure flour, baking powder, baking soda, and salt into a bowl and stir together.

In a separate bowl, stir sour cream and vanilla together.

In a mixing bowl, beat the sugar and butter together for three minutes at medium speed.

Add the eggs, one at a time. Beat well after each addition.

Alternate adding the flour and sour cream mixtures to the sugar, beating after each addition, until smooth.

Gently fold the fruit into the batter, distributing it evenly. Pour the batter into the baking dish.

Beat the topping ingredients until they come together in large crumbs. Spoon the topping over batter.

Bake 45–50 minutes. Test doneness by inserting toothpick in the center until it emerges clean. Cool completely before cutting into squares.

ACKNOWLEDGMENTS

I would like to thank Boothbay Harbor Police Chief Robert Hasch and Attorney Richard Hayes for the generosity of their time and advice about procedure and charges. All mistakes, inadvertent and intentional, are mine.

Thank you to Marilyn Mick and Carolyn Vandam for their insights into tourism, clambakes, and herding a crowd. Thanks to Olga Carito for being the reason I ended up with a Victorian house with the best view in the world in Boothbay Harbor, Maine—and for so many other things.

Thanks to my agent, John Talbot, for lighting the match, Sheila Connolly for supplying the fuse, and to my fellow Maine Crime Writer, Lea Wait, for handing me the explosives.

Thanks as always to my first readers, my fantastic writers group of seventeen years, Mark Ammons, Katherine Fast, Cheryl Marceau, and Leslie Wheeler. And with deepest gratitude to my second readers, Bill Carito, Kate Carito, and Sherry Harris, who all went above and beyond.

Thanks also to Bill Carito, the real foodie in our family, for all his help with the recipes and the food scenes.

Also to the Maine Crime Writers, Sisters in Crime New England, and the New England Crime Bake.

Finally, if this book leaves you with an urge for lobster and clams, there is a company that will take you on a boat ride to a private island and provide you with a real New England Clambake experience. The island, the family, and the business vary wildly from the fictional ones in this book, and even the menu is slightly different, but you'll have a fantastic time and I guarantee you won't be murdered. For more information on the Cabbage Island Clambakes see www.cabbageislandclambakes.com.